"Amazing—down to the last line. Bravo!"

Victoria Christopher Murray,
Essence bestselling author
of *The Ex Files* and *Sins of the Mother*

"It's easier to say 'if you see something, say something' than it is to decide what you will do when your family is affected. *Snitch* absorbed me to the point that I felt my life and the lives of my family were at stake. It's just that good. *Snitch* should be required reading for anyone with a pulse and a conscience."

Lisa Cortés, executive producer of the Academy Award–winning film *Precious: Based on the Novel "Push" by Sapphire, Shadowboxer,* and *The Woodsman*

"Captivating from start to finish. *Snitch* is a compelling tale about the psychic turmoil of upholding the code of the streets. Booker T. Mattison deftly interweaves psychological themes of depression, anxiety, and PTSD with the harsh realities of black urban street life."

Kevin Cokley, PhD, editor-in-chief, *Journal of Black Psychology*; associate professor of counseling and psychology, University of Texas, Austin

"Wow. Good stuff. I loved the interconnectedness of every character and the powerful, fresh, black male characters effecting positive change in the neighborhood. It reads like a movie."

Stephanie Allain Bray, producer of the Academy Award–winning film *Hustle & Flow, Black Snake Moan,* and *We the Peeples*

"Like many of us, Andre wears a mask but is convinced that he can just will himself through his inner pain. But his entire world and the fate of his family are closing in on him—fast—so the mask has to come off.

"Mattison turns a mirror on our community and takes an unflinching look at who we are. Gratefully, he doesn't stop there, because the characters in *Snitch* also show us what we will become—for better or for worse—in a world of change. Full of suspense that happens organically, *Snitch* will keep you on edge and will live in your head long after you've turned the last page."

Terrie M. Williams, au
Looks Like We're No
president of th

Books by Booker T. Mattison

Unsigned Hype
Snitch

SNITCH

A NOVEL

BOOKER T. MATTISON

Revell

a division of Baker Publishing Group
Grand Rapids, Michigan

© 2011 by Booker T. Mattison

Published by Revell
a division of Baker Publishing Group
P.O. Box 6287, Grand Rapids, MI 49516-6287
www.revellbooks.com

Printed in the United States of America

Library of Congress Cataloging-in-Publication Data
Mattison, Booker T.
    Snitch : a novel / Booker T. Mattison.
        p.   cm.
    ISBN 978-0-8007-3396-4 (pbk.)
    I. Title.
PS3613.A855S55 2011
813'.6—dc22   2010045751

Some Scripture is taken from the Contemporary English Version © 1991, 1992, 1995 by American Bible Society. Used by permission.

Some Scripture is taken from the Holy Bible, New International Version®, NIV®. Copyright © 1973, 1978, 1984 by Biblica, Inc.™ Used by permission of Zondervan. All rights reserved worldwide. www.zondervan.com

Some Scripture is taken from the New King James Version. Copyright © 1982 by Thomas Nelson, Inc. Used by permission. All rights reserved.

11   12   13   14   15   16   17   7   6   5   4   3   2   1

For my greatest earthly gifts: my beautiful wife Angela; my lovely daughters, Lee, Jean-Angel, and Justice; and my only begotten son, Truth.

*Death and life are in the
power of the tongue.*

Solomon

It's cold tonight. So cold that if you listen hard enough, you can hear the ice that's wedged in the cracks in the street expand and make greater fissures.

Dante is the only soul on the lifeless avenue. He draws his shoulders against his skinny neck in a vain attempt to ward off the howling wind that whips up his back. The sharp winter chill has little regard for his dingy New Jersey Devils coat. He shudders, quickens his pace, and focuses on the glowing O that floats above the frozen sidewalk two blocks ahead.

He considers the number of times he's been to the police station at this hour, and he's surprised that he never noticed that every letter in POLICE is blown out except for the circular, glowing vowel. He balls up an ashy fist and wipes the dribble from his nose before it crystallizes. He smiles.

Easiest job I ever had.

Andre yawns and maneuvers his empty bus onto Bergen Avenue. Fortunately, there are no squad cars parked in front of the police station, so he's able to comfortably clear the curb without blackening it with tire rubber. The lighted O on the sign affixed to the brick police fortress captures Andre's attention as it flickers its last and goes dark. He announces to empty passenger seats, "On your left, ladies and gentlemen, all of police is officially on the blink." He eases on the brakes and brings the full weight of the mechanized beast to a graceful stop at the light. A deserted intersection. The light turns green.

Since Andre has become a bus driver, he's gotten used to being his own audience. Not many people ride the bus after midnight in Greenville. Those who do, make him nervous. But what are you going to do? It's a gig, and a good one.

Occasionally Andre gets a talkative soul who parks in the first seat to his right and tells him more than he's comfortable hearing. But most midnight riders are the drunk and disheveled, stumbling to the back of the bus to sleep off life's malaise until Andre chases them off at the end of the route.

"Watch the cars. The lights ain't never killed nobody!" Andre is pleased with his Moms Mabley imitation as he looks both ways, presses the gas, and passes through the intersection.

Up ahead he sees a man dressed in black arguing with a skinny man in a New Jersey Devils coat. The skinny man punches the man in black in the face and takes off running. The man in black is bigger and easily gains on the slimmer man. Andre is almost upon them and, intrigued by the late-night spectacle, remarks, "Ain't this some—"

The skinny man lunges into the street and into the path of the bus. Andre slams on the brakes, but not before clipping the man with his right front bumper. The man rolls, springs up, and runs onto the sidewalk. The man in black almost smacks into Andre's driver's side window. Andre notices his weasely eyes floating around inside the darkness of a black hoodie. Fear creeps down Andre's back and burrows in his stomach.

The man in black peels his beady eyes off of Andre, steps onto the sidewalk, and watches the skinny man escape.

As he flees, he looks over his shoulder just as the man in black aims and lets off multiple orange blasts from his weapon. The skinny man wildly alters his flight pattern—bobbing and weaving, avoiding getting hit—until he drops. The weasel-eyed gunman looks back at Andre before he disappears into a crease between two buildings.

Andre pulls up to the rumpled mass splayed in the street. He kills the engine. When he depresses the air brake, the familiar *psst!* rips through the night silence and startles him. He slips off the bus and gawks at the motionless body.

He's . . . like . . . dead.

A glacial shudder swashes through Andre's veins.

The black hole between buildings that swallowed up the shooter stands empty. Looking up the three blocks to the police station, Andre notices that the O has found new life and is burning brightly.

Sandra's block is no walk in the park. The unemployment rate is easily 20 percent, and the other people are either retired, too young to have a job, or on work release. Andre feels guilty anytime he's over here, so he makes it a point to stay away as much as possible. However, tonight he can't think of any better place to go. Once upon a time when he and Sandra were a happy couple, 64 Martin Luther King Drive, Apartment 2F, was his address. That was before Sandra locked him out one too many times for him to feel comfortable in his own home.

Mr. Dibiasi, the landlord, let Sandra and Andre swap

names on the lease after he left for the last time. That was a year ago, and the front door that leads to the cold, dark hallway still dangles from the same rusted hinges. The buzzer has been broken for years, but even when it worked, the quickest way to get inside the building was to holler up at whoever you came to visit.

Andre skips the fourth and ninth steps on the way to the second floor without even thinking. It's too dark to tell, and not worth the gamble, to see if the steps were repaired. Mr. Burrell still bumps Bobby "Blue" Bland's "Ain't No Love in the Heart of the City" until the wee hours of the morning.

Some things never change.

When Andre reaches the second-floor landing, the sun is just starting to peek over the neighborhood's ornery skyline. Greenville is the other Jersey City, the part unspoiled by the trappings of urban renewal and gentrification.

The dirty hallway window lets in just enough light for Andre to see his face in the mirror that Sandra keeps posted on the front door below the peephole. The mirror allows her to monitor her makeup one last time before she steps out. What's interesting is that people in the building steal anything not nailed down, but no one has ever laid a finger on the oval looking glass.

On more than one occasion, Andre and Sandra caught neighbors, and even strangers, checking themselves out in the mirror. People's responses were always the same: "My fault" or "Pardon me."

Andre shakes his head. *Not even poverty and urban blight can blot out people's fixation with looking just right.*

The man in the mirror staring back at Andre could easily pass for thirty-five even though he won't reach that milestone for another eight years. Andre sighs. He is not aging gracefully. His finely trimmed goatee is seasoned with seven gray hairs. He got his first one at twenty, so he's averaging one a year. His cheeks are fuller than they once were, and the bags beneath his light brown eyes book-end a broad nose with flaring nostrils. An encroaching shadow of scrappy hairs has overtaken his head in places where permanent baldness hasn't set in. What Andre wouldn't give for those hairs to be gone. Then he would have the luxury of a shiny, maintenance-free dome.

He taps out his signature knock on the front door. *Tap-tap, tap-TAP.*

No answer. He pulls out his cell phone and dials Sandra's number. He hears it ring inside the apartment.

"Hello?" Sandra whispers.

Hearing her voice through the door and on the phone at the same time is disconcerting.

She must be sleeping on the couch.

"Hello?" she says, this time a little louder.

"Hey, it's me. I'm in the hallway."

"Do you know what time it is?"

Andre looks at his phone. "Five twenty-seven."

"I'm not letting you in," Sandra says.

"You have somebody in there?"

"I don't have to answer your questions, Andre."

"If you have somebody in there, just tell me."

"Goodbye."

Little Dre's cry roars through the house.

"See! You woke up the baby!"

She hangs up. Andre hears feet pattering through the apartment and back, and then the click-clack of four locks being released. When Sandra cracks the door, Little Dre stops howling instantly. He bumps through the opening and reaches for Andre, cupping his tiny fingers to his palms like a baby lobster. His smile beams behind a pacifier locked in place between two teeth on the bottom and gums on top. Sandra sighs and passes the baby to his father.

"What's up, little man? You need a haircut as bad as me."

Andre moves past Sandra and into the living room as he runs his fingers through Little Dre's tangled 'fro. He ignores Sandra's slamming the door and dotes on his son.

"Daddy missed his little man! How're you doing, sonny boy?"

Andre senses a cold stare and turns around. Sandra is watching him with her arms folded and a scowl fixed on her face. She enunciates each word as if to ensure that they don't come out as sour as she looks.

"I-have-somewhere-to-be-in-a-few-hours. Is-there-some-special-reason-you're-showing-up-here-at-five-o'clock-in-the-morning?"

The skinny man's lifeless face flashes in Andre's head. The image sends the creeps skittering across his torso like a host of tiny, biting mites.

"I saw a man get killed."

Sandra clutches one hand to her chest and twirls one of her long braids with the other. "What were you *doing*?"

"Driving my route," Andre says, put off by her accusatory tone.

Sandra sits and so does he. Little Dre looks up at Andre and gives him a big ol' cheese grin. Andre doesn't pay attention, so Little Dre grabs his bottom lip. Andre removes the tiny fingers from his mouth and says, "I was driving down Bergen and I saw these two guys fighting. One of them started running, and I guess he was trying to use the bus to separate himself from the other guy, so he ran in front of me."

Andre stops and looks Sandra in the eye. "The guy doing the chasing pulled out a gun and started shooting. The guy running was doing alright until he got popped."

"What'd you do then?"

"What could I do? I'm sitting in a lighted box for the whole world to see."

"He saw you? What did he look like?"

"It was dark and he had on a black hoodie, so I couldn't see his face."

Sandra grabs Little Dre and presses him against her chest. "How do you know he won't come looking for you?"

Andre gets up and looks out of the window onto the street. "I guess I don't know."

"Did you call the police?"

Andre rests his forehead against the chilly pane. "Yes."

"What did they say?"

"I didn't hang around to find out."

"Why not?"

"I'd rather not be involved like that."

"Involved like what?"

Andre turns and faces her. "Look. I saw his eyes. That's it. There was nothing else for me to say."

Clops is not sure how he feels. Although he has carried a gun off and on since he was fifteen, he has never had an occasion to fire one.

After the first two rounds went off into space, he firmed up his grip to accommodate for the Glock's recoil. That's when Dante dropped—instantly. Not like the movies where people slink to the ground in slow motion.

Boom and then boom, Dante was down.

What sticks in Clops's mind the most is that after Dante collapsed, he squeezed off three more rounds.

He feels the touchy strains of sickness rapidly advancing up his digestive track. He curls over the kitchen sink and heaves.

As his body attempts to forcefully expel every ounce of juice from his belly, he chokes on a dry, violent retch.

"Claymont?"

She must be 'sleep on the couch.

"I'm okay, Grammy Lee!" he hacks. He battles his breathing in an attempt to force it through his nose instead of his mouth.

He stores the .40 caliber Glock pistol with olive drab frame in a hole cut out of the wall behind the sink basin. He cups his hands, runs water in them, and for the first time notices that they're shaking. He splashes water on his hot face.

Clops tramps into the living room and into a flickering light that paints the room in extraordinary bursts of flash and shadow. Grammy Lee is reclined in her favorite chair in front of the television. He adjusts the blanket that covers her feet.

"You okay, Grammy?"

"Am *I* okay? You're the one in there spitting up the dickens. Have you been drinking?"

"No, ma'am."

"I've told you about keeping these late hours. Nothing good happens in Greenville after midnight."

"Sorry, Grammy."

"I don't want sorry, I want change. You're twenty-five years old. I shouldn't have to talk to you this way."

"I'm gonna change, Grammy. I promise."

He kisses her on the cheek, and she swats him on the back of the head. "Good night, Claymont."

"Good night, Grammy."

He climbs the stairs and stops at the top, draped in panic. *That bus driver looked right at me.*

He gets breathless as if he just might go to pieces.

But I ain't going to jail.

Clops considers the funk of a concrete cage populated with musty gangsters doing life with no parole. He shakes his head violently.

That ain't gonna happen.

2

Andre gamely paces about at the front of a loaded lecture hall. He makes eye contact with everyone in the room. His classmates are all suspended in silence and on the edge of their seats, so he begins.

> Darkness is my shroud,
> I lurk mysteriously beneath her cover.
> I knock once. I knock twice.
> I am here—her fresh, fly lover.

Andre pauses for effect, and as if on cue, coed giggling wriggles up to the rafters. Andre's teammates, a muscular wall of peacock blue jerseys, nudge each other and smirk.

> She welcomes me, obsessed,
> And then she melts into my arms.
> Eyes closed, tight embrace,
> Another victim of my charm.
> I give her what she wants
> And then I dash into the night.
> I have six more souls to please
> Before the coming of the light.
> I'm every father's nightmare
> And every daughter's dream.

The king at macking women,
And you too can be my queen.

Andre trains his eyes on Sandra, who doesn't meet his gaze—likely out of sheer embarrassment and the penetrating weight of his stare.

Be ye tall, be ye short,
Be ye dark, or be ye light,
I am here to bring you pleasure,
Within the shadows of the night.

Andre artfully crafts and holds a dramatic silence and then quickly takes a seat. Applause erupts. He coyly checks on Sandra. This time he got her attention.

Andre's eyes snap open. It was all so vivid.

But St. Peter's was a lifetime ago.

He rolls over and buries the thought before regret slithers in. Then he remembers that he's on Sandra's couch.

Everything is as it was the last time he was here. The gently weathered Manchester love seat set in rich earth tones and the matching couch he lays on, husky oaken end tables, and an oversized brown faux leather beanbag that serves as the coffee table. As always, the place is spotless.

The house is spectacularly quiet.

"Sandra!"

Andre's call echoes as he pulls himself up and strolls through the apartment. He peers out of the bedroom window and sees Sandra and Little Dre at the bus stop.

Sandra is huddled inside her flint-colored down coat with the metallic toggle front and standing collar—the expensive one he bought for her birthday two years ago. She is wearing a gray flannel skirt, dark tights, and smoke-colored knee boots. Her long, natural, auburn braids grow from under a slate-colored knit cloche hat, its Berber trim rimming her gentle face. Sandra is a pretty flower. Her balsa-wood complexion sparkles against a backdrop of drab brick buildings and spindly tree skeletons. Little Dre is bundled up and tucked under a clear plastic stroller cover.

Andre flips open his cell and says, "Sandra."

The phone dials. He watches Sandra retrieve hers.

"Hello?"

"Where are you going dressed up like that this early on a weekend?"

"Do I ever call you and ask you where you're going?"

"You have my son with you, so I have a right to ask you questions."

"This is getting really old, Dre. *We* are not together anymore. Haven't been for a year—your choice. But for some reason you feel like you can question me about who I'm with, where I'm going, and when and why I'm wearing nice clothes."

The bus creeps up.

"I'll talk to you later, Dre."

Andre flips his phone shut and watches Sandra hoist Little Dre out of the stroller, collapse it, strap it onto her shoulder, and mount the bus steps. The sight causes guilt to back up in his throat like heartburn. He swallows hard as the bus pulls off. He can see Sandra through the window of the bus, working hard to get Little Dre unbundled and settled into his seat.

Sandra looks up and catches Andre's penetrating stare just as the bus passes the building.

Staring out the window at me and I'm doing all this work. I should've put him out before I left.

20

Little Dre closes his eyes, throws his head against the seat back, and whimpers. Sandra breathes a commanding hush before the toddler flare-up erupts. Little Dre's whimper burbles into sniffles and then boils over into a clamorous screech. Every eye on the bus lands on Sandra. Even the driver cuts his eyes at her through the rearview mirror.

Disrupting my quiet commute!

If you can't control it, don't have it!

Baby Mama!

Shame!

Sandra is frisked by each of their thoughts and methodically glares back at every one of them.

Y'all don't know me!

She leans into Little Dre and spits a shushed, "Be quiet!"

He holds up his little hands and howls, "Co', Ma-ma. Co'!"

Sandra is gripped with guilt. She takes his tiny hands in hers and warms them with a vigorous rub. "Mommy's sorry, baby. I'm so sorry."

Little Dre climbs into her lap. Sandra wraps him in her arms and anxiously rocks back and forth, determined to ignore the huffy eyes that linger. Another block and she'll be off of this bus and on to the next.

<hr>

The fluorescent lights planted in the water-stained ceiling in the break room of the Greenville Bus Garage bathe the room in a gloomy, greenish glow. Andre mindlessly picks at a warmed-over turkey sandwich slathered with globs of Miracle Whip and mealy tomatoes. Tonto whisks in, unpacks his dinner, and flips on the television. He is lithe, tightly wound, and the color of red Alabama clay. His real name is François, but people call him Tonto because he's the spitting image of an American Indian. But Tonto is as black as

Andre is nervous when the lead story pops up on the eleven o'clock news.

Immediately Andre's eyes are drawn to the bright yellow crime scene tape snapping in last night's biting wind. Too-cold cops huddle around a lifeless lump zipped in a body bag. The B-roll video cuts to a reporter live on the scene.

"A brazen murder three blocks from a police station has a neighborhood that's accustomed to violence on edge."

A photograph of the skinny man dominates the television screen.

"Twenty-two-year-old Dante Stallworth was gunned down shortly after midnight."

Tonto shakes his head and speeds his chewing. "My cousin knew that cat. Said he'd been snitching for years."

Andre keeps quiet. He pushes away from the table and his now-cold sandwich.

Tonto squints and leans toward the television. "That's your route, Dre! He got blasted right around the time you hit Bergen if you were on time. You had to have just missed it."

"I guess so," Andre says.

Tonto shakes his head. "Every year it gets more crazy out here, man. I've been thinking about moving down South. I heard you can get a house down there for less than a hundred grand."

"Yeah, but you make peanuts."

"You're probably right."

"I'll catch you later. My bus should be ready."

"Alright, Dre," Tonto says, never moving his eyes off the television. "Be safe out there."

It's like this every night when Andre passes through the dusky garage between the dark, hulking busses. He feels as if he's meandering through a mechanized mausoleum. The lightless headlamps on the buses are mischievous eyes, the grills gnashing teeth. One of them—all of them—could be

22

roused from their slumber by his trespassing and devour him. He'd be defenseless against the diesel beasts as they gorged on his unlucky flesh.

Andre smiles uncomfortably.

Imaginative minds make men mad.

He removes a notebook from his shirt pocket, frees a nubby pencil from the spiral, and completes the couplet.

Trepidation is truth painted in glimmering shades of sad.

Andre pockets the notebook and pushes open the door to number 5201. The light that springs from the bowels of the bus chases away his cryptic blue funk.

Tonight Andre will be riding in style. Number 5201 is a 2011 Metro Suburban Compo Bus with a Cummins ISM engine and a Caterpillar C9 power train. If a forty-five-foot bus could be a hot rod, this would be it.

"Okay, bus. Let's take on the night."

Streetlights spill conical shafts of yellow light on the pavement, creating oceans of murky shadows between each pole—a perfect cover for an infinite number of unknowns. Andre's eyes bounce from sidewalk to sidewalk like pinballs in motion. Any movement on the block causes his insides to freeze, from the innocent reflection of traffic lights off of windshields to the more pernicious sight of men in dark clothing crossing the street.

Someone is standing at the bus stop ahead. Andre's heart pumps wildly as he eases on the brakes and brings the Metro Suburban to a gentle stop. Andre opens the door, and a hooded man in black climbs the stairs and cocks his eyes.

"Andre."

Andre doesn't answer. He just stares at the man, who is about his age with overlong dreads and a full Philly beard.

When the man sinks his hand into his pocket, Andre's heart drains.

"Hakeem Shabazz. St. Peter's College."

He pulls out his bus pass and pays his fare. Andre squints and looks closely at his eyes. The name doesn't ring a bell.

Hakeem tugs at his locks and points to his thick, neatly trimmed beard. "I didn't have all of this back then."

"Wait a minute," Andre says. "Logic and argumentation? With Doo-Doo Breath Dabrowski?"

"Exactly!" Hakeem chuckles. "Dr. Dabrowski had a stink cloud in his mouth. And that was when he *had* a tongue full of Tic Tacs." He sits in the seat next to Andre. "So how's everything? I see you're driving a bus now."

Andre glances at Hakeem but keeps a cautious eye on the street.

"Yeah, you know. For now. What about you?"

"I'm a counselor."

"At a camp or something?"

"No, psychological counseling."

"Oh." Andre gives him a short look, then returns to vigilantly searching the streets. The corners. The shadows.

Tonight is not as cold as last night, but the mounds of dirty snow packed in the gutters show no sign of melting. Andre marvels that something so beautiful and pure when it falls can become so filthy and vile mere moments after hitting the city streets.

"I started a practice on Communipaw."

Andre jumps out of his skin. He was so wrapped up in a defensive posture, looking out, that Hakeem slipped his mind.

"Are you this jumpy every night?" Hakeem asks.

"Who, me? Nah, it's just . . . you know . . . a lot going on right now."

"Anything you care to share?"

24

"Look, man. Don't try to run the head games on me, alright?"

"It's not about that," Hakeem says. "I'm just trying to help a brother out. This is my stop right here."

Andre eases on the brakes and Hakeem stands.

Bang!

Andre flinches. A sheet-metal-and-aluminum dust bucket had backfired and is stopped at the light.

"It's not healthy to be that easily rattled, Andre. Especially out here." He slips Andre a card.

HAKEEM SHABAZZ, PSYD. LICENSED PROFESSIONAL COUNSELOR.

Hakeem replaces the hood on his head and steps off into the night. "Nice seeing you, man."

"Alright, peace."

Andre wheels the bus back into the mirthless streets.

Andre checks the route assignment schedule and shakes his head. He moves to his locker, opens it, and does a bang-up job of acting as if he's reordering its scrambled contents. He keeps an eye on the locker-room entrance through the mirror posted inside his locker door.

He unearths the picture. It used to be his locker's main feature, prominently displayed so that all who passed could see how lovely Sandra was. Now he keeps it buried beneath a stack of *Sports Illustrated* magazines. In the photograph, Andre and Sandra are sandwiched between Bugs Bunny, Foghorn Leghorn, and Pepé Le Pew.

The picture was taken at Great Adventure Amusement Park the summer after Andre was kicked out of St. Peter's. It was Andre and Sandra's first real date. Sandra was a rising sophomore, and Andre, had he not blown it, would've been a week away from preparing for the beginning of the end of his lifelong passion—knocking around on the gridiron with twenty-one other men.

Despite All Metro Atlantic Athletic Conference honors three years running, and downfield blocking skills that earned him the nickname Bad News Bolden, Andre knew that getting drafted into the NFL was all but impossible. Even an invitation to a predraft camp would have been a long shot, barring a miraculous season. But Andre had tempered his dream of playing professional football the moment he accepted a scholarship to play Division II ball at Jersey City's own St. Peter's, the Jesuit College of New Jersey.

In the mirror, Andre sees Big Will finally arrive. Andre allows him to reach his locker before he eases over.

"Big Will. What's good in your world?"

"Yeah, I saw your girl yesterday," Will says. "That's what you came to ask me about, right?"

Big Will is Mr. Intensity, even when he's tying a tie around his big, beefy neck. Although ties are not a required part of the bus operator uniform, he chooses to wear one anyway.

"Come on, Will. You can give me more credit than that."

Big Will adjusts his knot and looks directly at Andre. "No, I can't. 'Cuz on the rare occasion that you do hang around after your shift, your agenda doesn't usually involve hollering at me."

For years Andre and Big Will have been two lions in the urban jungle, tentatively circling each other to protect their pride. Big Will was a standout linebacker at Lincoln High School, and Andre the star wide receiver at crosstown rival Dickinson.

Even though ten years have passed, Andre hasn't forgotten the "89 Banana, 42 Slant" pattern across the middle. It was overtime in the annual Jersey City Classic, which pits the two best high school football teams in the city against each other on Thanksgiving Day.

Lincoln scored on their first overtime possession to make the score 35–28. Now it was Dickinson's ball. Andre and his teammates had picked apart the Lincoln defense the entire game with their passing attack. Andre already had seven catches for 130 yards and had scored all four touchdowns. It was 4th and 10, and if Dickinson didn't get a first down on the play, the game was over.

When the ball was snapped, Andre exploded off the line of scrimmage. As soon as he passed the first down marker, he planted his foot in the turf and cut inside. The next thing he saw was rockets and a dizzying array of pastel colors in bloom. Big Will cleaned his clock as soon as the quarterback released the ball. Andre found out later from a St. Peter's teammate who was on that Lincoln team what had happened.

Big Will had told everyone on the sideline before overtime began that if Andre came across the middle, he was going to take his head off. He reasoned that he would rather knock Andre out of the game and take a fifteen-yard penalty than let him catch another touchdown and tie the score. But that was only part of the issue. Will had had a problem with Andre since Recreation Youth Football. In his mind, Andre had always typified the "diva receiver," self-centered and convinced that he was God's gift to the cosmos.

Conversely, Andre envied Big Will because he was recruited by several Division I schools and Andre wasn't. Big Will went on to ride the bench for a year at Penn State before he got homesick and returned to Jersey City.

"She got off at Ocean," Big Will finally says. "That's all I can tell you, other than she's still fine. You were a fool to let that go."

Andre decides to let *that* go. He got all the information he needs.

3

Ever since Greenville was founded as an independent township in 1863, it had money problems—mainly over an inability to improve its streets. That was the primary reason why in 1873 township residents voted overwhelmingly 261 to 45 to officially become a part of Jersey City, even as it maintained its townie gravitations. At that time, the problems with Greenville's streets were a public works issue. And 138 years later, Greenville still has problems with its streets, only "streets" is now code for "urban drama played out on an asphalt stage." Particularly the part of the neighborhood that grew darker over the years: east of Kennedy Boulevard, south of Communipaw Avenue—save for a scattering of exceptional blocks—to the Bayonne border.

As Greenville browned, its chocolate-colored souls functioned as one body, complete with eyes and ears that saw and heard, and that made everyone responsible for each other as a matter of survival. After all, big northern cities could be as viperous as small southern towns. Nevertheless, hopes and dreams were the heartbeat of this body, and common decency flowed through it like a life-giving fluid.

Now as Clops bops into Vittas Haberdashery, purveyor of quality men's fashion since 1923, a nattily clad white salesman looks up and seems to be alarmed at the sight of a black man less than half his age rolling in with all the pimp and bravado of a rap star. The salesman appears to expertly mask his alarm with what he knows best—the finest customer service in northern New Jersey.

"Sir, how may I help you?"

"I'm trying to get one of these suits."

The salesman sizes up Clops and says, "Forty-two Long."

Clops looks down at himself and smiles, showing two platinum-crowned incisors. "Your guess is as good as mine."

The salesman apparently takes that as an affront to his aptitude. "I'm certain of it," he snaps as he unstrings a measuring tape from around his skinny neck. "Remove your coat."

He helps Clops peel off his North Face, moves behind him, and presses each end of the tape to a shoulder. He then measures from the top of Clops's shoulder blade to his wrist and faces him.

"Chin up."

Clops does as he's told as the salesman measures his neck.

"Is this suit for the office, job interviews—a funeral?"

"Just looking for something nice."

The salesman's eyes narrow. He probes his pointy chin with a slender index finger and studies several suits. He grabs one and displays it as proudly as if he had tailored it himself.

"Brioni. Three-button. Notch lapel," the salesman says. He flips it around. "Center vents. Masterfully crafted. This is both modern and traditional. You can't go wrong with this one."

Clops studies the suit as if he has been buying them for years. "That's hot, but how much you want for it?"

"Eight ninety-five."

"*Eight ninety-five?* What you got in the hundred-dollar range?"

"With all due respect, sir, you'll find that at the Walmart in Secaucus. Is this your first suit?"

"Yeah, first one. What about two hundred? You got anything in here for that?"

The salesman furrows his brow, turns on the heels of his shiny Stamford Oxfords, and heads to the back of the store.

Clops takes in the space as Mozart's *Menuetto Trio* wafts lightly from hidden speakers. He feels like he's being watched and the culprits are everywhere. He looks out onto the street. No cops. He whirls around, and a host of mannequins in custom-tailored suits stare at him with vacuous indifference.

He smiles. *What am I tripping for?*

To the mannequins, "And what y'all dead-face fools looking at?"

The salesman returns. "Did you say something?"

"Just talking to myself."

The salesman holds up a two-button suit with no vents and a peak lapel. "Two ninety-five and I'll throw in a nice shirt and tie."

Clops pulls out a wad of large bills and thumbs through them. "A'ight, bet."

"Do you have shoes?"

Clops looks down at his brand-new black Timberlands. "Nah, I'm good."

"Surely you don't plan to wear those with this suit?"

"Why not? I'm only gonna wear it once."

"You must at least buy a coat. North Face and Burberry can't be spoken in the same sentence, much less worn on the same body."

"I got a coat. My grandpop left it for me. It's a classic."

Andre stands naked in the middle of Bergen Avenue. A wrecked, snarling bus speeds toward him. He struggles to get out of the way, but he's powerless to move. When he looks down, he sees that his feet are melded into the asphalt. The skin and muscle tendons around his ankles pull away from the bone each time he attempts to lift them. It's the worst pain he's ever felt. He screams in agony, but no sound ekes out.

The bus accelerates and is almost upon him. Andre closes his eyes and braces for impact. When he opens his eyes again, the weasel-eyed gunman is behind the wheel, his mouth stretched into an awful, evil smirk. Andre's parents are in the first two seats of the bus, their eyes closed.

Andre awakes, choking on his own fear. Even as he realizes that it was just a dream, anxiety pulses behind his temples. He had heard about people waking in a cold sweat, but he had always thought that was hyperbole. Now jots of ice drip from his pores and dampen his bedsheets.

Andre sits up and checks the time on his phone. Nine thirty p.m. He turns on the light.

His tiny one-room apartment features everything in miniature—a kitchenette with a mini microwave, a two-burner gas stove, and a sliver of a refrigerator. The only other thing that can fit is Andre's full-size air mattress and the plastic milk crate that he uses as a nightstand. The apartment is in the basement of an elegant nineteenth-century brownstone in a trendy neighborhood near downtown Jersey City. It has hardwood floors and exposed brick walls but is only three hundred square feet. It costs the same to rent as Sandra's apartment, which is three times the size. But that's Jersey City. The closer you get to Manhattan, the higher the uptick in rent.

Andre dials.

"Hello?" a voice says.

"Mr. Dominick?"

"Yeah, it's Dominick."

"Hey, it's Andre. I'm not going to be able to make it in tonight. I'm not feeling well."

"You sure you can't make it in? It's kinda short notice."

"Yeah, I'm sure."

"What, that you can't make it in, or that it's kinda short notice?"

"That I can't make it in."

"You're putting me in a tough spot here, Bolden. Now I gotta find a fill-in an hour before your shift."

"Sorry about that."

"You'll be in tomorrow night?"

"Definitely."

"Okay."

"Alright, bye."

Andre flops onto the air mattress and buries his face in his pillow.

Clops stands at the bus stop at the corner of Bergen Avenue and Wegman Parkway. His brand-new, tailored, $295 suit shows nicely through the opening in his tan, camel-hair topcoat. His black Timberlands may as well be Stamford Oxfords under the cover of night. Clops looks more like a businessman than a drug dealer with a record longer than the shadow cast by the streetlight overhead.

He looks at his watch—12:03 a.m. *Same time I stepped to Dante.*

Clops remembers because he looked at his watch just before he spotted him bopping up the block. *If he hadn't showed up when he did, we wouldn't have crossed paths that night.*

Clops didn't know how much longer he could wait because of the bitter cold. He reminds himself that he didn't intend to kill Dante. *But I had to let him know that the streets knew he was snitching.*

He also had to warn Dante to keep OGC out of his mouth unless he wanted to catch a piece of hot steel. Clops brought his gun along for no other reason than to punctuate the threat.

Then he had to go and catch me in the eye and run like a punk.

After that, Clops felt he had no other choice but to blast.

He looks up the block and chafes inwardly at the sight of the approaching bus.

Big Deaks and Brother K talk about murkin' like it's as easy as making a baloney sandwich. Clops shakes his head. *Killing ain't supposed to be that easy.*

The hair on his neck raises and a hint of sickness tickles his stomach when the bus brakes. He cuddles the olive drab Glock tucked in his belt.

A leather-faced white man with an eye patch opens the door.

"You getting on?"

"Nah. Wrong bus."

"This is the only one that stops here."

"Yeah, I know."

The driver slams the door shut.

4

Little Dre seems to be regressing. Sandra thought he was on the verge of finally sleeping through the night, but now he pops up like clockwork at 4:30 a.m., sniffing around for milk. She rolls over and pops a bottle in his mouth.

"Ma-ma," Little Dre says between swills.

Sandra manages to wrestle free from the depths of her fatigue, but her eyes are still too heavy to open. "Little boy, Mommy's tired. Lay down and go back to sleep."

Dre ditches the bottle and reaches through the bars of the crib. "Ma-ma."

Sandra forces herself up, lifts him out of the crib, and tucks him in bed beside her. "Your grandmother would kill me if she knew you were sleeping with me—"

The rest of her mother's declaration sweeps through her head. *Especially a boy without a full-time father.*

Statements like that never bothered Sandra until the things her mother said started to come true.

"A woman can raise a boy to be a good citizen," her mother said, "but she can't raise him to be a man."

The room blurs as Sandra's eyes well up with tears. This is not where she thought she would be at twenty-five. Nevertheless, here she is, trapped—a single mother in Greenville.

"Ma-ma."

Little Dre is all gums and two bottom teeth. Sandra smiles back at him through tears.

"Mommy loves you."

She kisses him squarely in the mouth. He grabs both of her ears, opens his mouth, and slobbers all over her nose. Sandra practically drowns in sweet baby-boy juice.

"You can't eat Mommy. Then who's going to take care of you?"

Dre stops and stares at her. "Dah-dah."

Moments like these give Sandra the chills because it seems that Little Dre understands things beyond his fourteen months. He grabs his pacifier and looks up at her with eyes as big as toy saucers.

"Yes, you do have your daddy."

With that, Little Dre pops in his pacifier, snuggles against her warm body, and passes off to sleep.

Sandra's eyes remain open.

Am I really going to be able to do this by myself for the next seventeen years?

Sunlight blazes through the lazy split between the black curtains that Andre uses to block out daylight and the foot parade of nine-to-fivers slogging to their Manhattan commutes. The only problem Andre has with living in a basement apartment is the ankle-eye view of the world that his one window provides.

But it's the weekend, so the block is at rest.

Andre drops to the floor and forces himself into crunch position. He looks across the surface of his chest at the flesh beginning to gather around his abdomen. He sucks it up and pumps out fifty hard-fought crunches. After forcing twenty more, the delicious pain of throbbing abdominal muscles ripples through his core. He clenches his teeth and strains out number one hundred. With sweat running down the ridge between his pecs, Andre releases his strength and relaxes into the floor. He jabs at his six-pack obscured by a layer of flesh.

"A hundred of those a day and you'll be back."

He focuses on the milk crate nightstand, which is jammed full of stuff stacked and half straightened. The bruised, burnt-orange binder buried at the bottom captures his attention.

He reaches over and carefully slips the notebook out without disturbing any other pieces of the pile. The cover has "Dark Poet" scrawled across it in graffiti. Andre opens the notebook and is greeted by the handwritten draft of the first poem he ever gave to Sandra.

> Once gray skies.
> Cloudy.
> Ominous.
> Made my days dark as nights
> And my evenings black as shadows.
> I hid my face in misery's toil,
> Depression was my daily yield.
> What has life prepared for me?
> A seat at death's table?
> Shall I sup with travail endless?
> The light of life did flicker when I looked on your
>   face.
> As the sun burst forth, bringing radiance and nour-
>   ishment for the soul.
> You are the curator of my newfound joy,
> The heat that melts the icy confines of loneliness.
> I welcome you to my world as dusk welcomes dawn
>   in all its glory.
> You alone know the secrets of my heart, my most
>   sacred place.

Andre stares at the wearied handwritten paper and smiles. He recalls how terrified he was when he slipped Sandra the bright red envelope with the typed poem inside after humanities class.

"This is for you," he said before ambling off with a carefully orchestrated, toplofty bop.

The next week in class, Sandra acted as if nothing happened. That confused Andre because his poetry usually melted away the wall of unfamiliarity that exists between a man and a woman when they first meet.

After Sandra ignored his poem, Andre second-guessed his decision to be so forward with his poetic advance. So he avoided her for the rest of the semester. His embarrassment and desire to prove to Sandra that he was "the man" is what inspired the end-of-semester poem that he performed in humanities class that finally got her attention.

That was the life.

He picks up the phone and dials.

Sandra's phone buzzes. She sees that it's Andre and ignores the call.

Andre is camped out in a window booth in Café Loco on Ocean Avenue. He checks the time on his cell phone. Ten thirty-seven a.m. Sure enough, Mr. Intensity is right on time. Big Will is all smiles as Sandra and Little Dre get off the bus. Sandra is clueless as he zeros in on her shapely bottom while she bends over to shake out Dre's stroller and straps him inside. Andre's head is thick with jealous ire.

Sandra turns and waves, and Will pulls off. Andre cranes his neck and follows her down the block until she passes from view. He makes his way to the door, but not before a pearly haired waitress drops into zone coverage.

37

"Don't try scramming out of here without paying." She crouches slightly and thrusts her palms out, fully engaged for the bump and run.

"That wasn't my intention, ma'am. Really."

The little old lady is tough as nails and not buying it. She stuffs the check in Andre's breast pocket and pats it as if to say, "Take that."

Andre presses a five-dollar bill in her hand.

By the time Andre is on the street, Sandra and Little Dre are gone. He canvasses the block and peers through each store window, then crosses at the corner. The first shop he encounters is a hardware store. Beside that, a newly renovated storefront with a sign that says NEW JERSEY TRUTH. It is without windows, so Andre opens the door and steps inside. He is met by two well-dressed black men in their late twenties who look like members of the Fruit of Islam. One extends his hand and gives Dre a firm handshake.

"Welcome, brother. We can let you inside in a minute."

"Is this your first time here?" the other man asks.

It takes Andre a moment to realize that he's been asked a question because he's busy searching for Sandra through the beveled glass lodged in the wooden doors before him. "Yeah, but I'm not staying. I'm just looking for somebody."

"We can help you, brother," the man who shook Andre's hand says. "Who is it you're looking for?"

Andre feels like he's being quizzed. "I can check myself when you open the doors."

The young man looks through the glass pane, and before he opens the door he says, "We'll stand at the back wall. And if you see who you're looking for, point them out and I'll pass on a message. I'm Fredrick, by the way."

"Andre."

Fredrick opens the door and escorts Andre into a room that

is larger than he expected. There are at least 150 people seated in folding chairs with peacock blue cushions. The carpeted floor is the same color as the chairs and gently slopes down to a polished teakwood stage. It looks strikingly similar to a St. Peter's College lecture hall. Andre scans the entire space, and in the middle of the fourth row from the front, he spots Sandra with Little Dre in her lap.

A sturdy man who exudes a ferocious air steps onto the stage. He reminds Andre of a good fullback: solidly built, low center of gravity, and prepared to bowl you over. Andre's curiosity is piqued.

"Do you see who you're looking for?" Fredrick whispers.

"Yeah, but I'll just stand back here for a minute."

Fredrick says, "It looks like all the seats are taken, but hang on."

The speaker never introduces himself, he just plows right in. "Death is a process, not an instant. You're not alive one minute and dead the next. Death happens in stages."

Andre crosses his arms, presses his back against the wall, and facilitates a face of disengagement.

"Within ten seconds of your heart stopping, brain activity ceases. Then a doctor shines light in your eyes, looking for a response. There is none, so you're clinically dead. But nowadays it's not unusual for people to be brought back from clinical death. And two out of ten report having consciousness when they're dead. Some remember, word for word, conversations doctors had over their dead bodies. Others see a bright light or find themselves on the highway to heaven in a naked bodysuit with a drop-seat flap."

The gathering laughs, but Andre doesn't. He loosens his arms and eases up off the wall.

"But the window of opportunity for life to return to your body is short, because within five minutes of your heart stopping, the body starts to deteriorate. And here's the gruesome truth. Our community is showing all the signs of clinical death. The light is shining in our eyes, but there's no response even though our consciousness is aware of everything that's going on around us.

"Brothers. Ladies. Our body is decomposing and our consciousness is rotting with it. Turn to Leviticus chapter 5, verse 1, and I'll show you how we're complicit in our own death."

Andre sucks his teeth. *One of those Bible dudes.*

Little Dre starts to fuss. Sandra attempts to plug him with the pacifier, but he swats it away. An older, heavyset woman is seated beside them. She offers to take Little Dre, but Sandra seems reluctant. However, Sandra swiftly complies when Little Dre continues to emphatically express what's on his tiny mind.

Immediately Little Dre gives the heavyset woman a "who are you?" look.

"I'm Grammy Lee." The woman speaks softly. "And you better settle your little self down." Little Dre quickly quiets.

Andre isn't comfortable with people he doesn't know handling his kid. The two things he fears most are Little Dre calling another man "Dah-dah" or some other man disciplining his child. Yet he knows that once you're out of the house, anybody can come in and be over your son.

Andre sours.

Maybe you shouldn't have left.

Fredrick returns. "Here's a chair," he whispers.

"That's alright. I'm not staying. What time is this thing over, anyway?"

"Twelve thirty. Can we talk outside?"

Andre pushes through the door into the lobby and spins around with an attitude stoked as much by his buckled relationship status as with Fredrick's dickering. "What's up?"

40

"Brother, don't take this the wrong way. I'm trying my best to accommodate you, but your response seems to be a dismissive one."

"You don't know me well enough to decipher where I'm coming from," Andre retorts.

"You're right. But we have all kinds of people coming through here. And I'm sure you know that guys get crazy when it comes to their wives, their girlfriends, and their colors."

"Well, I didn't come in here with a hatchet and death on my mind, so you can let all the hot air out of your balloon."

Fredrick smiles. "That's pretty funny, actually. Andre, right?"

"Yeah."

"Some of the men get together on Wednesdays for the Realness. We talk about whatever's on our minds and try to get a truthful perspective on it. And, oh yeah, there's hot wings on the house."

"Nah, I'm good."

"It's a standing invitation."

Fredrick holds the door open for Andre, and once he's back on the street he's bent out of shape and not exactly sure why. He smirks.

Hot wings. Everybody's got a gimmick.

5

Another bone-chilling Jersey night. Andre freezes when he sees a black Crown Victoria parked in front of the bus garage with its rear tire straddling the curb.

You're being paranoid, Dre.

He curls his hands together and blows on them to keep warm.

Inside, two men who possess all the swagger and sloppy chic of undercover DTs are in Dominick's office. Mr. Dominick, Andre's supervisor, tips the scales at a fleshy 375, and is spread out in an oversize chair behind a messy desk. The two men sit across from him. Andre hides himself and pays attention.

"So this guy, he drives the 22?" the white detective inquires.

"Yeah."

The black detective follows up with, "And according to your driving logs, all of his runs were on time that night?"

"That's correct," Dominick says, "but nobody reported hitting anybody. And not reporting an accident is immediate cause for canning."

The black detective flashes a toothy grin. "Usually? What's reported and what happens don't have much to do with each other." He lightly backhands his partner in the chest. "That's why we have jobs."

Andre lowers his chin and heads for the locker room. The white detective spots him.

"Who's that?" he asks Dominick.

"The guy you were just asking about."

Andre is scarcely out of his jeans when Dominick and the detectives enter the locker room. The white DT is scary in the worst way. He's a diminutive man, and his pale, plain-featured face is not the least bit intimidating—but his eyes. They're ice-blue and as lifeless as a baby doll's. The black detective is chocolate brown and brawny.

"Andre, this is Detectives Jackson and Carollo from the JCPD."

Andre works hard to maintain a calm veneer as he rises. "Gentlemen, nice to meet you." He heartily shakes hands with both men.

Jackson smiles. "Andre, how are you tonight?"

"I'm great."

"Good. We'll make this quick so you can get on with your shift. Just a couple of questions." He whips out a pen and notebook, licks his thumb, and flips to an empty page. "Two Sundays ago. You were working, right?"

"Right."

"And your route that night went down Bergen?"

"Yes."

"Past Wegman Parkway?"

"That's correct."

"According to the driving logs, you were on schedule, so you arrived at that intersection around midnight?"

"About that."

Jackson dutifully scribbles notes without looking up. Carollo keeps his lifeless eyes parked on Andre but doesn't move an inch.

Andre starts to perspire. "Excuse me," he says. "Can I put on my pants before we continue? It's a little weird standing here in my underwear."

Jackson smiles. "No problem, buddy. You go right ahead."

Andre slips on his dark blue slacks. "Okay, I'm good now."

"So'd you see anything out of the ordinary that night? Say, a vehicular accident? Maybe even a shooting?" Jackson smiles again.

What's with all the smiling? Andre wonders.

Detective Jackson's sarcasm makes Andre nervous. He knows that he doesn't have to answer without an attorney present, but he'll look as guilty as sin if he refuses, especially with Dominick tonsil clocking.

"Nothing out of the ordinary. No," Andre says.

Jackson licks his thumb again and snaps a business card from his breast pocket.

"If you remember things differently, give me a call. I know from experience that memory and dirty diapers have a lot in common."

Carollo, Dominick, and Andre all look at him.

"Always changing," Jackson says. He beams at the genius of his punch line as Carollo's eyes show the first signs of life.

"Don't quit your day job," Carollo swipes.

A light moment, but Andre knows the drill. Jackson is granting him the opportunity to come to the precinct to talk without Dominick hovering—just in case things went down differently than his present recollection.

Tonight Andre is in the belly of a dinosaur, a 1997 MCI Detroit Diesel Series 60G. From the moment he started the engine, the rattling old bus has steadily ramped up the tension in his head. On a normal night, after driving several miles Andre would no longer notice. But tonight the shaking has whipped up a headache that crouches behind his left eyeball and dances on his optic nerve. His left eye waters.

What could those detectives possibly know?

Andre wipes his eye. Suddenly he's cloaked in panic.

He pulls into the garage, throws the bus into park, and roots through his wallet. He finds the business card and stares at it. After he punches the number into his cell, he checks the time before he hits SEND.

Six fifty-five a.m. I can just leave a message. SEND.

"Hakeem Shabazz."

Andre's tongue sticks to the roof of his mouth.

"Hello?" Hakeem says.

"Yeah . . . this is Andre. Andre Bolden."

"Hey, how are you, man?"

Andre hesitates. "Iffy."

"Well, it's good you called. You should stop by. We can chat informally and I can let you know how I work."

Andre processes what Hakeem says. It all sounds cool, but he is still a shrink, no matter that they both suffered under Dabrowski's doo-doo breath.

"I don't know. I guess I'm not even sure why I called," Andre says.

"Hey, I'm aware of the stigma associated with seeing a shrink in our community. But look at it this way. If you saved my card and you called despite the stigma, that's a pretty good indication that you need to talk to someone. The longer you wait, the easier it is to convince yourself that you can handle things on your own. We humans have the unique ability of thinking more highly of ourselves than we ought to."

45

Andre is surprised at how easily Hakeem seized upon his thought processes without any prompting.

"Are you open right now?" Andre asks, half joking.

"No, but I will be by the time you get here. Use the bottom buzzer."

Second thoughts crawl up into Andre's head the instant he hangs up, and when he sees the building that matches the address on Hakeem's card, it takes everything in him not to turn and walk away.

The two-story brick structure at 674 Communipaw Avenue is hidden behind scaffolding and stumped between two rusty fences. A used-car dealership is to one side and an auto parts store with inventory harvested from junked cars is on the other. The parts of the building that can be seen between the scaffolds are spray-painted with phrases colorful enough to make a sailor blush.

Andre presses the bottom buzzer.

"I'll be right down," crackles through the intercom. After a moment the door swings open. "Andre, welcome."

Hakeem's office is the entire first floor. Partially unpacked boxes outline office furniture wrapped in plastic and positioned in slapdash fashion.

"Still under construction," Hakeem says. "I've only been here two weeks, but since I live upstairs I had the contractor start on the living quarters first."

The inside is freshly renovated with blindingly shiny hardwood floors, and the exposed brick walls are adorned with oversized black-and-white portraits in chunky mahogany frames. "I recognize two of them," Andre says, pointing to the pictures of George Washington Carver and Benjamin Banneker, "but the others I don't know."

"Maybe not their faces, but I'm sure you're familiar with their work. They're all scientists and inventors."

Hakeem approaches the first picture. "This is Benjamin Bradley. He developed a steam engine for use on American warships back in 1850. He couldn't get a patent for it because he was enslaved, so he sold the technology and used the money to buy his freedom."

Hakeem moves to the next frame. "Lewis Latimer invented the electric lamp and the carbon filament in lightbulbs. He was the only black person who worked in Thomas Edison's engineering laboratory."

"Where'd you get these?" Andre asks, marveling at the illustrious black faces that stare back at him.

"Banneker and Latimer were gifts from my dad, but the others I hunted down at different archives and collectors' shows. It's a hobby my dad and I do together.

"This next one is Patricia Bath. She founded the American Institute for the Prevention of Blindness, and she also invented the Laserphaco Probe, which treats cataracts."

Hakeem stops in front of the final picture. "And this is Mark Dean. He led a team of scientists at IBM who pioneered the technology that made personal computers crazy-fast. He also led another group of IBM scientists who created the first one-gig processor chip."

"Why'd you put them down here instead of upstairs in your house?" Andre asks.

"So that all who enter can see what a healthy black mind can accomplish."

"Good idea," Andre says, completely at ease now. "Are you from Jersey City?"

"Born and bred."

"What part?"

"Bergen Square."

"So you went to Hudson Catholic?"

"As a matter of fact, I did."

"I went to Dickinson. We didn't get a chance to stomp y'all rich boys because you were under parochial protection."

Hakeem laughs. "I've never heard it put that way, but you're right, we didn't play the public schools. But I didn't play football. I was on the swim team." He motions to Andre. "Let's go over to my desk. I'd like to put your contact information in my database if that's okay."

"Sure."

Andre studies the titles of the many volumes shoehorned in the bookcase behind Hakeem's head. *The MMPI-2: An Interpretive Manual*, Second Edition. *Reading Statistics and Research*, Fifth Edition. *Introduction to Personality: Toward an Integrative Science of the Person.*

"So what was it that made you call?" Hakeem asks.

"Well. Sometimes I get the feeling that I'm trapped in life's crosshairs."

"Spoken like a true poet. You still doing spoken word?"

"I don't write as much as I used to, but I still have it in me."

"Cool. And I'm sure New Jersey Transit insurance covers psychological treatment, but check with your HR rep to be sure."

Psychological treatment. The thought of it makes Andre's ego crawl.

"So here's how I work," Hakeem says. "Basically, I have two jobs. The first is to help you arrive at the truth about yourself, no matter what it is. The second is to help you accept that truth. And that's where we have to begin. Because only then can we determine what we need to do in order to get you headed in the right direction. Once that happens, we assess what your needs are at that time and then determine if we need to continue to meet. In my line of work, success is determined by how many *former* clients I have. Any questions?" Hakeem asks.

"I guess not."

"So if you're up to it, we can set an appointment for next Tuesday around this time. What do you think?"

Andre kicks around the idea of an actual appointment. "Why not," he says.

What do I have to lose?

6

By day, the exterior of 674 Communipaw Avenue is showing signs of life. By night it's still a horror, fronted by a riley bunch of juvenile offenders dressed in black.

Every several minutes a car pulls up and legal tender is exchanged for tiny vials of white rocks. Capitalism. The street corner variety.

Sentries with smartphones are posted at the top and the bottom of the block to ensure that the gang knows precisely when the JCPD pops the curb. The young capitalists scatter like roaches when headlights from an unmarked car shine light on their dark deeds done beneath the scaffolding.

Above it all, Hakeem peeks through an upstairs window and follows the black Crown Victoria with his eyes as it disappears around the corner. He sees a man relaxing on the stoop of the building, his head caught up in a puff of marijuana smoke. Foot soldiers reappear from the shadows and return to working the street.

The man looks startled and lowers his blunt when Hakeem opens the front door. He scoots to the side to allow Hakeem to descend his own steps. Hakeem offers a hand.

"What's happening, fam? Hakeem Shabazz."

The man snuffs out the blunt on the freshly repaved steps and stands. He contemplates Hakeem's hand before he shakes it.

"Cyclops."

Hakeem smiles. "That's an original name."

Clops is not so easily disarmed.

"I'm sure you brothers noticed that I moved in a few weeks ago," Hakeem says. He gives Clops space to respond, but he doesn't. "I'm a psychologist. I bought this building to establish a counseling center here in the neighborhood."

Clops looks up at the scaffolding. "I see that. And I've been meaning to have a word with you because you erased my sign."

"Sign?"

"OGC," Clops says and points to the sandblasted bricks. He taps on the shiny brass plate beside the front door that announces Hakeem's name and title. "What if I moved your sign?"

Nothing in Hakeem's "Psychological Interventions: Ethnic and Racial Minority Clients and Families" class had prepared him for this.

"I'm 'a ask you something," Clops says. "You put that gold plate up there to let people know this is where you do business, right?"

"Right."

"And that's why I had OGC spray-painted up there two years before you got here, you feel me?"

Hakeem chooses silence. He recognizes that he's losing control of the conversation.

"You ain't from the hood, are you?"

"No, I'm not," Hakeem answers.

"I didn't think so 'cuz you don't seem to know who OGC is."

"Original Gun Clappers."

Clops pauses, looking surprised.

Hakeem sees an opening and seizes it. "Smif-n-Wessun, 1994. That was my favorite song when I was in sixth grade."

51

"Yeah, you know the song. But what you *don't* know is that OGC run these blocks," Clops says.

By now two of Clops's teenage lieutenants, Rahjaan and Smooth B., have gathered around. Rahjaan pokes his chest out and says to Hakeem, "OGC, nigga. Whassup?"

"With all due respect, young bro. Calling me that is worse than cursing me out," Hakeem says.

Rahjaan looks to Clops as if to receive guidance. That was apparently not the answer he expected.

Hakeem motions to the door. "I want to show you brothers something." He leads them into his office and stops in front of the Benjamin Bradley photograph.

"This man was enslaved, but he invented technology that's still in use around the world to this day. Can you imagine how many times he was called *nigger* and couldn't do anything about it?"

Rahjaan looks at Clops again.

"When we call ourselves *nigger*, we're willingly drinking the same poison we were forced to swallow back in the day. And that kind of poison kills your self-worth whether you realize it or not."

Clops speaks up. "We ain't down for no history lesson, bruh."

"That's cool," Hakeem says. "But can I holler at you for a minute?"

Clops nods, and Rahjaan and Smooth B. step out and close the door behind them. Clops traipses freely through the newly minted space.

"Looks good." He turns to Hakeem. "I see you put those fancy bars on the windows, though. That's gonna jack me up in the summer 'cuz this is where I bring my feminine tenders to do my Marvin Gaye."

"That's why I wanted to talk to you—"

Clops raises his hand. "If this is the part where you ask me to be a good neighbor and move my operation, you either smoking that white or you need some counseling yourself."

Hakeem chooses silence again, only this time the choice is strategic.

"Listen, bruh," Clops says. "We doing business out of the same location. But any smart businessman listens when he's made an offer he can't refuse, you feel me?"

"No, I don't."

Clops spreads his arms wide with palms turned upward. He smiles big, and the track lighting that Hakeem installed above the photographs reflects off his two platinum-crowned incisors. "Make me an offer I can't refuse," he says.

Hakeem sorts through several approaches, all the while maintaining a cool countenance. "How about you relocate, and in return I give you a year of counseling sessions free of charge."

The joy of expectation drains from Clops's face. "Nig—man, you *are* crazy. You think I'm gonna trade my flagship location for free sessions from a dreadlocked shrink?" Clops's words ricochet off the exposed brick walls and dissolve into the shiny wood floor. "I'll tell you what. Since you a positive brother, I'll move across the street. That's about all I can offer you." He heads for the door. "Welcome to the hood."

Andre doesn't like police stations. It's the way people look at you. Whether it's a cop or a suspect, everyone's eyes seem to say the same thing. *You in here, so you must be guilty of something.*

And that's precisely the look that Detective Jackson gives Andre as he leans back in his chair and kicks both feet up on his desk.

"So you're telling me you hit the guy. *With your bus*. But he got up and kept running?"

"That's what I'm saying, but *hit* is too strong a word. Really, I only grazed him."

"Why didn't you tell anybody then?"

Andre carefully considers his words. "Because snitching can be dangerous."

Jackson looks exasperated. "I don't get it. I just don't get it."

Andre is not sure what Jackson doesn't get, but he's not asking any questions.

"And you have no idea what the shooter looked like?"

"It was dark."

"I gotta tell you, Andre. I appreciate you coming in, but what you're saying doesn't really add up, and here's why." Jackson leans over the coffee-stained blotter on his desk. "If you didn't see what the shooter looked like, then how would it be snitching if you reported the accident?"

Ice coats the walls of Andre's stomach as he realizes that what he's saying doesn't exactly amount to good sense.

"What're you hiding?" Jackson presses.

"Nothing."

"I want to help you, Andre. But we have to be willing to help each other. Your boss finds out you were in an accident that you didn't report, and that could be curtains for your job. And New Jersey Transit's a good gig, especially for a brother in this economy. But I need you to be honest with me."

"I'm telling you everything I know."

"Clipping someone who runs in front of your bus isn't a crime. So I'm still not getting why you didn't report the accident."

"I was scared."

"Of what?"

"I saw a man get killed. How am I supposed to think

straight after seeing something like that? After I didn't report the accident, I couldn't just go back to my boss and say, 'Oh, by the way, I had an accident the other night.' And that's the truth."

"Truth is, law enforcement is about give-and-take. You *give* me something that I use to *take* crooks off the street. But you're not doing that, Andre. And I can't have you walking around freely and you know something you're not telling me. The rule of law can't survive like that. And that's the long and short of it. You feel me, bro?"

Okay, now he wants to play the "brother" card.

"Look, I'm from Greenville just like you," Jackson continues. "Been here my whole life. So let's work this out because I come to work every day to improve these streets." He extends his hand across the desk to Andre and smiles. "I'm here when you need me."

Andre scoots out of the office.

———

Jackson rubs his callused palms into his eyes.

I need one of those cushy private security gigs babysitting Park Avenue rich guys under house arrest.

He rises and studies the precinct map of Greenville on the wall. Clusters of red dots vividly depict the neighborhood's hot spots.

But then you'd be left to the Carollos of the world that don't give a what about you.

He touches the map and pronounces under his breath, "Greenville, I love you, but you're killing me."

———

Back in front of the police station, Andre looks toward Wegman Parkway. He blows slowly through pursed lips and dials Sandra to release the anxiety that bubbles in his chest.

"Hello?"

"Can I come see my son?"

"I have a meeting to go to and I was going to take him. But if you're coming right now, I can leave him with you."

"You sound excited."

"I am. See you when you get here."

She's off the phone before Andre can ask why.

Andre is out in the cold. He stands on the fractured pavement in front of Sandra's building and looks up at her silhouette flitting back and forth behind the drapes in the living room window. He can tell by her lively hand gestures that she's in the middle of an animated phone conversation.

She's still on the call when she opens the door. She actually smiles at Andre and directs him in with a nod. Little Dre is asleep in the playpen in the center of the room.

Andre takes a seat on the couch and observes his little man. He's a miniature gentleman, complete with a button-down dress shirt, sweater vest, blue jeans, and tiny Timberland boots. His pacifier dangles from his bottom lip and he cracks a dreamy grin while he sleeps. Andre smiles.

"I don't have one yet, but I'm definitely going to get one when I get paid next week," Sandra is saying. "Okay, I'll get that version. See you in a bit, bye. Hey, Dre. How are you?"

"Not as good as you." Andre hasn't seen Sandra this bubbly in a hot minute. "What are you so happy about?"

"I'm making new friends. And one of them invited me to a group at his house."

"*His* house?"

"Yes. And the other people who are going to be there are all—"

"So you're going to some dude's house and you were going to take my son?"

"It's not like that, Dre."

"Men can't be friends with women. Especially a woman who looks like you."

"Thank you for the compliment. And you know I don't agree with you. But as I was saying—"

"Where'd you meet this guy?"

"At work, but I'd appreciate it if you'd let me at least get halfway through my sentence before you cut me off."

Andre sinks deeper into the couch.

"This group is something called a home cell, and what they do is—"

"I don't want you taking my son to no dude's house. I don't care what you're going over there for."

"You know what, Dre? I'm trying to be nice, and you come over here with your stinky attitude, trying to get me upset because something's bothering you."

"Did it ever occur to you to ask me how I'm doing?" Andre asks. "Do you even care how I'm feeling? You just go into telling me how happy you are because some dude invited you to his house."

"There you go twisting my words around."

Little Dre starts to stir, and without missing a syllable, Sandra continues her rant in a razor-sharp whisper.

"I'm trying to get on with my life, Dre. And you don't seem to be happy about that. You just want me to be sad and miserable and sit around here waiting for you to call. Why, Dre?"

Sandra's eyes well up with tears. Andre hates to see her cry, but at the same time, he can't bear the thought of her slipping away.

For the first several months after their breakup, Sandra seemed to exist under a dark cloud. Something about that made Andre secure. Knowing that she was having a tough time living without him was oddly empowering. Andre convinced himself that Sandra forced his hand, and that's why he chose to break if off with her. But deep inside he knew that wasn't true.

"I'm sorry," he says.

"Well, I'm going to be late. He has two bottles in the refrigerator, and I fixed you a plate if you want it. It's in the oven."

Sandra slips on her coat and out the door. Andre can hear her rustling around on the other side. He pictures her in the mirror as she dabs her eyes with Kleenex, retrieves her eyebrow pencil and lipstick brush, and repairs her tearstained makeup.

Andre lifts Little Dre from the playpen, and he sprawls onto Andre's shoulders and squeezes his back with tiny hands. Father takes pleasure in son pressed against his chest and rocks him, feeling high off of Little Dre's baby-powder scent.

"Daddy loves you so much . . . and I know it might not seem like it, but I love your mother too."

Beyond the front door, Sandra is astonished at what stares at her from the oval looking glass. She smiles and whispers softly as if afraid to even say it. "Forgot I was beautiful."

She notes the bleak, colorless walls that surround her. *But my life isn't.*

She disappears down the stairs.

7

The scaffolds and graffiti that cleaved to the front of Hakeem's building just last week are gone. Andre surveys the architectural significance of the structure that is constructed of red brick and limestone. A steep stone stoop located in the center of the first floor leads up to a strong mahogany door framed by a segmental stone arch. Decorative roof cornices run the length of the building. Last week the shoddy edifice blended perfectly with the surrounding decay, but now it looks stunningly out of place.

Inside, Hakeem is more serious than he was on Andre's initial visit. The two are seated on opposing leather love seats separated by a glass coffee table. A stack of Styrofoam cups and three large bowls of cereal await them. One bowl is loaded with Lucky Charms, the second with Raisin Bran, and the third with Honey Nut Cheerios.

Hakeem points. "Please. Partake."

Andre chooses Lucky Charms as Hakeem scoops up Raisin Bran with a plastic serving spoon. They munch their cereal trail-mix style.

"Even though we had a class together, the truth is, we hardly know each other," Hakeem says. "And even if we were best friends, it's been nine years, so we have to get reacquainted and build a level of trust so that our time together will be productive. Does that make sense?"

"Sure."

"So tell me. What three words would best describe you?"

Andre weighs the question, and in the absence of a definitive answer, his mind diverts to the sound of the cereal crunching in his ears. "Three words? That's tough."

"Let's try this then. I'll say a word, and if you think it describes you, I'll write it down."

"Okay."

"Hungry."

Andre gets the joke and smiles.

Hakeem continues. "Content. Happy. Cross—"

"What do you mean by *cross*?"

"Easily aroused to anger."

"No, that's not me. Go ahead."

"Creative—"

"That's one," Andre says.

Hakeem writes it down. "Loving. Determined. Negative. Depressed . . ."

Andre fixates on "depressed." In his mind, that has always been a loaded word because it proved that a person was unable to deal with what life threw at them. So Andre never latched "depressed" onto himself. It would signal that life had finally gotten the better of him. He resurfaces from the bounds of his thoughts when Hakeem stops talking.

"You tuned out," Hakeem says. "Right after I said 'depressed.'" He stares at Andre and waits for a response that never comes. "What is it about 'depressed' that grabbed your attention?" Hakeem asks.

"Depressed people tend to be weak."

"Why do you say that?"

"Because that's not a normal way to live."

"I would agree with that. Have you ever been depressed?"

"That depends on how you define it."

"A state of feeling sad, marked especially by inactivity or difficulty in thinking and concentration. Feelings of dejection and hopelessness, and sometimes suicidal tendencies."

"I think everybody has felt that way at some point," Andre replies.

"Do you feel that way now?"

"Well . . . I mean, not the killing myself part, but it's a lot going on in my life."

"Anything you're comfortable sharing?"

Andre takes a deep breath. "Me and my girl broke up a little over a year ago. We have a son together, and . . . I just can't be in the relationship the way she wants me to be."

"How does she want you to be?"

"Well . . . she's a really good woman. Smart, beautiful, takes excellent care of our son. Excels on her job, keeps a clean house. I don't have any complaints. But now she's developing a new life."

"Did she break it off with you or did you break it off with her?"

"I broke it off with her. But I pay my child support and I'm there for my son, so I'm not a bad guy."

"Does she think you're a bad guy? Because I don't know enough about the dynamics of the relationship to take a position either way."

"It's just that sometimes I feel guilty about the way everything went down."

"What is it that keeps you from being in the relationship?"

"She wants to know where I am all the time and who I'm with. She doesn't trust me."

"Why not?"

"Because I'm not perfect. We were together seven years."

"Andre, I'm not getting straight answers from you. You seem to be on the defensive. You have to realize that I'm not the enemy. I'm on your side. But that doesn't mean that I want to just get you in here to make you feel good about yourself. What we're after is truth. But let's shift gears a minute. I know you're creative, so let's use that. Could you write a poem that describes you before our next session?"

Andre smiles. "I should be able to do that."

"But don't hold back, and be true to yourself. Bear in mind that what we discuss here stays here."

"No doubt."

"Let's stop here. Since this is our first session, I want to keep it short. Do you have any questions?"

"No, I'm good."

Hakeem stands and extends his hand. "So I'll see you next week?"

Andre shakes his hand firmly. "Same time."

When Andre steps out of the office, he sees two teenagers across the street. *Those young brothers should be in school right now.*

Smooth B. keeps watch and Rahjaan gives Andre a nod that says, "If you're looking, I'm holding."

Andre looks away, confused.

Why would Hakeem open an office across the street from where people sling?

Andre slips into Torch & Basil, a sassy dining establishment stashed among luxury high-rises in downtown Jersey City. Andre is almost upon Sandra before she looks up and says in her West Essex County lilt, "Good evening and welcome to Torch & Bas—"

Andre smiles and produces a blue iris and pink tulip bouquet.

62

"What are you doing here?" Sandra asks.

"I just want you to know how much I appreciate you and all that you're doing with Little Dre."

Sandra accepts the flowers and noses their aroma. "Every time you gave me flowers, it was because you either messed up or you were trying to keep me from leaving. What are you up to now?"

Sandra's words skid across Andre's face like hot tire rubber. A formally attired, middle-aged white couple enters the restaurant. Andre notices that Sandra is impeccably dressed in a black jersey dress with a ruche bodice that flows into a swingy skirt that stops just above her knee. He has on his bus uniform. He measures himself against Sandra and the couple and feels especially out of place.

Sandra seems to observe Andre's awkwardness and gently touches his hand as his gaze sweeps the floor. She whispers, "I'll call you later."

Andre stands outside of the restaurant and peers in at Sandra through smoked glass.

This is her world. Not mine.

In an instant, Andre sees Sandra the way he did when he was first taken by her in humanities class: a beautiful gem from a different world that he desires to have and to hold.

She's as far out of my reach now as she was then.

———

Sandra spies Andre out of the corner of her eye as he turns away and trudges up the block.

8

Sandra's emotions are tied in a butterfly knot. Her mother hasn't spoken to her the entire drive because she's apparently as uneasy as Sandra is. Little Dre is a welcome distraction, and he occupies both of their motherly graces on the eighteen-mile ride from Martin Luther King Drive in Jersey City to Upper Mountain Avenue in Montclair.

By the time Mrs. Horton creeps through the foothills of the Watchung Mountains, Little Dre is spent from all of the correction in coo-speak. Mrs. Horton parks her 2011 Mercedes E550 beside a spotless 1993 Dodge Dynasty LE. The circular driveway and stately Italianate Victorian are lorded over by mature oaks that populate an ample-sized lot. Mrs. Horton is out of the car and unsaddles Little Dre before Sandra has a chance to move. Sandra closes her eyes before heading inside.

Please let there be peace tonight.

Mr. Horton's face brightens the instant Little Dre appears. Mrs. Horton holds him in front of her as a weapon of conciliation.

"Come on over here and see ol' Gramps!"

She hands him off.

Sandra leans in the doorway of the parlor with Little Dre's

baby bag slung across her shoulder. She watches her parents smother Little Dre with affection. Mr. Horton pauses and says, "Baby Love, are you just going to stand over there the whole night?"

"Happy sixtieth, Daddy."

"Thank you, Baby Love."

Sandra places a small gift box on a plush table that showcases a menagerie of tiny framed photographs of Sandra at different stages of her life.

Snaggletoothed Sandra minus two front teeth.

Sandra at her first dance recital.

Sandra in her Montclair High School cheerleader uniform.

Sandra graduating high school with a yellow satin honor stole draped around her neck.

She takes a seat in what was her favorite chair when she was growing up, a turn-of-the-century occasional armchair that rests on casters. She looks around the parlor.

Nothing ever changes here.

The mantel of the baronial oak fireplace features colorful wax flowers under glass domes. Mr. Horton is perched in his domain, an Italian, fruitwood, upholstered sectional with handmade doilies draped across the arms. The thick floral carpet blends seamlessly with the wild floral highlights on the striped wallpaper.

"Daddy, turning sixty is a big deal. Don't you think you should've invited some people over?"

"Baby Love, you're here. And that's the best present I've had in a long time. Besides, with people come their problems, even when they're the bearers of birthday wishes. Wilda, take that young fella in the kitchen and get him some of those goody bars I made."

Mr. Horton removes a neatly folded kerchief from his breast pocket and cleans his bifocals. He is quite handsome once you get beyond the black square glasses, receding hair-line, and ample folds in his raw umber face.

"So tell me, Baby Love. How are things with you?"

Sandra hasn't seen her father in sixteen months, despite the fact that Mrs. Horton babysits Little Dre here at the house on nights when Sandra works. So she knew that he was going to isolate her at some point during the visit. She just didn't expect it to happen so soon.

"Daddy, are you really interested in how I feel?"

"Of course I am. Why would you ask that?"

"Because if I tell you things are good, you won't believe me. And if I tell you things are bad, you'll say I told you so."

Mr. Horton replaces his glasses. "I'm extending an olive branch. Why are you rejecting it?"

Sandra holds her peace as she sifts through the mental list of offenses that she has kept over the last seven years.

"How about we start with you not letting Mommy have a baby shower for me?"

"Do you know why I didn't let her have the shower?"

"And I'm not just going to forget that, Daddy. Now you try to act like you love Little Dre so much."

"Baby Love, you didn't answer my question. I said, do you know *why* I didn't allow your mother to have the shower?"

Sandra shakes her head.

"You chose to start a family in a way that was contrary to how you were raised. And having a baby shower would be honoring that and celebrating the consequences of the sin that you *chose* to get into."

Sandra closes her eyes tight.

I will NOT cry in front of him.

She takes a deep breath and says calmly, "Andre is a baby, not a sin."

Mr. Horton touches Sandra's chin and gently guides it toward his. "Andre is my grandson, Baby Love. And no human life is a sin. But fornication is. And this has never been about Little Andre. This is about you and his father."

"You can stop talking about me and his father, because we're not together anymore."

"So now what, you're just another statistic? Your mother and I poured our whole lives into you. And you throw it away on a lowlife who doesn't have the decency to marry you and then leaves you?"

Sandra stands, but not before a tear sneaks out. "Mommy, I'm ready to go."

Mrs. Horton appears. "What's wrong?" She looks at Mr. Horton. "Dewey, what did you say to her?"

Mr. Horton looks deflated. He says softly, "If she wants to go . . . go ahead and take her."

Little Dre's wide eyes go back and forth between his grandfather and his mother. He finally lays his head on his grandmother's shoulder and says, "Pa-pa. Ma-ma."

Sandra swipes him from her mother's arms and leaves the room. In an instant she's back to snatch up Little Dre's baby bag.

"Baby Love, you know I love you," Mr. Horton says.

"Goodbye, Daddy."

Andre fingers the bumps on the inner arc of the steering wheel of number 5201. When he slips the key in the ignition and turns, the bus quietly springs to life. He releases the gearshift and the transmission glides into drive. Together, Andre and the bus are ready for the wiles of the night.

Tonto raps on the door. "Dominick wants to see you."

Andre hesitates.

"Everything cool?" Tonto inquires.

"Yeah."

"I hope so because y'all interrupting my dinner."

Andre trails Tonto into the building. Dominick doesn't look up when Andre knocks on the door. "Sit down," he says.

Andre does. He can't recall ever conversing with the top of a meaty, balding head. Dominick has strategically stretched several wisps of hair across the brown splotches flecked across the surface of his pink scalp.

Dominick looks up. "Why didn't you tell me you hit somebody?"

Andre is blindsided.

"Bird got your tongue?" Dominick asks.

Andre rehearses what he said to Detective Jackson. "Mr. Dominick, I was scared. I wasn't thinking straight. A man got killed right in front of me. I realized later that I needed to report what happened, but I thought it would only get me in more trouble since I didn't mention it right away."

Dominick toggles his noggin from side to side. "This whole thing is putting us in a very bad light, Andre. The JCPD thinks a driver of mine is withholding information related to an unsolved murder. That's why we have protocols in place, to prevent this kind of thing."

Andre is quiet.

"Automatic suspension. Two weeks. No pay. You're a hard worker and I like you, and that's the only reason I'm not firing you. But rules are rules and I have to follow them. You got anything to say for yourself?"

Andre doesn't.

"I need your keys."

Dominick sticks out a king-sized paw and accepts Andre's key ring.

Tonto's head pops out of the break room as soon as Andre steps out of Dominick's office.

"Yo, Dre, I forgot to tell you. That night you didn't come in? A guy in a snappy suit stopped me in front of the garage and started asking me a bunch of questions about your route. Said he was your cousin. He must think I'm stupid because he never said your name. What's up with that?"

"I don't know," Andre says.

"Dude creeped me out with his eyes, though," Tonto says. He peers closer at Andre. "Everything cool in there?"

"No." Andre turns up his collar and steps onto the street. He shudders from apprehension more than cold as he searches up and down the block. Streams of light from the streetlamps suddenly run together. He tastes tears at the corners of his mouth. Andre wipes them clean and steels himself.

On the bus ride home, Andre opens his tiny spiral notebook to a blank page bookmarked with an ATM receipt that shows a balance of $1,287.23. His $800 rent is due in six days and the $500 for Sandra will be automatically transferred into her account the week after that.

Andre scratches out a verse.

When he gets home, he splits open the Dark Poet notebook and transfers the rough lines of the fledging poem. Next, he forces his way into cordoned-off portions of his mind and drags out stanza after stanza. When he is finished, Andre does something he hasn't done in a long time—he stands in front of the mirror and gives life to his words by speaking them.

> I look at life through the eyes of one who has danced
> with misery.
> I am death. Waltzing with vexation—serenaded by a
> dissonant dirge in a minor key.
> My world is not my world—but terror remains real.
> And laughter is but temporary respite from a tan-
> gible gloom.
> But I cannot take my own life.

What prevents me?
The sea of tears my son would cry,
Seeing his father lowered in the ground with his own
    blood on his hands.
So I press on.
Steer clear of my person—you that are wise,
Lest you too be afflicted by my reckless masquerade.
The tears are all gone now.
Escaped on the wings of aborted youth.
There is no life here.
Only eternal darkness and the flame
Of a cold shame. That never ceases.

Hakeem delicately places the poem on his desk. Andre tries to shroud his face in a tenuous, emotionless gaze.

"Wow." It's the shortest sentence Andre has ever heard Hakeem speak.

Andre looks down because he has never been sure of how exactly to accept praise. At the same time, he expected his work to be applauded. If it wasn't, he became palsied by a deep-seated insecurity.

He wants to scream. The oppressive frustration of constantly being ripped between conflicting emotions is taking a toll on his mind.

"What inspired such dark, powerful words?" Hakeem asks.

Andre distends his cheeks and expels all of the carbon dioxide from his lungs. "I lost my parents when I was nine."

Hard-boiled pity is never the reaction that Andre desires. Rather, he hopes, even against hope, that someone can help him return to the life that he knows is gone forever. So he monitors the reaction of Hakeem, who stares back at him without a trace of pity.

"What happened?"

"An accident."

"You want to talk about it?"

"No."

"Any particular reason why?"

Andre sorts through the many.

Does it still hurt? Yes.

Will discussing it make it any better? No.

However, it's too late because the mere mention of the accident gives Andre's mind license to drag him back to the night.

He recalls the smell of gas and the eternal wait. Still and all, it wouldn't have mattered because his parents were dead and he knew it. Andre never cried because his father always told him to be solution minded instead of problem focused.

He unstrapped his seat belt and tried the back doors. Jammed. He crawled to the front and those were stuck too. He was relieved because it would have been too scary to venture out into the dark by himself.

What if there were monsters out there?

So Andre huddled between his parents' mangled bodies. One of his mother's hands was twisted behind the seat, but the other was free, so he held fast to it. He lay on his father's lap and closed his eyes so that he could block out the sight of their injuries. He wanted to remember his parents as they were.

"Would you want to talk about it if it were you?" Andre says curtly to Hakeem.

"I don't know," Hakeem admits.

Andre sits silently for longer than what feels comfortable. "It's the images."

More silence.

Finally, Hakeem asks, "What kind of an accident?"

"Auto."

"Where did it happen?"

"Virginia. The Dismal Swamp Canal. A two-lane road that runs alongside the water."

"You ran off the road?"

Andre nods.

Hakeem doesn't fill in the long pause with words. "How did you feel when help eventually came?" he asks finally.

"Like I was alone in the world."

Hakeem looks down at the poem. He reads through it again and unconsciously drums his index finger on the desk. "I am death," he says and looks up at Andre. "What did you mean when you wrote that?"

"That's how I feel."

"Describe that for me."

"It's like . . ." Andre smiles in an attempt to lighten the heaviness that has settled in the room.

Hakeem notices. "It's okay for you to feel uncomfortable. You lost something that you can never replace. But death, even when it's tragic, doesn't have to keep you from rebuilding a full life."

9

Andre lies on his air mattress, fingers locked behind his clean-shaven head as he stares into the darkness that clogs his tiny apartment.

The accident.

His phone buzzes. It's Sandra. He lets it go to voice mail, but the suspense of why she called gets the better of him.

"Hey, Dre. It's Sahn. I wanted to see if you could watch the little man tonight. I have a meeting and I want to make sure he's not getting into everything. Call me if you can do it. Bye."

"Sahn" is the love name Andre gave Sandra when they were still in college. He calls her right back.

"Hello?" she answers.

"Is this Sahn?" he asks sarcastically.

"Sorry, that kind of slipped out. Can you do it?"

"What time do you want me to be there?"

"You can come now if you want. I figured I'd cook you something as payment for your services."

"You don't have to pay me to spend time with my son. I'm off for the next couple of weeks, so you can tell your mom that I can watch him while you're at work."

"You're on vacation?"

"Something like that."

"Why didn't you tell me?"

"Now who's quizzing who on what they do?"

Sandra's giggle tickles Andre's ears before quiet drops in. To him, the silence is reminiscent of the soundless communication that turned their phone calls into all-night affairs when they first got together. Just knowing that the other was on the line was enough to keep them wide-eyed for hours.

Sandra breaks the whimsical silence. "I'll see you when you get here."

Andre painstakingly irons his Daniel Hechter V-neck jumper sweater with stitched harlequin diamonds up the right front. His black flannel dress pants hug tighter than they used to but still look sharp. A touch of Joop behind each ear and the box-sized apartment is spiced like a perfumery.

Andre watches himself in the mirror, and the man who smiles back at him looks like the old Dre. Suddenly he's intoxicated by the giddy pleasure of pursuit.

Andre taps his signature knock on Sandra's front door. *Tap-tap, tap-TAP.*

A smooth-faced, slender brown man with thick eyebrows and wavy hair answers. Andre recognizes him as the hot-wing peddler from New Jersey Truth and experiences the sensation of being punched in the stomach—hard.

"Hey, how's it going?" Fredrick says. "I met you a few Sundays ago."

Andre pushes past him and searches the apartment for Sandra, Little Dre, and any flimsy excuse to swing on the wing man. Sandra comes out of the bathroom holding a naked-bottomed Little Dre and seems to notice the ruin in Andre's eyes.

She quickly explains, "The baby got stinky all over his

clothes and I had to clean him up in the bathroom, so I couldn't get to the door."

"Dah-dah!" Little Dre glows and twists from Sandra's arms into Andre's grasp.

"What's he doing here?" Andre demands, jamming a thumb at Fredrick.

"He's part of the group that's—"

"What does that have to do with him answering your door?"

Fredrick steps in. Andre pushes Little Dre back into Sandra's arms and squares off.

"I'm going tell you once to back up off me."

"Andre, I'm telling you, it's nothing—"

"You don't know me, so don't say my name!" Andre balls up both fists. "And I *said* back up off me!"

Fredrick throws his hands up in surrender.

"And I advise you to step outside!"

Fredrick backs out of the door with his hands still raised while Andre turns his attention to Sandra. "I knew something was up, talking about 'this is Sahn.'"

"Dre, you are really out of line right now, so I'm going to ask you to leave."

"Why? So you can run off to your meeting with pretty boy while I'm here watching Dre?"

Sandra draws back to smack Andre but stops. "The meeting is here!" she screams. "And Fredrick came to help me prepare since this is the first one I'm hosting!"

Andre's canine psychology kicks in.

Yeah, right.

He's struck by how naive women are when it comes to discerning a man's true motive for helping them with anything.

Sandra grabs the phone. "I said get out, Andre, or I'm calling the police!"

Andre suspects that Sandra's threat is just another case of emotional high jinks, but he's not taking any chances. The last thing he wants is to wind up back at the police station.

"Sandra, hold on."

When Andre opens the door, Fredrick is seated on the hallway steps. Andre waves him in and mumbles a rootless apology, but he doesn't trust the wing peddler any farther than he can throw him across the room and through the window onto King. He extends his hand to Fredrick, who ignores it and reenters the apartment.

For the next half hour, Andre huddles in the bedroom with Little Dre. Between countless encores of "Itsy Bitsy Spider," "If I Was a Great Big Bumble Bee," and "Old McDonald," he strains to capture dashes of Fredrick and Sandra's conversation. Fredrick's slick baritone carries farther than Sandra's dainty soprano, so Andre can only scrape together Fredrick's end of what's being said.

"You're not leading the conversation, you're just facilitating it . . . Your experience is your experience, and that's what everyone is interested in hearing . . . The question is how did it affect *you*? No one expects you to be a scholar . . ."

All of this makes Andre crazy.

Why wouldn't she like somebody like him?

Fredrick is magazine handsome, refined, and graced with a natural athletic build. Moments like these are when Andre regrets not having a degree the most.

After twenty minutes of Andre's tone-deaf serenades, Little Dre is out cold on Daddy's shoulder, rocked to sleep on a bellyful of warm milk.

Andre feels extraordinarily reduced—sequestered in the back room of what used to be his apartment, babysitting— while Sandra yuks it up with a smooth dude and a company of strangers. It's bad enough that he drives a bus for a living.

But I'm not even doing that now.

It occurs to Andre that he must be nice to Sandra since the shortfall from the suspension will affect his child support payments.

I still don't regret flipping the way I did.

He just wishes he hadn't done it in front of Sandra. Andre hoists his chin high.

The wing man needs to know that Sandra isn't some lonely damsel who needs to be whisked away on his white horse.

There's a knock at the door. Andre opens it. It's the stocky dude who controlled the stage at New Jersey Truth.

"What's happening, brother? I'm Rock."

"Andre."

They engage in an equally firm handshake.

"When Sandra told us you were back here, I thought, 'What's he doing back there? He should be out here with us.' Care to join us, brother?"

Andre wavers between curiosity and embarrassment. He's not sure what Sandra or Fredrick told the others about their encounter, but even if they said nothing, Andre has never been comfortable in situations where he didn't know anyone or where he wasn't in control. Nevertheless, curiosity wins.

Seven people are sorted throughout the living room. In addition to Fredrick, Sandra, and Rock, there's a young Latino couple, an attractive African American girl who looks like she's fresh out of high school, and the other usher that Andre encountered at New Jersey Truth.

Everyone stands to shake Andre's hand as Sandra introduces him as "Little Dre's father." Something about that hurts. Sandra doesn't acknowledge anything more from their seven-year connection.

But is there still a connection?

Lately, Sandra hasn't demonstrated any interest in Andre

other than his services as a babysitter. Even so, he has functioned under the illusion that he could have her back at any time. That may have been true in the early stages of their breakup, but now?

Resentment wrestles Andre into his seat. He notices that everyone has a Bible, a notebook, and a pen. He feels like a beast among the meek. Rock slips him a small Testament and whispers, "We're talking about the law of sowing and reaping."

Andre stares at him blankly.

"Galatians 6:7?" Rock queries.

Andre has no idea what Galatians is or where to find it. Rock leans over and gives him a clue. "Table of contents."

"Right."

Do not be deceived, God is not mocked; for whatever a man sows, that he will also reap.

"Andre, we're going around the room and everyone is giving an example of how they've seen the law of sowing and reaping play out in their lives," Sandra says. "Rock is next."

"Oh, it's on me?" Rock asks, looking around. "Okay. Well, the biggest one for me is probably my greatest regret. I started a gang fifteen years ago, got locked up for ten, and when I got out my nephew was running it. Now when I try to tell him about life and how I've changed, he doesn't want to hear it. Why? Because he learned how to thug by watching me."

Now the ferocious air that Rock gives off makes sense. Andre is surprised that a man of the cloth started a gang and did a dime in the clink. Even more surprising is that he openly shares it with a roomful of people.

I wonder how much of our situation Sandra has shared with these folks?

By the time it's Andre's turn to speak, his wonder has hardened into annoyance. "You all may attribute sowing and reaping to God, but that's the same thing as karma, and that has nothing to do with God. Why do Christians try to make God responsible for things he has nothing to do with? And that's assuming God even exists in the first place."

Andre is careful not to peek Sandra's way, because he can sense the blast of fury emanating from her eyes. He smiles on the inside because everyone in the room seems to be searching for an appropriate response.

"My brother," Rock calmly replies, "on the one hand you say that Christians put God in places that he doesn't belong, but then you question the existence of God. Which do you believe? Because it doesn't sound like you're sure what you think."

Andre's inner smile turns downward. He didn't anticipate a response, much less one that he couldn't readily smack down. He ponders Rock's question, and rather than answer, he turns the tables and tosses a question back at him. "Can you prove to me, right now, that God exists?"

"Of course not, 'cuz you're committed to not believing."

Andre is thrown. He expected a verbal joust.

"Anything else you'd like to say before the young lady continues her discussion of sowing and reaping?" Rock asks.

If black people could turn red from embarrassment, Andre would look like Tonto. For the rest of the meeting, he stews in silence.

At the end of the night, Andre loiters in the kitchen and waits for the last person to leave. On his way out, Rock slips Andre a card and says, "Call anytime. I like debating. That's all we did in the pen." Andre looks at the generic white business card with blocky black type.

ROCKY JENKINS, SERVANT LEADER. NEW JERSEY TRUTH.

He slips the card in his pocket, closes the door, and notices that the large dent that Sandra kicked in it years ago is still there.

Behind him, her laughter erupts and bounces around the kitchen like a ball of flames.

"What's so funny?" Andre asks, even though he knows exactly why she's laughing.

"I'm sorry." Sandra seems to be having a tough time getting her hee-hawing under control. "You came over here acting like a—" Her snickering explodes again.

I can't believe I let that dude silence me like that in front of my girl.

Sandra catches her breath. "You came over here acting like a complete fool, and by the end of the night you looked like the biggest fool in the room. You sowed foolishness, and that's exactly what you reaped!"

Andre is ready to move on—to the more serious matters that he stuck around to discuss.

"But I'm glad I can find something to laugh about, because you embarrassed me twice tonight," Sandra continues. "And if that's the way you're going to act with my friends, I can't have you around anymore."

Andre gets down on one knee and takes her hand. "Sandra, I was an idiot a lot in the seven years we were together. Even tonight I showed out. But you and Little Dre are the only good things in my life, and the thought of you being with someone else makes me crazy. I want to try and make it work between us."

Sandra covers her mouth and Andre braces himself.

Please don't start crying. I haven't even said anything yet.

Nevertheless, Andre's insides get warm because his charm still works. He hadn't planned to bow the knee, but at this point he's prepared to do anything to get Sandra back. And he's relieved because he was starting to think she had lost her love for him.

Sandra uncovers her mouth and clasps Andre's hand in hers. "Dre . . . I don't know what to say. But it's not like that with us anymore. I'm sorry."

10

The Jersey City Free Public Library is a four-story, Italian Renaissance building on the corner of Jersey Avenue and Montgomery Street. The elaborate lintel detail along the roofline looks like a row of patina-green afros set ablaze.

Andre climbs the palatial marble steps from the first to the second floor. He's not accustomed to being out at this hour on a weekday. He spots the perfect place to write, an empty table drenched in midmorning sun. The light that cascades through the large window warms Andre's face despite temperatures outside that are barely above freezing.

He produces his notebook and is confronted by the dilemma of the blank page. In search of inspiration, he looks to the street. A New Jersey Transit bus turns off Montgomery onto Jersey, and all of a sudden Andre feels free, like his whole life is ahead of him and his future is pregnant with possibility. The thought is so full of life that it gives Andre pause, because he's not sure where a notion so fanciful would come from.

Auntie Cheeks appears in his mind, and it's as if she's sitting directly across the table from him. She flashes that wry smile that reveals her three missing teeth. She launches into what she always said before she left him. "You don't have to be afraid, because God'll protect you. But don't open the door for nobody."

The image makes Andre numb, so he invokes more comforting thoughts of his grandmother. He can almost feel her gentle hand rub his head while she sang:

> Grandmother's little baby.
> Grandmother's little sweet baby boy.
> Grandmother's baby is Grandmother's boy.

Andre covers his face. Tears bleed through his fingers as he whispers the words of the song behind the privacy of his palms. "Why?" he asks softly. He doesn't expect an answer, but something deep inside of him forces the question up from the depths of his yearning.

He wipes his nose with a finger and a sniff. The library has lost its allure, so he heads back to the street.

Rock stands on the large porch of a well-maintained house on Warner Avenue, two blocks from Sandra's apartment on Martin Luther King Drive. Most of the proud, working-class families Rock grew up with have been replaced by renters. The new landlords are Rock's former playmates. They grew up, moved to other cities and states, and inherited the homes they grew up in after their parents died. Most of them had no desire to forsake the privileged middle-class lives they had built for themselves to return to Greenville, so they carved the homes into rooming houses to maximize the income on their Schedule E's.

In less than a generation, the block went from a cozy family haven of manicured yards, where the entire village raised the children, to a hovel of dismembered denizens blindly going their own way in search of cheap rent. Unfortunately, the attendant problems that accompany such metastases are now as common on Warner as the grassless yards that Rock observes as he somberly looks up the street.

First crack, then Section 8.

Grammy Lee finally opens the door. "I'm sorry, baby. I didn't even hear the doorbell ring."

Rock gives her a hug and a kiss. "That's okay, Momma. Where's Claymont?"

"I don't know where that boy is half the time."

"Stop calling him a boy. He's a grown man."

Grammy Lee belts Rock on his broad shoulder. "That's a figure of speech and you know it. Did you try him on his cell phone?"

"He never answers when I call. I'm telling you, Momma. It's time for you to put him out. He's twenty-five years old."

"He's also my grandson. And at least if he's here, I know he's not somewhere dead in the street."

Clops walks in. "What's poppin', Unc? How long you been here?"

Rock looks at his watch. "You're late."

Clops flashes a platinum-toothed grin. "Better late than not at all."

They hug, slap backs, and head to the basement. Each man selects a pool cue from the rack on the wall and chalks up.

"Age breaks," Rock says.

"You the only one that play by that crazy rule."

Clops racks and Rock scatters the balls with a devastating first shot.

"Claymont, I practically raised your dusty behind. So you're more like my little brother than my nephew—"

Clops jumps in, probably because he's had this conversation before.

"Did I tell you I was thinking about taking a class at Hudson Community College?"

"What class?"

Clops hesitates in nothing flat. "Business."

"How many times do I have to tell you that you can't out-slick the slickster? But here's the deal. I'm not asking you to move out anymore, I'm telling you."

"Unc, why you tripping? This is the only home I ever had."

Rock makes a bank shot in the corner pocket and tosses Clops a compassionless gaze.

Clops tries another angle. "Why should I move out and pay Jersey City rent when I have the perfect setup right here?"

Rock places his cue on the table and abandons all tact. "Because you're living foul, that's why. When I started OGC, we just sold weed. And not that I'm trying to justify that, but you're selling crack. That's a whole 'nother level. What happens if somebody runs up in here blazing, trying to take you out? 'Cuz if anything happens to Momma, I'm blaming you."

"Blaming me? I'm handling *your* business. You OGC for life no matter how righteous you try to act now. Look at your hand."

Rock doesn't have to. The crude OGC initiation tattoo that he personally designed is still stamped on the web between his right thumb and pointer finger.

"And you must be crazy all up in my face right now, Unc. I ain't no little kid no more!"

Rock hardens. "I'm gonna make this easy for you, 'cuz this is not a debate. Either you leave tonight, or I'm dropping a dime. I'll *be* a snitch."

Clops breaks his pool cue across the table with a crackling *thwack*. He holds the bottom half in his hand like a splintered spear.

Rock gets in his face. "Oh, I'm supposed to be scared now? I broke up cats ten times harder than you in the joint. Try me, Nephew. I'll snap you in half just like that stick you holding."

Clops slams the broken cue to the floor. "You foul, Unc."
He passes Grammy Lee on his way up the stairs.

"Rocky, what's going on down here?" She notices the shattered wood on the floor.

"Claymont's leaving."

"Where's he going?"

"Not our responsibility. That's for him to figure out."

Hakeem's elbows rest firmly on his desk, and his fingers
are clasped in a two-handed fist. He pays particular attention
to Andre's every word.

"Rough week." Andre sighs. "I get to my girl's house and
a dude answers the door."

"So you're back together?"

"No, same deal. So I show up—"

"Andre, I have to stop you right there. If you and—what's
her name?"

"Sandra."

"Sandra Horton from St. Peter's?"

"Yeah."

"Y'all were together all those years?"

"Yeah, long time."

"Wow. Okay. But still. If you and Sandra aren't together
anymore, you have to stop calling her your girl."

Hakeem's demand jars Andre as much as someone telling him
to no longer call himself Andre. He slinks back into his chair.

"Like I told you last week," Hakeem says, "my primary
goal is to get you to arrive at the truth about yourself, and
that starts by acknowledging the truth about your relationships, especially with the people closest to you."

Andre feels dizzy, as if all the vital fluids in his body have
dried up. He continues his story, albeit with less panache.

"Supposedly she met this guy at work. He opens the door, and I'm ready to straight smash him."

"Let me make sure I'm remembering correctly," Hakeem says. "You broke up with her, right?"

"Right."

"Andre, believe me when I tell you that I'm familiar with a man's impulse to try to control his girlfriend, even his ex-girlfriend. I'm not proud of it, but I've been guilty of that myself. But my question is, is that reaction ever justified?"

"Hakeem, you're killing me with all the questions. I'm just trying to lay it all out for you."

"Okay, go ahead."

"I didn't swing on the guy, even after he interrupts my conversation with Sandra. And then she threatens to call the cops on *me*." Andre's eyes are wide, and he's waiting for Hakeem to express similar alarm. "Can you believe that?" he asks finally.

"How tall is Sandra?"

"I don't know, five eight, five nine."

"And you're what, six feet, 205?"

"One ninety-five."

"And how big is this guy?"

"A little shorter. A little slimmer."

"If you would've lost control, would Sandra have been able to stop you from hurting him, her, or even yourself?"

"Probably not."

"So then, do you think she was justified in preparing to call the police?"

Andre considers. "Maybe. But at the end of the night, I tell her that I'll meet her relationship demands and that I want to work things out."

"What did she say?"

"She said no. But I think it's because of that dude."

"Are those her words?"

"Man, women don't admit to that kind of stuff. To let them tell it, they never like anybody. Then six months later, you see them at the mall pregnant by the guy they supposedly weren't feeling."

Hakeem smiles. "Andre, let's establish a ground rule. No sweeping generalizations. You can't speak about every woman because you haven't met them all."

"You sound like Dabrowski."

"Anyway. So what else happened?"

Andre narrows his eyes. "I go to the library to write and I get this vision of my aunt and my grandmother. That messed me up."

"Why?"

"After my parents died, I came here to live with my grandmother. That's how I wound up in Jersey City from down South. When I first got here, the only way I could go to sleep at night was if my grandmother sang this song she made up for me. It was like I could feel her hand rubbing my head. Her singing was the only thing that made the images go away." Andre looks at Hakeem. "A year after I got here, she died too."

"How?"

"Diabetes." Andre sucks in every oxygen molecule in the room and lets his breath out slowly.

Faint voices of fury can be heard outside. Hakeem parts the curtain to take a look.

Across the street, Rahjaan and Smooth B. jeer at each other, their faces twin violent visages. Clops wedges himself between them.

"Chill!" he says.

Rahjaan lunges at Smooth B., but Clops flips him to the ground and puts a knee in his chest. "I *said* calm down!"

"I told him not to say nothing else to me!" Rahjaan woofs.

"How you gonna hold down a block without talking?" Clops lets Rahjaan up, and as soon as he's on his feet, he levels Smooth B. with a devastating right cross.

"I'm 'a kill you, son!" Smooth B. snarls. He leaps up from the ground and rushes Rahjaan.

Clops pulls his gun. "I told y'all to calm down! Now who wants to get it?"

The young lieutenants stand at attention.

"Y'all must've forgot what you out here for. We're here to occupy. Do business."

Two of Jersey City's finest round the corner in a marked cruiser.

Clops tucks his weapon and announces, "The beast."
So keep cool and they'll just roll on by.

Clops, Rahjaan, and Smooth B. walk composedly toward the police, because to flee or look nervous would be akin to screaming, "We're shady!"

His session now complete, Andre slides down the stoop outside Hakeem's building just as the cruiser passes Clops, Rahjaan, and Smooth B. The two officers and three OGC engage in an ocular chess match—I stare, you stare, and I dare you to do something.

Andre heads in the opposite direction, clueless as to how close he came to meeting the weasel-eyed gunman face-to-face.

11

Fredrick is at the maître d' desk inside Torch & Basil, outfitted in a dark blue wool suit, crisp white dress shirt, and burgundy bow tie. Sandra can't look him in the eye.

"I'm really sorry about the other night," she says.

"Not your fault. Men are territorial. It's in our DNA. That's the same impulse that drives us to protect our homes and families."

"That still doesn't make what he did right."

"Of course it doesn't. But if I was in his position, I probably would've done the same thing."

Sandra smirks. "Sure, Fredrick. I can hear you now." She does a spot-on thug imitation, complete with hand gestures and screw-face countenance. "Yo, I'm about to get street on you, son! Wall Street, ya heard!"

Fredrick smiles. "Trust me, men are men when it comes to women, regardless of their tax bracket."

"*Any*way," Sandra says. "I need to get back to work before my boss starts wondering why you stop up here every time you come in."

"Don't worry about Trizonis. I helped put together some of the financing for this place, so we're cool. But you should invite Andre to the next home cell."

"So he can pull more of his 'debate the world' antics?"

"No, so he can have a place where his questions can be answered."

Sandra considers. "I don't know. I'm trying to get myself right. Him being there would be a distraction."

"At least consider it."

Silence settles between them. The kind of quiet that comes when there's a break in a conversation that neither party wants to end.

"By the way," Sandra says, "do you *ever* cook?"

"Why should I when I have one of the best restaurants in Jersey City right downstairs?"

Fredrick's unintentional charm quickens the arid degrees of Sandra's passions, though she has already determined that her fondness for him is not romantic but rather an antidote to the Andre-inspired gall that sloshes around her heart like a disease.

Let me stop smiling before he gets the wrong idea. Plus I know any man that looks, walks, and smells like him has swarms of bees trying to get his honey.

"I'll see you Friday," Sandra says.

"See you then."

Sandra disciplines her eyes so they don't follow Fredrick out the door.

All of Sandra's life, it was drilled in her head that a suitable mate was someone like Fredrick. It started with her parents and was subtly reinforced by the clubs and organizations that a young lady of her social standing was expected to join. Before Andre, Sandra had dated only the scions of the African American power elite in Montclair.

But at St. Peter's College, the handful of African Americans who attended naturally fused together—rich and poor, academics and athletes.

Sandra unconsciously curls a braid around her finger.

The way Andre twisted me around, I should've stuck with the "bougie blacks only" mantra my girlfriends swore by.

Mr. Trizonis saunters over to Sandra, wearing a smile as big as his aggravated sense of self-regard. He is a fit, dashing, middle-aged Greek man with perfectly coiffed, jet-black hair. Sandra, along with every other patron and employee, suspects that he dyes his treasured locks, but none would dare ask.

He leans in close. "So. You and Fredrick. You two like each other?"

"We're just acquaintances."

"And I'm Pete Sampras. Here's some expert advice. Fredrick's a taker. Your other boyfriend?" Trizonis sucks his teeth. "Lacks polish."

Sandra opens her mouth to respond.

"Ah, ah, ah," Trizonis interrupts. "Andre's like Diddy. Fredrick's like Obama. Who do you think is a better example for your son?"

Trizonis's words touch Sandra in places that are off-limits. Her response swiftly passes her lips before she can filter it. "My personal relationships are not the business of my employer. Now if you'll excuse me, I'll get back to doing what you hired me to do."

Trizonis looks startled by the tart response from "sweet little Sandra," but he's apparently no less resolute. "I call it as I see it," he says. "I'd tell my daughters the same thing."

Sandra nervously twirls a second braid as he walks away, because she's surprised at how instinctively she barked at Trizonis when he disrespected Andre.

But his words hurt.

Sandra recalls how supportive everyone was of her relationship when Andre was a fixture on the back page of the *Jersey Journal*. And how fast that ended when the front-page story ran that announced his dismissal from the team. She can still hear her bougie friends: "Things to avoid in college—dumb jocks and hard rocks." In the minds of Sandra's friends, the allegations against Andre confirmed that he was both.

Mr. Trizonis returns. "I'm sorry if I upset you."

"Thank you. I accept your apology."

And I'm going to be by myself for a while so no one will ever be able to tell me "I told you so" again.

Andre sees *Torch & Basil* come up on his cell phone as he heads into the bus garage.

Probably wants me to babysit.

He tucks the phone in his pocket and lets the call go to voice mail.

Once again Andre finds himself seated in Dominick's office, only this time he's not staring at the top of his meaty head. Dominick's eyes are practically hidden beneath the convergence of his tangled, furrowed brows.

The four-page application Andre filled out almost three years ago is spread across his desk.

"On August 3, 2004, you were convicted of felony drug possession with the intent to distribute."

From the moment Andre grazed the skinny guy, he knew this moment would come. He can't meet Dominick's gaze.

"Is that true?" Dominick asks.

"Yes."

"On your application, which you filled out September 19, 2008, you checked that you'd never been convicted of a crime."

Andre nods.

"I need you to look at me, Andre."

When Andre does, Dominick's face has loosened somewhat. "Why'd you lie, Andre?"

"If I would've checked yes, my application never would've made it out of HR, and you know it."

Now it's Dominick's turn to lower his eyes. "You're probably right," he says.

"I'm not a drug dealer, Mr. Dominick," Andre continues. "Never was. I made one stupid mistake, lost my scholarship, and got kicked out of school because of it. And I'm not making excuses for what I did, but if I would've known it was going to follow me for the rest of my life, I never would've done it."

Dominick spins the application around and slides it toward Andre. "Read what I underlined."

Andre knows the section well. He never paid attention to it before he got in trouble, but now the paragraph sneers up at him like a nasty smear campaign.

"I hereby certify that the foregoing statements are true. I understand that if I provide any misleading or incorrect information during the employment process, it may render this application void and result in my immediate termination if the misleading or incorrect nature of the information is discovered if and after I am employed."

Andre pushes the application back across the desk with his chin held high. *I will NOT wallow in the mire of self-pity.*

"You're one of my best drivers, Andre," Dominick says. "And I think you're a good kid. But I don't have a choice. I have to let you go."

Dominick's words transport Andre back to suite 129 on the first floor of Dineen Hall at St. Peter's. Father Turchini, the dean of students, said the same phrase almost verbatim. "Andre, I know you're a good kid. But unfortunately, we don't have much of a choice. We have to let you go."

Andre was in jail three days before his creative writing professor raised enough money from among the faculty to bail him out. Andre acutely remembers the terror he felt when he was locked in the filthy holding cell at the Essex County Jail with twenty-two other men. He wasn't afraid of an attack because he had played Little League football with many of the inmates, and word quickly spread to the others that he was a "college football star." Andre's fear was that he would remain incarcerated until his hearing because he didn't have anything approaching the five-thousand-dollar secured bond the judge set, or family to help him string it together.

Dominick stretches a corpulent arm across the desk to shake. Andre stands and gives him a firm grip.

"Take care, Andre. Good luck."

Once Andre is on the street, a pall of terror blankets the sky. He shuts his eyes and ransacks his mind for something—anything—good to hitch his hopes to, but the only thing he sees is velvet darkness. And he's trapped in it. It swallows him whole and squeezes him down into its saucy belly.

He keeps his eyes shut, searching. And the epiphany that rocked him at the library claws back from the depths and blazons, "YOU'RE ALIVE!"

I am not death.

When Andre opens his eyes, the night sky is clear.

12

Hakeem peers through the wrought-iron hook-and-lattice work on his office window. Rahjaan is already out, shivering, glancing up and down the block.

Why is he out there this early every morning?

The two of them make eye contact. Hakeem nods, Rahjaan coolly throws his chin out and head back in one smooth motion.

Hakeem crosses the street. "How come you don't go to school?" he asks.

"Because I work."

"You call being out here at nine o'clock in the morning, freezing to death, working?"

"Yep. 'Scuse me."

Rahjaan approaches a car that pulls up. Hakeem can't see what transacts because Rahjaan's back blocks his view. The young white man behind the wheel of the Escape, Yankees cap shunted backward, suspiciously eyes Hakeem when he pulls off.

Rahjaan steps back on the curb. "You can't be over here, man. He thought you was the beast."

"How long have you been doing this?"

Rahjaan looks askance at Hakeem. "Why you asking me all these questions?"

"Because I was once your age and I'm hoping you'll be my age one day."

Rahjaan smiles. "Negative. I'm only sixteen, so it'll take me forever to get as old as you."

"Play your cards right and twenty-eight will be here before you know it. What do you see yourself doing in the next twelve years?"

Rahjaan shrugs. "I don't know. Have my own crib. A job maybe."

"What kind of job?"

Rahjaan searches Hakeem's eyes. "If I tell you, you promise you won't laugh?"

"Why would I laugh?"

"'Cuz in the hood it ain't cool to say you want to be certain things."

"Like what? It couldn't be worse than being a shrink, could it?"

Rahjaan grins. "Nah, it ain't that bad." He concentrates on his Tims. "I want to be a park ranger like Smokey the Bear or something like that." He quickly looks up to catch Hakeem's reaction.

"That's actually cool," Hakeem says. "You like animals?"

"Well. I been to the zoo a few times when I was in elementary."

"You have to at least have a high school diploma to be a ranger, you know that, right?"

Rahjaan looks stumped. "Never really connected school to a job. I just thought it'd be nice to get out of Greenville. Work around mountains and trees. Seems like less drama in the jungle than out here, you know?" Rahjaan smiles. "And in the jungle the beasts don't wear badges."

"I hear you. Hey, you like hot chocolate? It's freezing out here."

Rahjaan's face darkens with unease. "Nah, can't risk Cyclops coming out here and not seeing me on my post."

"The other guy you're usually with, he's not out here yet," Hakeem reasons.

"Yeah, but he don't have no responsibility. I'm the one in charge of this block."

No deed, doesn't live on this block but says he controls it.

Hakeem catches himself before he shakes his head. Instead he asks, "How much is your average sale?"

"I don't know, around twenty bucks."

"So how about you come in and warm up for a few, and for every car that goes by, I'll give you twenty bucks?"

Rahjaan cautiously looks from one corner to the other. "I guess that could be okay."

An SUV slows but pulls off before Rahjaan can reach it. Rahjaan looks at Hakeem and smiles sheepishly. "That's twenty bucks."

Hakeem smirks and digs in his pocket. "Okay, the rest will be five dollars. And that's only for ones that come to a complete stop."

Andre sees one of the teenagers from across the street on the stoop with Hakeem when he arrives for his session.

"Dre, this is Rahjaan," Hakeem says. "Rahjaan, this is Andre."

"Nice meeting you," Rahjaan says.

"Same," Andre replies and extends his hand. The two of them shake.

Hakeem stands. "Alright, Rahjaan, I'll catch up with you later. And you can holler at me anytime. I mean that."

"Cool." Rahjaan hands Hakeem his mug and turns to Andre. "See you around."

"Alright. Peace."

Hakeem waits until Rahjaan is out of earshot before he speaks. "Dropped out last year and he's been slinging ever since. He's been OGC since he was twelve."

Andre knows many people who started out like Rahjaan, only to wind up as career menaces, in prison, or cold in a box before they were legally old enough to buy a forty-ounce.

"Probably has a sixth-grade reading level," Andre says.

"Try fourth. I was able to get him to come inside and talk for a few minutes, and I asked him to read what was on the back page of the *Journal*. I told him I was too busy to find out who won the Nets game last night. He barely got through it."

Inside, Hakeem leads Andre to the twin love seats. "I want to build a relationship with young people like Rahjaan because many of them have undiagnosed issues that they're not even aware of. But anyway, how was your week?"

"I'm unemployed."

"Unemployed?"

"Fired. So I can't even get unemployment while I look for another job."

"What happened?"

"They got me on the job application."

"Let me guess, you never told them about the arrest when you were at St. Peter's?"

"Right."

Wait a minute. Why do I come here every week and discuss my personal business with a guy I barely know?

Andre pushes past the thought, because he has to admit that when he leaves Hakeem's office, his head is always clearer than when he came.

"So what ever became of that situation?" Hakeem asks.

Andre's insides fold, and not because of the drug charge—Hakeem already knew about that. It's the weight of knowing that for the rest of his life he'll be a living example of the very stereotype that he fought so hard to defy.

Black man and drugs.

In Andre's experience, many link them together as comfortably as peanut butter and jelly, soap and water, lock and key.

"Possession with the intent to distribute."

"How does a scholarship athlete get caught up in that?"

"Long story."

Hakeem looks at his watch. "We have time."

***

The view of the ratty apartment through the water-filled plastic bag bent and bowed like images in a fun house mirror. Dink stood up over Andre and grinned.

"Easiest job you'll ever have."

Andre wasn't convinced. Ever since he was twelve, Dink had tried to get him to do runs. His favorite refrain was, "You a star. Ain't nobody gonna suspect you."

The annual St. Peter's College President's Ball was less than a month away, and Andre hadn't rented a tux, reserved a limo, made dinner reservations, or bought the two fifty-dollar tickets that, according to the previous week's *Pauw Wow*, were almost sold out. His reason? No money.

Of course, Sandra didn't know any of that. The word in the locker room was that she was a bougie girl from Montclair whose dad owned several car dealerships. When Andre heard that, it made sense that she ignored his poem. She was probably used to getting wined and dined at expensive restaurants by guys who had cars.

Andre had conjured up his costly idea because he thought

that approach would best appeal to a bougie girl's sensibilities. He was convinced that the only reason Sandra gave him the time of day was because of his offer of an all-expense-paid trip to the President's Ball—a rare feat for a freshman, no matter how fine she was.

Andre passed the plastic bag that held the exotic fish back to Dink, who continued the hard sell. "The only thing you have to do is get *ten fish*"—he spread his skeletal fingers apart for emphasis—"through baggage check. That's it. The airline staff will load 'em on the plane. And for that you get this." He pulled out six crisp hundred-dollar bills.

Andre looked at the ten plastic bags in the red Igloo cooler, each holding a different-colored fish. "What am I delivering? Because if you're paying me six hundred dollars just to drop it off at the airport, I know you're making a whole lot more than that."

Dink frowned. "You don't need to know all that, Dre. You know why? 'Cuz the less you know, the less you can say."

"If I get caught," Andre finished.

"It's fish in plastic bags," Dink retorted.

Andre stood and towered over Dink, who used to seem so tall, but that was eleven years ago.

Dink was Auntie Cheeks's boyfriend when Andre moved to Jersey City. Andre was nine, Auntie Cheeks twenty, and Dink twenty-one. Andre remembered because Dink was old enough to legally buy the "knotty-head" gin that he and Auntie Cheeks mixed together with orange juice and sucked down in the basement. Their clandestine benders ceased once Grandma became ill—after she was confined to her bed, they were free to do whatever they wanted openly, anywhere in the house.

Andre had always liked Dink. Even after he and Auntie Cheeks broke up, he still came by the house on weekends to check on Andre. Dink was one of the few people who knew that Auntie Cheeks left him alone. Looking back on it, Andre was convinced that Dink continued to come by because he felt responsible, since he was the one who turned Auntie Cheeks on to things harder than knotty-head and Newports.

Two years after Grandma died, Dink started in on Andre. By that time, Auntie Cheeks would leave the house early Friday morning and sometimes wouldn't return until late Monday night.

Andre never told Auntie Cheeks what Dink pushed on him because he wasn't sure how she would react. Maybe she wouldn't have cared, but Andre didn't want to risk anything happening to his friend. After all, it was Dink who stopped by to make sure that he was alright when there was a violent storm or when drama broke out on the blocks around the house.

The signature *tap-tap, tap-TAP* that Andre adopted as his own, he learned from Dink. That was the cue that Dink used to let Andre know that it was safe to open the door.

Auntie Cheeks had sufficiently spooked Andre with, "Don't even look out the window 'cuz it could be anybody out there! You don't have to be afraid, because God'll protect you. But don't open the door for nobody! You hear me?"

Little Andre would drop his head and say, "Yes, ma'am."

Apart from Dink's signal, the door remained sealed while Andre imagined the horrifying things that lurked on the other side. Most chilling was the almost nightly blare of police sirens—a graphic reminder of the accident, the images, and the monsters lying in wait in the Dismal Swamp Canal.

Still, Andre never did a run for Dink because he didn't want anything to jeopardize his NFL aspirations. Professional football was his way out of a life of terror and uncertainty. Besides, he saw firsthand what drugs were doing to Auntie Cheeks.

On the morning of the airport drop, Andre showed up at Dink's house at eight a.m. sharp. It was an unseasonably hot Saturday in early May, and when Andre knocked, the door swung open immediately, like Dink had been spying through the peephole awaiting his arrival. Dink's eyes were as big as quarters and he looked skinnier than usual. Andre swore that he could see the veins in Dink's neck pulsating as blood coursed to his coked-up brain.

"What took you so long?" Dink demanded.

"You said eight o'clock and it's eight o'clock."

"Being on time is late 'cuz you don't give yourself no time to prepare."

It never ceased to amaze Andre how people who used drugs all seemed to believe they were sages. Maybe in their minds, espousing wise sayings made up for their being trapped in user prison.

Auntie Cheeks was no different. Every night before she left, Andre's ten-year-old mind struggled to figure out how she could be so sure that "God would protect him." *Can an addict know God? And if she does, then why's she leaving me in this house by myself?*

Though Andre at first dreaded it, as he grew older, he came to like having the house to himself, especially after he discovered the mystery of girls.

Dink lit up a Newport, grabbed Andre by the shoulder, and pulled him inside. The house stank of ammonia.

Dink lifted one of the bags from the cooler. A fancy-looking fish stared at Andre through the plastic barrier. It could have been the stirring water or Andre's imagination, but the fish appeared to shake its head no.

"Once you get back here, you get the rest of the money," Dink said. He slid three hundred-dollar bills into Andre's breast pocket. "You don't gotta count it, but you should." He smiled. "People in drugs can't be trusted."

Andre took the money and counted it. He thought about finally getting a date with Sandra, he thought about his parents, he thought about his grandmother, he thought about his fading shot at the NFL.

Ten fish.

Dink gave Andre the keys to his 1999 Mitsubishi Eclipse. "Now get out of here. The flight leaves at 9:30. Be sure you wait until you see the cooler loaded on the plane. And don't mess with me, Andre. I got a lot riding on this. If that cooler don't make it to Norfolk, I'm gonna have problems, then you gon' have problems. Get me?"

Even though Andre could twist Dink up like the pipe cleaner that he resembled, there was something chilling about his words. In all the years that Andre had known Dink, he had never threatened him.

Suddenly Andre was eaten alive by alarm. *What happens if I get caught?*

He gave Dink the keys back. "I'm having second thoughts."

Dink planted the keys onto Andre's chest. "Naw, Dre. I got people waiting."

"I'm starting to have a bad feeling about this."

"Each of these bags is a grand, Dre! Liquid cocaine. Do the math. You not backing out." He said it with finality as if Andre had no say in the matter.

"I could lose my scholarship." Andre heard how weak he sounded, like he needed Dink's permission to kill the deal.

"Scholarship?" Dink scoffed. "What's that scholarship doing for you besides keeping you busy and broke? You on lockdown during the season, weights in the spring, and training camp in the summer. They won't even let you have a job!" He gave Andre a once-over and sneered with the cigarette teetering on the ridge of his bottom lip. "Got on that same busted outfit every time I see you. I got junior high cats working for me that dress better than that."

Dink had hit a sore spot. Andre would never admit it, but he resented being one of the most popular students on campus yet not having enough money to buy nice clothes like some of the other players on the team.

"If you was at a D-I program, you'd have boosters giving you a little pocket spending change," Dink said. "But look at you. As soon as your financial aid check run out, you broke again."

Dink's words lashed across Andre's face like a cat-o'-nine-tails, but Andre remained silent.

"Dre, how you gonna get caught?" Dink gave Andre a fatherly pat on the cheek. "Tell me. How you gonna get caught?" He pulled out three more crisp hundred-dollar bills. "Take it, Dre. You know you need it. That fancy girl ain't gonna stand for being stood up." He closed Dre's hand around the balance of his pay and the keys to the Eclipse.

Terminal A at Newark Airport appeared to rise up out of the shimmering heat that danced above the blistering hot asphalt. The building had ground-to-roof arabesque windows and concrete columns along its facade. Andre was surprised by the functional beauty of the structure. He hadn't noticed it the only other time that he had been to the airport, in his sophomore year. At that time, Andre was so excited about leaving Jersey for the first time that he hadn't noticed much of anything.

The occasion was an invitation for St. Peter's to fly to Boston College for a Beantown beatdown on a crisp Saturday afternoon. Midget schools like St. Peter's jumped at the chance to get mauled by Division I opponents because they collected six-figure sums that covered their athletic budgets for the entire year. An additional perk was that the bludgeoning usually took place on national television, so tiny schools got exposure they would never receive otherwise. Andre remembered the president coming to the locker room at halftime when they were down 44–0. He "encouraged" the team by saying that the sacrifice of their bodies on national TV was "an excellent recruiting tool for the Jesuit College of New Jersey!"

Andre shook his head at the memory as he guided the Eclipse into short-term parking and took a ticket. When he grabbed the red chest from the trunk, his head felt weightless. He dropped it and squatted, but the fuzzy sensation continued to spread through his head. He lowered his face between his knees, heaved, and forced himself up. He pounded his chest twice—the same way he pumped himself up after a jarring collision on the football field.

Ten fish.

Andre took a deep breath and walked confidently toward the terminal.

No one in the airport eyeballed him strangely, even though he felt like a walking felony as he made his way to air freight. Andre was pleased to see an attractive young woman manning the desk. He relaxed into what, in his mind, was an appealing pose—elbow on the counter and his self-assessed, gorgeous chin resting in his cupped hand.

"Shipping to?" the young woman asked without looking up.

"Norfolk, Virginia. Long morning?"

"Yes," she said, clicking away on her computer, eyes sealed to the screen. "ID?"

Andre slid the fake ID that Dink had made for him across the counter. "Sweetheart, you're a prime candidate for CVS," he said.

The woman stopped typing and looked up. "Prime candidate for what?"

"Computer Vision Syndrome."

She rolled her eyes and locked again into her work. Andre looked around to see if anyone saw him get dissed as hard as he did.

"And what are you shipping today, sir?"

"Ten fish. Exotic."

"Up here, please," she instructed as she patted the scale.

When Andre placed the cooler on the counter, the woman turned up her nose at the pungent odor of ammonia that violated the ether. "You said it's fish in this container, sir?"

She spotted the drizzle of juiced cocaine sluicing through the hairline fracture in the cooler the same time Andre did. She grabbed her walkie-talkie.

Andre's impulse was to take off, but he was convinced that if he ran, his fate was sealed.

A security agent approached with a German shepherd that barked once, sat, and anxiously swished its tail back and forth across the polished floor.

"Sir, could you step over here?"

An order pronounced as a question.

Andre's lightning-quick first step enabled him to effortlessly scale the velvet rope that penned in the stunned public. He turned up the blazing speed that made him an all-conference wide receiver. The middle-aged men with guns had no chance of catching the young gazelle shot through with fear.

Andre reached the terminal exit and heard voices for the first time.

"DEA! TSA! Freeze!"

It was no matter because Andre was the wind as he exploded through the exit, leapt over two cars, and skidded to a stop at the parking garage. He strained to remember where he parked and then foolishly retrieved the ticket from his pocket.

"Move another muscle and I'll shoot!"

The thought of a barrage of small missiles tearing through his back and piercing his chest was intoxicating. Extinguished, snuffed out like a wick. It aroused Andre in a way that was almost sexual.

In an instant, Andre experienced the sharp pain of being rammed through the pavement. He was set upon by a thousand pounds of weapon-wielding officialdom. His face skidded across the concrete as his wrists were twisted behind his buttocks—clamped. A knee was driven through his back. Kicked. The dark danger finally subdued.

Andre's mind was filled with everything and nothing at the same time. Sirens took over and screamed a life-ending lullaby.

What is Sandra going to think of me now?

Andre relaxes into the back of his chair.

"So what did you do after you were kicked out of school?" Hakeem asks.

"Other than being homeless?"

"I thought you were living with your aunt in your grandmother's house?"

"By the time I was a senior in high school, I was basically on my own. I was still in the house, but Auntie Cheeks had stopped coming around altogether. The last time I saw her was after my last high school game. I think she planned it that way."

"Why didn't you just go back to the house after you got kicked out of St. Peter's?"

"Because the city condemned it the week before I graduated from high school." Andre smiles and shakes his head. "This doesn't even sound real, does it?"

"No, it doesn't," Hakeem says. "I never would have guessed

that you were going through all of that. You seemed like the quintessential big man on campus."

"People going through drama are the best actors."

"And your life sounds like a made-for-TV movie."

The weight in the room lifts on the strength of their spontaneous laughter.

"So how did the house wind up condemned?"

"It was already an old house," Andre says. "But when my grandmother died, it went down even further. The deeper Auntie Cheeks got into drugs, the less she was concerned about anything, especially the house. I cut the grass and shoveled the snow, but in the winter of '01 a storm took part of the roof off. After a year, the city noticed that it hadn't been repaired. They left notice after notice, and they kept piling up.

"When Auntie Cheeks was home, I'd tell her about the notices, but she'd just wave me off with that hand that always had a Newport dangling between her fingers. She had her issues, but she's the only family I have."

13

It's as if the blinking cursor on the library computer monitor dares Andre to lie. The question radiates off the screen like a flash of blinding light.

Have you ever been convicted of a crime?

An inquisition. Strategically placed like a Rubicon that, once crossed, irrevocably commits you to every keystroke. Andre lustily works through the rest of the online application despite knowing that he must go back and answer the third degree.

New York City is hiring day-shift bus drivers, and if Andre gets one of the coveted positions, he'd net a third more pay, better health coverage, and a higher pension than he had with New Jersey Transit.

With his index finger suspended above the mouse, Andre fancies himself sleeping through sunrise instead of witnessing each day break above barren blocks. And how wonderful it would be to rid his apartment of those Delphian black curtains that shut out daylight, that symbolize his station in life as a night imp, coursing through the arteries of Jersey City in a diesel beast.

The frustration of four weeks, seventy-three applications, and not a single phone call drives Andre to left-click a lie.

No, I have not been convicted of a crime.

He sends the application through before he can change his mind.

Virtue for life can be found in hard work.
Lying or starving, what's worse?

Andre records the line in his spiral notebook just as his session expires.

"Sir—"

"I'm going," Andre says as he stands and pockets his notebook.

The librarian who doles out computer chits is firm in purpose. Before your thirty-minute session is up, she's up. And she times it so that her face hovers above your monitor the instant you time out.

Andre is certain that she was gorgeous in her day. Even now she's a looker if you're into sharply dressed, middle-aged white women. The permanent scowl she wears is only rivaled in intensity by the wicked pumps, a different color each day, that add two inches to her chipper frame.

"Any luck today?" she asks.

Andre is startled because she never so much as shot him a glance in the four weeks since he started coming to the library to apply for jobs. "That remains to be seen," Andre says. "But I hope so."

"See you tomorrow then?"

"I'll be here."

Andre takes the long way home, even though the temperature outside is starting to tank. He is in no hurry to get to his apartment, which lately has become a hollow chamber absent of all life and substance. Futility seems to ooze from the walls and coat the floor, and he has to trudge through the muck to get to the bathroom, to cook, to move.

He steels himself against a rising tide of pointlessness, stuffs his hands in his pockets, and shudders as he turns onto a tree-lined block decorated with an array of handsome brownstones.

Andre hasn't seen Ms. Rutigliano, his landlord, in several months. That's not unusual because she spends most of the winter in a cabin that she owns in the Great Smoky Mountains. Which is why Andre is surprised to see lights ablaze on all three levels of her house above his basement apartment.

Andre slides his key in the lock, but it won't turn.

A window on the second floor blows open, and Ms. Rutigliano's hoary head dips out. The rubbery skin that hangs from the bottom of her arm shimmies as she stabs a bony finger down at Andre.

"You're two months behind, Andre. When I get my money, you get your stuff."

She slams the window.

"Ms. Rutigliano!" Andre shouts up.

Silence.

"Ms. Rutigliano!"

The second floor goes dark.

Andre races up the stoop and zings the buzzer. No answer. He rings it again.

A third-floor window flies open.

"I'm not having this conversation with you, Andre. When you're ready to talk two months' rent plus late fees, we can tête-à-tête. Until then . . ."

The window slams shut.

Andre spins around and catches a host of mugs slip behind sheers shut suddenly. He licks his lips, but that does nothing because his mouth is bone dry. In order to not look as foolish as he feels, Andre whips out his phone.

"Sandra," he says as he peeks around to see who's still watching.

"Hello?" she answers.

"Can I come see the little man?"

"That's fine."

Andre hangs up, and instantly the dark sky opens and mirth cascades from the heavens.

I can move back in with them.

There's an extra bounce in Andre's step at the thought of shacking with his family, and the idea that he once lived with them seems too good to have ever been true.

Two busses pass. Andre scans each vehicle out of the corner of his eye and is glad that he doesn't recognize either driver. He is certain that by now everyone knows he got canned because he lied about a felony drug conviction. Andre is sure that no one celebrated his demise more heartily than Big Will.

When Andre arrives at the apartment, Sandra opens the door with Little Dre in one arm and the phone cradled between her ear and other shoulder. She drops Dre into Andre's arms.

Although it's difficult, Andre determines not to ask Sandra who she's talking to. He forces all of his focus on baby Dre, and the little one demonstrates that it's past his bedtime because he writhes and twists in a vain attempt to break free.

"I'm not letting you go, little man," Andre says.

Little Dre gives Andre a solid pop in the eye with a minikin fist. And it hurts. Little Dre laughs through his pacifier while Andre blinks to relieve the pain and watering.

"That's not funny. You don't hit Daddy."

Little Dre clobbers him again, this time in the other eye.

"No hitting Daddy, Andre!"

His sharp tone causes baby Dre to drop his head onto Andre's shoulder.

Andre fights off a laugh. "You know I love you, little man, but there's a way to play and some things you just don't do. Hitting your father is one of them."

Andre kisses him on the ear. Dre giggles and wiggles free. Andre goes to grab him but he's gone. Little Dre tucks his chin to his chest and zips. He pumps his arms, and his miniature feet spin like wheels. Even so, he covers about as much ground as he would if he were running in place.

"You have to move a lot faster than that if you're trying to get away from me, little man," Andre says, laughing.

Junior Dre is undaunted as he wheels his way around the corner and makes a dash for the bedroom. Andre allows him to feel empowered by his speed before he scoops him up and into the air, which causes Little Dre to laugh so hard that his pacifier falls to the floor.

"Daddy's going to eat you up!"

Andre nuzzles his face into Little Dre's neck and gnaws. Dre screams with delight.

"This bite is with a large order of junior juice!"

Andre nuzzles—Little Dre squeals.

"And this one is with chocolate baby boy seasonings!"

Little Dre laughs until he loses his breath.

Andre cradles him into a bear hug, looks into his eyes, and plants two daddy-sized kisses on his chubby cheeks.

"Daddy loves you, little man."

"Wuv oo too," Little Dre says in vintage baby bluster.

"You're in a good mood. What's going on?" Sandra asks.

Andre turns about and is taken by the totality of Sandra's delicacy. She is wearing a baby-doll T and sweatpants that showcase her slender waist, perfect curves, and shapely hips— the kind of outfit that she would never wear outside. Nevertheless, in the dead of winter, the radiators in the apartment get so hot that you have to practically strip to get comfortable.

The "hot times," as Sandra and Andre call them, usually correspond with when Mr. Dibiasi, the landlord, is home. Otherwise, the heat is kept at the minimum legal limit required by the state of New Jersey.

Sandra notices Andre noticing her and looks down at herself. "Sorry. It's hot."

"You don't have to apologize," Andre says, ogling still.

"Well . . ." Sandra disappears into the bedroom and reappears with a loose-fitting T-shirt that shelters her graceful curves.

Andre's mind flashes back to times when they were intimate. *I wonder if she's wearing anything under there.*

Sandra interrupts his delicious thought and asks, "What's got you so giddy?"

"I'm just happy to be here with my family."

"Ohh-kay . . ." Sandra twirls one of her braids around her finger. Little Dre's gaze alternates between mother and father.

"The locks were changed on my apartment, so I came here to be with you two since I have nowhere else to go."

Sandra is silent. Little Dre smacks the top of Andre's shiny head and disrupts the quiet.

Andre flips him upside down and tickles him senseless. "I told you, no hitting Daddy!"

Sandra shifts her weight from one foot to the other. "So what happened with Ms. Rutigliano?"

"I haven't paid the rent in two months."

"But you've only been out of work for a month," she says.

"Instead of paying the rent last month, I held on to it for you and Dre in case I wasn't able to get a job by now."

"How's that going?"

"It's not. I've filled out tons of applications and haven't gotten a single call back."

Sandra bites her lip and looks down. "Somebody will call."

It never occurred to Andre that Sandra was his biggest fan until he found himself alone without a cheerleader.

I took her for granted, but I don't know how to say it the way I feel it.

"Sahn, I still love you," he blurts, and regrets it before the words are fully off his tongue.

Little Dre claps his hands. "Yay!"

Sandra's golden cheeks become flush. "I don't even know how to respond to that, Dre."

Andre turns away. "Forget I said it."

Little Dre seems determined to pull his parents into his party. "Yaaayyy!" He claps determinedly.

Andre and Sandra face him, poker-faced, and applaud.

14

A jacked-up house on the corner of Warner and Rutgers Avenues, three blocks from Sandra's apartment, appears to lean against the darkness that surrounds it. Were it not for the sturdy gable porch trusses, this ramshackle arrangement of bricks and beams would fold up and call it quits.

A well-organized system of man and opiate operate within the cheerless, paint-peeled walls. In the kitchen is a long table covered with fortuitously shaped slabs of white gold. Six young men dressed in black use meat cleavers to chop the product into nickels, dimes, and quarters—but small change is nowhere in sight. OGC provides first-class trips to the moon—you just choose the size of the spaceship to get you high.

Clops pulls Rahjaan aside and holds up a white rock. "You ever smoked this stuff?"

"Nah."

"The moment you do is the moment you're no longer OGC. Understand?" Clops tosses the chunk back onto the pile and eyes each foot soldier. "That goes for all of y'all." He turns again to Rahjaan. "Come here."

They have a seat in the living room on the house's lone decor, a slovenly couch that hasn't seen good days since the first Bush administration.

Clops stares Rahjaan in the eye. "We family, right?"

"No dizz-out," Rahjaan exclaims.

"And family takes care of family?"

"I'm saying, though." Rahjaan slaps Clops five.

"Let me see your hammer."

Rahjaan hands over a shiny, nickel-plated .38.

Clops smacks him over the head with it. "What's wrong with you?"

Rahjaan wrenches his face into a confused grimace.

"Never hand your gun over to anybody!" Clops says. He locates the short barrel between Rahjaan's eyes. "Now what you gonna do?"

Rahjaan seals his peepers shut.

"You ready to die?"

Rahjaan swallows hard and shakes his head.

"Then you ain't ready to advance, young bruh. 'Cuz if you ain't ready to lose your life, you ain't ready to take somebody else's. What determines a bullet's course?"

"I don't know," Rahjaan mumbles.

"Physics or fate," Clops says. "So when the sun rises, it's either your day to go or it's not. But you gotta be ready either way. Science and destiny, young bruh. That's what life is all about."

Rahjaan opens his eyes and seems to absorb the weight of Clops's wisdom. His youthful face hardens. "I'm down for whatever."

Clops lowers the gun and slaps him five. "My man. Now listen. We gotta find somebody. And this dude's gotta go the way of the earth 'cuz he's seen some things. And I don't want him talking about it. You understand what I'm saying to you?"

"No doubt."

There's commotion on the front porch. From outside, one of the watchmen yells, "The beast!"

Clops springs up and shouts through the house, "One time!" He grabs the two bags of uncooked 'caine from the kitchen.

He looks at doe-eyed Rahjaan. "Let's go!"

They sprint down the basement steps. Clops gives Rahjaan the two bags of snow. "Lay low and wait for me to call you."

Clops and Rahjaan scramble through the basement window and into a backyard overrun with bony trees, an abandoned Buick, and cast-off household appliances. They dust over a partially collapsed chain-link fence and scatter at different angles as the JCPD crashes through the yard from the street. Luminance from the officers' flashlights slice through the night like razors, but Clops and Rahjaan are ghost, absorbed by waves of eventide shadows.

To this day siren blasts still jolt Andre's viscera and set all five of his senses on edge. When he peeks through the window and sees three cop cars race toward Warner, he shudders. Images of the accident enkindle his mind, and he remembers the smell of gas and how sick it makes him. The metal-on-maple bomb of a collision explodes in his ears.

Little Dre is startled awake by the ruckus. Andre can hear Sandra in the bedroom calming him. She appears, strains her eyes, and stares at her watch.

It's 12:03 a.m.

"You're still here, Dre?"

"Yeah."

"What time were you planning on leaving?"

"I was hoping I could stay."

Sandra sighs big. "You can stay tonight, but that's it."

"What am I supposed to do after that?"

"Andre, I'm sorry. But you staying here doesn't look right."

"Doesn't look right? This was my apartment. *You* moved in with *me*. I didn't say that when you didn't have any place to go."

"*I* could've gone back to my parents' house. I just chose not to. But that was then—"

"And this is now, so what's the difference?"

"The difference is that I should've never been with you in the first place, Dre. What has it gotten me besides a baby and a busted apartment?"

Sandra's words force all the wind out of Andre's sails.

She touches his arm. "Sit down." They sit. "We can't live together if we're not married," she says.

"So let's get married."

"You're not in any position to be anybody's husband. Especially mine."

"This is about the pretty-boy wing man, isn't it?"

"The who?"

"Your man from the home group."

"I'm trying to get my life back in order, okay? This has nothing to do with Fredrick."

"And I'm Boo-Boo the Fool. You weren't saying all of this when you used to let me—"

"NO!" Sandra holds up one hand and clenches her other fist. "You will *not* beat me over the head with what I used to do!"

Her crazy-eyed countenance and tightly held fist deliver shock waves through Andre's middle.

"I'm a different person, Andre. And you don't have to believe it, but I will not be disrespected. Not by you."

She's dead serious.

Andre retreats and looks onto the street. A shaft of light sweeps through the window and momentarily brightens his face. A Jersey City Police helicopter scours the muted Greenville blocks.

Clops slinks over the fence and crawls military style, one elbow in front of the other, toward his house. The husky pattering of the copter's rotor blades buzzes overhead. The searchlight splashes into a corner of the yard and spreads toward Clops like a flash flood. He rolls between the fence and the detached garage in the back corner of the yard an instant before the light gives him up.

He can feel his heart beating in his ears, and from where he's holed up, he has an unobstructed view of the street. A Jersey City black-and-white passes quietly with cherries flashing. Every house on the block is awash in an eerie red silence.

Clops's cell phone screams. He twists and adjusts in the tight space to get to it. *Rahjaan* blinks on the display. Clops ignores the call.

Clops huddles beneath several paint-splattered canvas tarps stashed behind the garage. He's still asleep, and his mind is racked with a shifting series of slumber-land phantasms.

Seven snarling police dogs with inconceivably long fangs pin Clops against the back of the garage. He wants desperately to fight them off, but he has no arms. The savage pack morphs into black bears, and the largest beast moves in for the kill. Its fangs glisten with saliva that drips to the ground and forms a blood puddle that reeks of rotting flesh. The bear crouches to attack, transforms into a lion, and lunges for Clops's throat.

Clops awakes and shakes off the tarps as if they were aflame. He jerks his head around and searches to see if the beasts are still upon him. Growls continue to reverberate inside his head until he whacks his attic and jars them loose.

Grammy Lee has been up all night in her favorite chair in front of the television, save for intermittent winks between worries of where Claymont is and regrets of how she went wrong. Yes, Rocky is on the straight and narrow, but it took the harrows of prison to uncoil his crooked ways. Now the police are asking about Claymont. Grammy Lee has a sneaking suspicion that last night's sirens and searchlights had something to do with him. The flurry of police activity happened not five minutes after the officers left her house. From what Grammy Lee can see, prison is in the cards for Claymont too.

A light knock.

She strains to hear and it comes again.

Grammy passes through the room, parts the curtain, and there is Claymont looking like a forlorn little puppy. She cracks the window, and a blast of morning air wraps her in its icy embrace.

"Was all that police business last night about you?" Grammy asks.

Clops drops his head.

"What are you into, Claymont? The whole neighborhood was crawling with officers."

Clops blows it off. "It'll be back to normal in a week. The beast don't stop crime, they just disturb it."

"But you're running like a fugitive slave. You need to turn yourself in, Claymont. It's the right thing to do."

"I'm not going to prison."

"Worse things could happen. Rocky went to prison and look at him now."

"Right. Soft preacher man. If I ever decide to meet God, I ain't going to the pen to do it."

121

"Keep up what you're doing and you're going to meet God, alright. People go to hell every day."

"I'm in hell now."

"You're in a world of trouble, but you're not in a lake of fire."

Clops is not willing to even entertain such a thought. *'Cuz it ain't no need fearing going to a place that ain't real.*

"Turn yourself in before it's too late," Grammy continues. "Pay your debt to society. Get right with God. You're too young to go to hell. And I refuse to get mixed up in this mess you're in, so I'm not letting you in here. But I'm praying for you because that's about all I can do for you right now." Grammy turns her back on her only grandchild, and the disappointment in her eyes as she lets the curtains fall crushes Clops.

He blinks his beady eyes twice, experiences the foul taste of fear, and swallows it whole. It settles at the bottom of his stomach and makes him queasy. He looks around and wonders who's watching him through the rear windows of the houses that surround him.

Snitches.

The windows appear to wink as a wave of morning sun washes over their panes. Clops hustles around the corner and out of sight.

Andre wakes but cannot breathe. He is smothered by a layer of polyethylene film. He takes in a noseful of the sweet, intoxicating smell of a Pamper. Anytime Little Dre catches Andre asleep on the couch, he clambers up, parks his bottom on Andre's unsuspecting whiffer, and wiggles to wake him.

"Nothing like starting your day with your boy's butt in

your face," Andre says, smiling. He lifts Little Dre off of him. "Good morning, little man."

"'Ey, Dah-dah."

For a moment, Andre forgets the iron set of circumstances strung around his neck. Sandra comes out of the bedroom and twists one of her long braids into place.

"Hey, Andre."

"Hey."

Reality seeps in on the heels of Sandra's beauty and chases away the bliss of comfy couches and fresh-scented baby bottoms.

"I'll be out of here in a minute," he says.

"Are you having breakfast?"

"I have to get to the library. Little man, I'll see you later."

Little Dre erupts into ear-piercing yowls when Andre stands. "Dah-dee! Dah-dee!" He stretches his arms upward, and Andre scoops him off his slippered feet.

"Daddy'll be back, little man."

Andre glances at Sandra. She releases a deep, audible breath as doubt arises and does violence to her lately held convictions. Her mind is awash with fresh questions.

Doesn't a son need his father around full-time? If Andre and I aren't a couple, is it still wrong for us to live together? Andre has been acting different lately. Hasn't he?

"Dre," she says.

Andre turns, and Sandra sees what he has been able to expertly mask since he was nine—the shade of sadness that abides behind his light brown eyes. A mawkish sentiment brushes across Sandra's bosom as she recalls how she stumbled and fell for the dark poet from the wrong side of the rusted Class 1 railroad tracks in Greenville Yards.

Not much got past Dewey Horton. Even though Sandra made it clear to her father that her escort was "just a guy I had humanities with," Mr. Horton wanted to know everything there was to know about him.

"Baby Love, if he's just a guy you had a class with, then how'd he get a date with you to the biggest event of the year? You know I took your mother to the President's Ball—"

"Three years in a row." Sandra finished the sentence with Mr. Horton and rolled her eyes. "Daddy, you've told me that story a thousand times."

"Add that to it and make it a thousand and one. What do you know about his family?"

"Daddy, I don't know anything about his family. He asked me to go and I said yes. It's not that deep."

Mr. Horton shook his head. "I don't understand you young people today. We're talking about the President's Ball here. And you're going with somebody you barely know?"

Sandra wasn't comfortable sharing with her father how she conducted her personal straw poll. *Because everyone knows that freshman year is when you establish your credibility and then build on it for the next three years.*

So Sandra went with what appeared to be a can't-lose visibility bonanza. Andre Bolden was a junior, nice-looking with a nice body, and the most popular athlete on campus. Second place was Malik Walker, a cute senior from Englewood Cliffs who was vice president of the Student Government Association. Andre seemed like a better choice because he was St. Peter's all-time scoring leader and, during football season, a regular on News 12. Malik Walker was cool, but people in student government didn't get the respect on campus that athletes did. Besides, Andre was offering dinner and a limousine, and Malik was driving his own car, a ten-year-old Jetta in okay condition.

And I'll look infinitely more elegant flowing out of a limo than a Volkswagen in a Tiffany gown.

The only person whose offer came close to Andre's was Hip Hop Harold, a guy who had liked Sandra since high school.

But he's only a sophomore AND a rapper, so basically—no.

Sandra found out that Andre had gotten arrested the same way everyone else did—on News 12. After that, it was *the* story on campus and *the* story on her parents' lips. When he saw the news report, Mr. Horton remembered Andre's name and immediately soured on his existence.

Back then, the way her father felt about Andre didn't matter because Sandra was as bitter toward him as Mr. Horton was. Besides, with the elegant dress and accessories she had chosen, Sandra could have showed up with Hip Hop Harold and still established herself as one of the women to watch at St. Peter's. But because of Andre and his arrest, Sandra never made it to the ball.

When Andre called after he was released, Sandra debated whether or not to pick up the phone. She was as mad as she was curious. In other words, she was dying to hear what he had to say.

"Hello?" She tried to sound uninterested.

"Sandra? It's Andre Bolden."

She remained silent to make Andre feel as uncomfortable as she did when she realized that she was going to get stood up for her first major collegiate social affair.

"Sandra?"

A frosty, "Yeah?"

"I know you heard about what happened."

An earful of silence.

"You're probably pretty upset, and you have every right to be. But I want you to know that I've never been involved with drugs in my life."

Sandra strangled the phone with one hand and flailed the other through the air in concert with each syllable that she spat. "Never been involved with drugs? It was *on the news*! I can't believe you have the nerve to call me and say something stupid like that!"

Before Sandra realized it, she had slammed the phone into its cradle. She recognized that her fury stemmed as much from her frustration with Andre's attempt to present himself as a poster boy for Partnership for a Drug-Free America as from her humiliation.

The phone rang again. It was him.

Sandra marveled because she never would have imagined that she would be twisted up in drama with a drug dealer from the hood. Despite her anger, a peculiar sensation in her chest moved her to answer.

"Hello?"

Andre spouted as quickly as an auctioneer, "Don't-hang-up-until-you-give-me-a-chance-to-explain-myself!"

Once more, Sandra whipped out the silent weapon.

"I'm not saying I didn't do it. What I'm saying is that I've never done anything like that before. Not even close. And the only reason I did it was because I wanted to make your night at the President's Ball unforgettable."

Sandra's silence became a sort of noiseless awe that motivated the peculiar sensation in her chest to snake around each of her ribs. Nevertheless, she replied crisply, "Sitting in my dorm room in a ball gown waiting for a limo that never came is something I'll never forget."

"I'm really sorry. And I'd like the chance to make it up to you."

Sandra sensed an opportunity to satisfy her inner emotional voyeur. "So you thought that going out with me was worth risking jail?"

"Obviously, I didn't expect to get caught."

"But you did," she snipped.

"Maybe if you wouldn't have ignored the poem I gave you last semester, things would've turned out different."

"You're kidding, right?"

"Well. You dissed me. I'm not used to that."

"And that's exactly why I dissed you. You parade around campus like you're unique to the universe."

"If I was rolling with you, I would be."

Sandra was caught off guard by the tightness of Andre's game and was glad he couldn't see her blush. Or the peculiar sensation that continued to crawl around her ribs then slither across the surface of her heart.

Until then, Andre was just one of several guys jockeying for Sandra's attention. And it wasn't that she thought Andre was unappealing. But all the guys she dated were noted and in demand. Therefore, a man had to have a dash of extra verve to get her undivided attention.

He must really be interested to put his future on the line for a chance to take me out.

Sandra turned down a budding smile because she recognized the oddity of finding any part of Andre's decision attractive. Still, his story coupled with his game sparked the emotional tipping point that piqued her interest.

"I was thinking about you when I was trapped in that dungeon, so I wrote something. You want to hear it?" Andre asked.

"Okay."

Andre cleared his throat to buy some time. This was different from a packed poetry slam at the student union. This was Sandra Horton, so close that, were it not for the phone, his lips would brush her ear when he spoke.

Andre closed his eyes and imagined he was doing just that. And the words flowed.

> Some things in life can't be tested by time,
> Others slowly blossom like the fruit of the earth.
> Still others are left to rot on the vine
> Because the labor of the harvest outweighs their
> worth.
> Not so your value, it exceeds degrees—
> Measureless, like the light of the sun,
> And neither time nor space can convince me other-
> wise.
> I think that you're the one.

15

Andre kicks open the broken door that leads to the street. He steps into the cold and heads toward downtown. Clops rounds the corner and moves briskly in the same direction.

Andre sulks down the block and notices that he's wearing the same clothes he had on yesterday.

Clops sees Andre from behind.
Can't be a undercover. Too early.

Andre casts off his concern because no one in the library pays him enough attention to notice what he wears anyway. He imagines that the computer Nazi will have on another snazzy outfit with a different pair of matching pumps.

The stretch between Andre and Clops whittles away with each step.

A shiny black-and-white pops the curb. The officers see Andre first and give him a menacing visual shakedown.

Clops peeps the interaction between man and beast.
Oh, sh—!
He quickly ducks into a bodega.

Andre glares back at the officers with equal menace, frustrated that his only crime is cruising down King. He recalls a white co-worker from Bayonne telling him that profiling is the price that law-abiding black citizens must pay if they want their neighborhoods to be safe. Andre sniffs at such a notion and leans into the cold.

The Yemeni man behind the counter studies the floor the moment he and Clops make eye contact. He knows who Clops is, and he knows what's been afoot since last night, but his official line to the cops was, "I don't know nothing and I don't see nothing."

Because I didn't come to America to start business to get caught between the war of the police and the blacks.

That keeps life peaceful for him and his family.

Clops's cell phone goes off. It's Rahjaan.

"Where you at?" Clops answers.

"At my mom's house."

"You a'ight?"

"Well . . . I guess."

"Your mom's cool with you being there?"

"She ain't here. I came in through the fire escape."

"Hold tight, I'll be there in a few."

Clops parks himself in the door of the store and monitors the block through glass almost completely covered with advertisements for malt liquor, New Jersey Mega Millions, and neighborhood watch. He turns to the man behind the counter, whose gaze drops to the floor again. Clops bunches his eyebrows together. "Whatchu lookin' at?"

"Nothing, nothing. No problem. No problem."

"Well, you need to stop looking at me 'cuz *that's* a problem!"

Clops pulls on his black hoodie and skulks out the door. As his eyes dart up and down the street, he scoffs at Grammy Lee's suggestion that he's a fugitive slave. Yet the comparison would neatly explain the driving tension, irritability, and fatigue that seethe beneath the surface of his skin. He crosses his wrists and scratches his forearms beneath his coat sleeves. Now if only he could silence the sound of his breathing. Magnified, it bounces around his head and flares off into the dark corners of his mind.

Is this what my mother felt like?

He stops scratching and fingers the dog tags strung around his neck.

Clops's mother, Jarda, was a gunner, and the rare woman to "man" a turret-mounted MK 19 grenade launcher atop a Humvee. She was the only female in the 105th Military Police Unit, but she worked harder than the men because she felt that she had something to prove. And like any Jersey Girl, she wasn't about to be outdone by anyone.

On the night that the 105th was deployed to monitor a rash of oil well fires set near their base in Rumalia, the glare from the flames made it impossible for the unit to see even with their Humvee lights set to high beam.

Two miles from the base, the unit was showered with heavy artillery fire. The Humvee hit a crater, and Jarda was vaulted from the gun turret when it flipped. Critically injured and disoriented, Jarda managed to crawl a half mile through the darkness in a confused attempt to elude capture. Members of the Iraqi army systematically tracked her down and put her out of her misery with a single shot to the back of the head.

Jarda was the older of Grammy Lee's two children. Her plan was to serve three years, cash in her GI Bill, pay for college, and use her VA loan as a down payment on a house in Florida because she hated cold weather. A fantastic idea at the time because the country was at peace. But the hawks were set to fly. President George H. W. Bush declared war three weeks after Jarda finished basic training.

Clops was already staying with Grammy Lee and Rock because Jarda knew that her mother and brother would provide the best care for four-year-old Claymont.

Clops recalls the last time he saw his mother. She stayed at the house the week before she deployed to Iraq. Clops's memory of her is that she smelled of pink cotton candy and jingled when she walked because she wore wrists full of bracelets that gathered in steel tangles at the top of each hand.

Clops's eyes dim.

What if she would've lived? Bought a house near Disney World and went to one of those black colleges? I bet I would've been different if I would've grown up in a friendlier place.

A place with citrus trees and ceaseless sunshine.

Clops focuses on the vapor clouds that pass his lips like frosted mirages and swiftly fritter away in the crisp morning breeze.

A black Crown Victoria materializes at the top of the block. It's Jackson and Carollo. Clops turns away, squats, and acts like he's tying his Tims. He can feel the DTs' eyes burning through the back of his bubble goose. When the heat dissipates, Clops checks over his shoulder and sees the car turn off of King. He's dizzy from the pressure, and white spots frolic in his sight as he unstops his breath.

This is crazy.

When Clops arrives at Rahjaan's mother's building, he positions himself just outside the door beside the buzzer. In the hood, it's proper etiquette to let a person in a building who doesn't live there even if you don't know them. To do otherwise would suggest that you think the person is up to no good (even when you know they are).

A young black man exits and holds the door open. "What up, OGC?" he asks.

"Science and destiny. All day every day."

"All day every day," the young man says and gives Clops a pound.

Clops trudges up the five flights in the weathered tenement, attuned to the audio-sensory shifts that occur on each landing. A baby screams on one, a man and woman bicker on two, the smell of fried chicken sticks to the walls of three, hip-hop and the scent of incense mix on four, and Gospel praises go up on five.

When Rahjaan opens the door, Clops's heart sinks. The white of Rahjaan's right eye is bloodred, and the same side of his face is purple and swollen. Rahjaan looks down.

"What happened?" Clops asks.

"I caught a bad one from the beast."

Clops notices that Rahjaan's front tooth is missing. Disgusted, he throws his arm around Rahjaan's shoulder. "You said you were okay on the phone."

"I'm cool except for this." Rahjaan fingers the black hole where his tooth once was. "Now the girls are gonna think I'm homeless or something."

Clops smiles. "Your face is jacked and all you can think about is girls." He turns serious. "So, where's my stuff?"

Rahjaan's one good eye gets wide. "I ditched it when they started closing in on me. I hit you on your cell to ask you what to do, but you didn't answer."

Clops's eyes decrease in size by half, and Rahjaan's eye darts wildly. "I didn't want to get caught with anything on me. But I can pay it back. I promise you."

Clops clamps his hand on his forehead and attempts to massage the madness from his temples.

Rahjaan scrambles to talk his way out of trouble. "I can—"

"Shut up," Clops says. He brings his thumb and pointer finger around to his eyes and rubs them roughly. He opens them and stares at a wide-eyed Rahjaan. "If it was anyone else . . ." Clops imagines the horrible things he would do. "But I'm gonna remain calm and try not to think about my five-thousand-dollars' worth of product in someone else's clutches."

The door swings open and Rahjaan's mother tumbles in. She doesn't notice them until after she has locked the door and landed on the funky couch.

"How'd you get in here? And what happened to your face?" She gives Clops a venomous gaze. "You no good mother—"

"I promise you I had nothing to do with it, Miss Pincus," Clops says quickly.

"Yes you did or you wouldn't be here. You just a punk. Recruiting young boys to do your dirt."

"That King Cobra must got you twisted 'cuz I don't recruit, I attract volunteers," Clops says.

A loud *thwack* as Miss Pincus swats Clops across the face. "Yeah, I'm drunk, but you a *crack dealer*." She spits the words off her tongue as if they were poison.

"I promise you, Miss Pincus, if you put your hands on me again, it won't matter whose momma you are."

She practically crawls into Clops's ample eye sockets. "Get out my house before I call the police."

Clops doesn't move.

"I said get out!"

Clops turns to Rahjaan. "Let's go."

Rahjaan looks to his mother.

"You can't stay here, Rahjaan. Family Services will say I'm in contempt." She touches the bruised half of his face with motherly affection.

"I got in a fight. I won though," Rahjaan says.

134

"You need to stop that fighting 'cuz it ain't gonna do nothing but get you in trouble. And I'm gonna get myself together so you and your brothers can come back and stay with me."

Rahjaan has probably heard that before. "Okay, Moms."

"Come here and give me a hug." She kisses Rahjaan on the neck.

"I'll see you around, Moms."

Rahjaan follows Clops, who balls up three twenty-dollar bills and drops them on the floor on his way out of the apartment.

16

Three-point-one miles separate Sandra's apartment from the main library downtown. What would have taken Andre ten minutes on a New Jersey Transit bus amounts to a thirty-five-minute hump on foot. He turns right onto Grand Street, and instead of continuing to Jersey Avenue where the library is located, he splits right on Prior and hangs a left onto Colden.

The neighborhood sign says BOOKER T. WASHINGTON APARTMENTS. JERSEY CITY HOUSING AUTHORITY. At the bottom of the sign is the phrase "Building communities, creating opportunities, transforming lives." Andre is staggered by the irony, for this is one of the most notorious housing projects in Jersey City.

"AhhhnnnDRE!"

Andre would recognize that voice anywhere.

"Whassup dere, boy? Ain't seen you in a *long* time! Got somethin' for ya."

Before Andre can turn around, June Poon has plastered a fluorescent orange sports jacket with faded lapel onto his chest.

"Don't let it fall! You gots ta *feel* that thang 'gainst your body!" June Poon insists.

Andre holds the jacket to his chest, flesh crawling at the

horror of not knowing where it came from. June Poon steps back, scrutinizes with head cocked, and takes pictures with fingers rectangled into an invisible camera. He even makes the "chick-shh" sound with each imaginary exposure.

"Das you, boy! Das you! O'inch is yo color. Twel' dollas!"

Andre holds the jacket in front of him with two fingers and releases his held breath. "June Poon, I'm not in the market for a sports coat, but thanks."

June Poon balls his face into a fist. "Don't you need a job?"

"Well—"

"Well? You *gots* to have a sports jacket if you wants to be hired!"

Andre can't help but laugh. "What makes you think I need a job?"

"No time for us quizzing each other on wha's obvious. The question is, is you gonna look yo best on the inna-view?" June Poon furrows his brow and reconsiders. "Assuming you even get one, since you a felon and all."

Andre shakes his head as June Poon rummages through a dingy suitcase tucked into the trunk of his 1977 Chevy Monte Carlo with white landau top.

"Besides, you know that word on the street travels faster than a tweet."

"June Poon, what do you know about Twitter?"

"The same thang you knows about unemployment. Enough."

June Poon whips out a wrinkled houndstooth sports coat. Andre stops him before he's smothered with any more frowsy apparel.

"I'm not buying any clothes today. And if I had it, you know I'd slip you a few dollars. But right now things are tight."

June Poon rubs his bushy head and folds his arms across his chest. Standing there, he looks exactly as he did when he showed up at Dickinson High School from the mountains of East Tennessee in Andre's sophomore year—lanky, ashy, and country. As far as Andre can tell, June Poon's elevator has never gone all the way to the top. And no one ever got the complete story of how he wound up in Jersey City, but it had something to do with moonshine, firearms, and a crazy uncle named Fee Fee.

"So you admittin' you ain't got no job then," June Poon says.

"I'm not saying anything."

"Fine." June Poon slams the trunk. "Good to see you, man. Still lookin' good. And if you ever need anything, give me a call." He forces a business card with crimped, dirty edges into Andre's hand. "And if I don't have it, I can get it," he says with a wink. "Don't matter, whatever it is."

June Poon slaps Andre five and shuffles on.

Andre stands in the middle of the street for several moments. The last time he was in Booker T., the result was not good. He looks around at the collection of nine three- and four-story brick buildings with lime green fire escapes.

Bullet town. That's what they call it. Andre gazes at the Goldman Sachs tower less than a mile away that scales through clouds. It dominates the skyline of downtown Jersey City's celebrated Gold Coast. He wonders what it would be like to have a job in a building like that.

His next thought is more menacing. *Would I be able to see anything pop off down here from my office window?* He dismisses the notion.

Andre trudges across the empty basketball court in the middle of the complex. Spray-painted at center court in big splotchy red letters is an enamel memorial that says, "RIP Stink Man."

He arrives at number 76 and knocks softly. No answer. He

knocks again, this time more forcefully. When there's still no answer, he's relieved. *What am I thinking?*

He turns to walk away and the door creaks open. He looks back and sees Dink peering at him through the security chain. In a raspy voice that Andre doesn't recognize, Dink says, "Come on back, I'm here."

Andre is astonished at how frail Dink has become in the seven years since he last saw him. His skin is gray, and what was once thick, tightly curled hair is now close-cropped fuzz with bald spots throughout. Dink was always skinny, but now he looks depleted by last agonies as he awaits the final call to nevermore. Every other sentence he speaks is punctuated by chest-splitting coughs that rock his entire frame.

"Can I get you some water or something?" Andre asks.

Dink waves him off as he recovers from another seismic ahem. "So what brings you around here?" he whispers. "Ain't seen you since the last time I seen you."

"I was on my way to the library so I decided to stop by to see what was up."

"Making it. Did you know I retired from the game?"

"No, I didn't."

A clumsy silence settles between them.

"Well, I'm glad you stopped by because there's something I been needing to tell you," Dink says.

"What?"

Dink licks his cracked, discolored lips and pauses for what seems like an eternity. "Last winter, the police found your aunt in Lincoln Park."

Andre attempts to swallow the hunk of horror lodged in his throat.

Dink drops his head and sobs. "She froze to death, man."

The nerve endings that cover every inch of Andre's body stand on edge, but none fire.

The last time Andre saw Auntie Cheeks, she was in the stands on the fifty-yard line, where she sat for every Dickinson home game. Andre would point the ball to her each time he scored a touchdown, and she would acknowledge his gesture with a nod and a smile.

After the game, Auntie Cheeks pushed her way through the crowd of teenagers gathered at midfield and hugged Andre around the neck.

"I love you," she said.

Andre thought she looked happier than he had seen her in a long time. "I love you too, Auntie."

She flashed that wry smile that revealed her three missing teeth. "You're going to be just fine. I know it," she said.

Andre thought that losing teeth should be enough to make anyone get clean, but it wasn't until years later that he realized that vanity was no match for addiction, even when personal beauty was at stake.

Because it was Friday night, Andre knew that he wouldn't see Auntie Cheeks again until Monday evening. Typically, she showed up around nine p.m., showered, and got dressed for her overnight shift at the General Pencil Company.

But something about that night was different. As Auntie Cheeks disappeared into the blithesome crowd, Andre had the sobering feeling that he was now officially on his own. She turned one last time and waved. Andre shook off the omen, waved, and went back to celebrating his final game as a high school baller.

Now the sight of Dink's face swells the anger and disgust that roils Andre's insides. He thinks about Dink and Newports, Dink and knotty-head, Dink and drugs, and Dink and jail.

Andre explodes out of the chair, locks his fingers around Dink's chicken neck, and snatches him off of his feet. "Why didn't you tell me!"

Dink's eyes bug out of their sockets as Andre shakes him like a sack of dirty laundry.

"Why didn't you tell me!"

Dink's wretched head lolls onto one shoulder. He hangs limp in Andre's grasp but Andre continues to squeeze. When Andre finally releases him, Dink drains into a chair and doesn't move. Andre gapes at the pile of crumpled flesh wadded into the seat.

Man. I killed him.

Dink chokes up rust-colored phlegm and hawks it into a handkerchief. He cracks his bloodshot eyes and clears his throat loud and long to loosen his vocal folds.

"I didn't know how to find you," Dink whispers. "And I didn't think you'd deal with me after what happened at the airport."

Andre sinks into a chair and buries his face in his hands. Dink struggles to his feet and massages Andre's shoulders. "It's alright, Dre—"

"Don't touch me, man!"

Dink shrinks back to his seat. "There's something else I need to tell you, Dre."

Andre looks up.

"Your aunt and I had a baby when we were in high school. So you had a cousin right here in Jersey City that you didn't even know about." Dink's eyes get misty. "We gave him up to my people to raise 'cuz me and Cheeks weren't ready for no baby, man."

Dink closes his eyes and jogs his head from side to side as if to shake loose the scabs of many unpleasant memories. "If I had to do it over again, I'd do something different with my life. Play some ball like you did. Open a barbershop or car wash or something."

Andre heads for the door.

"Dre."

Andre turns.

"Your cousin—" Dink drops his head. "He was murdered on Bergen two months ago. It was OGC. They said he was snitching." Dink swallows hard and looks up with bitter eyes. "Dante was my son, man."

Unable to absorb any more, Andre floats out of the house.

Once he's downtown, the idea of propelling himself into the chocolate murk of the Hudson is tempered by the image of his bloated, bacteria-eaten body ballooning up from the depths when the weather first breaks in spring.

But is that any worse than being hunted down and shot by OGC?

The thought of Dante's lifeless face gives Andre the creeps, and their cold, hairy tendrils scurry up his stomach, across his chest, and around to his back.

My cousin.

Andre imagines Auntie Cheeks, alone, cold, and dying by herself in Lincoln Park. He drags his nails back and forth across his bald head, takes out his phone to dial Hakeem, but remembers the young guys posted across the street.

OGC.

He flips the phone shut and stares at the glancing towers of lower Manhattan across the river. He focuses on the sky above them, closes his eyes, and drops his chin to his chest. The weight of his life has finally made it impossible for him to keep his head up.

Andre looks back up at the sky. Blue and empty.

He curses everything, removes the dirty card from his wallet, and dials.

"Whassup dere, boy?"

"I need a four-pound."

"Why you need that for?"

142

"Do you always ask your customers this many questions?"

"I only ast you one question, Dre."

"All I need to know is, can you get it?"

"I can get it."

"Cool."

June Poon grins like a used car shark when Andre sits beside him on the bench at the basketball court in Booker. T. He pulls out a shiny, nickel-plated .38.

"This isn't a .45," Andre says. "And it's a revolver. What do you think this is, *Gunsmoke*?"

"'S all I could get on such short notice. You give me more time and I can get you a grenade launcher if you want it."

Andre takes the gun, turns it over in his hands, and looks back at June Poon. "How do I know this thing works?"

"I fired it myself. Twice."

"When?"

June Poon rolls his shoulders back and beams like the headlamps on a beat-up Chevy. "All June Poon's merchandise is qual'ty tested. But go on 'head and shoot it. It's loaded."

Andre looks at the one or two people milling about in the courtyards between buildings. "Right here?"

"It's alright. You gotta have bodies on the ground for the cops to show up in Booker T."

Andre snaps out the cylinder and spins it around to make sure the chamber is stocked with six shots. "I'll take your word it works."

17

Thirty-two dollars gets you one night in a four-by-six room with arched Gothic ceilings at the Jersey City YMCA on Bergen Avenue. Despite the building's architectural significance, it has the rank, musty odor of a space that has been around since 1924.

The only illumination in Andre's room is the egg-shaped spill from a banker's lamp that sits on a small table shoved in a corner. Andre is hunched over it, concentrating on the words that he commits to paper. He balls up the sheet and tosses it onto the growing pile on the glowing tile floor.

Andre shifts his focus from the empty page to the .38 that rests on the cot-sized bed. He takes the gun, places it on the table, and leans in to carefully consider the interlocking parts of the weapon before he tips his chair back and rocks on his toes. He gently brings the legs of the chair to the floor, seizes the firearm, and stares down the barrel.

Then, carefully, Andre moves the snub nose of the gun onto his right temple. The sensation of the cold metal on his skin sends shock waves of poison intent through his veins. Andre puts the pistol down, thrusts back from the table, and stands. He dries his palms on his jeans and sits on the edge of the bed.

Staring at the gun, he grabs it again.

Andre looks up to the ceiling and places the barrel in the soft pocket under his chin. His trigger finger trembles, his body convulses, and out of his mouth spills a frightening, guttural sob. Andre sucks in his breath, clenches his jaw, squeezes his eyes shut, and pulls the trigger.

Click.

Instantly, Little Dre's chubby cheeks blaze across the surface of Andre's addled conscience. He recalls his own words.

> But I cannot take my own life.
> What prevents me?
> The sea of tears my son would cry,
> Seeing his father lowered in the ground with his own
>   blood on his hands.

Andre throws the gun across the room.

Blam!

The universe goes silent except for the piercing, high-pitched frequency ringing in his ears.

Seconds of irritable stillness give way to the requisite sounds of life. Hurried footsteps approach the room, so Andre flops on his belly and gropes around on the floor until he finds the spent shell under the bed. Voices are outside the door.

"Is everything okay in there?"

Knocking.

Andre tucks the gun in the small of his back, opens the window, clambers down the fire escape, and drops to the street. A brisk two-step and he's around the corner. He checks over his shoulder even though he knows that OGC wouldn't be caught dead in the Bergen Hill neighborhood. No one from the Y tails him either.

Andre fumbles through his wallet, locates another business card, and dials.

"This is Rock."

"Hey, it's Andre Bolden. I met you a few weeks ago at Sandra Horton's house?"

"Yeah, what's going on, brother?"

"I need some help. I don't have anywhere to go and I'm thinking about twisted things."

"Brother, that's a great place to be."

Andre is fuddled by Rock's easy response. "What do you mean?"

"Where are you now?" Rock asks.

"Jewett between Bergen and Kennedy."

"Stay right there. I can meet you in about five minutes."

"Can't stay on this block. I have to keep moving."

"Alright, meet me at the fountain in ten."

The fountain in Lincoln Park is a fifty-three-foot marvel of early twentieth-century largess, complete with water-spouting frogs and creatures that most certainly go bump in the night. At least that's what Andre always thought. He and Auntie Cheeks used the fountain entrance to get to the playing fields where he first established himself as a gifted football player in Little League.

Andre has never been here at night, so he cautiously peeks over the rim of the fountain to see if the frogs and fiends look as frightening as he figured. They don't. Real life is scarier than any fountain, so the dead eyes peering up at him render the stony creatures harmless. Andre is relieved and disappointed at the same time.

He realizes that he thrives on fear. It has been with him so long that without it he feels incomplete. So he seeks it out beneath every rock and hard place that he has encountered in his hopeless life.

He slips the gun from his waist and stares at it.

Nothing works for me.

He hears a noise behind him and spins. Rock's hands shoot up when he sees Andre holding the gun.

"It's me. Rock. Put the gun down, Andre."

Andre smiles nervously. "Sorry, man. I wasn't pointing it at you. You caught me off guard."

Rock doesn't lower his hands as he eases forward. "Just put it away and we can talk about whatever's on your mind."

To Andre, Rock moves like a crisis negotiator attempting to talk someone off the edge of a bridge. But then he recalls his frantic call. *I'm thinking about twisted things.*

Self-conscious now, Andre pushes the gun back in his waist.

"You have a good job and a baby boy—why would you want to jeopardize that by carrying an illegal firearm?"

"How do you know it's illegal?"

"Because you can only get a concealed weapon permit in Jersey if you drive a armored car or you're a retired cop."

"I need it for protection."

"From who?"

"People."

"What people?"

Andre peers into Rock's eyes. "Just people, alright?"

Rock smiles and extends his hand to shake. "It's okay, brother. Bottom of the night to you. I didn't get a chance to properly greet you because of the way you were holding that gat."

Andre shakes his hand and the two men sit on the basin of the fountain. Neither says anything for several minutes.

"I can't believe I just tried to end everything." Andre monitors the reaction of Rock, who doesn't so much as flinch.

"Things must be pretty bad if you tried to take yourself out," Rock says. "Self-preservation is one of the strongest motivations humans have. What happened with what you just tried to do?"

"The gun didn't work."

"You pulled the trigger?"

"Yeah."

"Where'd you get the gun?"

"One of my contacts."

"So he beat you?"

"No, it fired after the fact."

Rock smiles. "Providence. It wasn't time for your hourglass to top out."

"Rock," Andre says, frustrated, "I'm really not interested in philosophizing right now."

"Philosophy went out the window when you tried to pull the plug on yourself, Dre. If you would've been successful, you'd be in front of God *right now*. With no more opinions and no more chances to get it right. So I'm here to challenge you to make finding out who God is your top priority. 'Cuz, brother, if you don't serve God in this life, you can't live with him in the next. Basically, you go to hell. That's just the way it is."

"But how do you know that?" Andre asks. He tries to sound gruff, but it squeaks out as if he's nine years old all over again.

"The way I know won't help you because you don't believe what I believe."

Andre gazes into the surrounding darkness. He stands and extends his fist to give Rock a pound.

"Alright, Rock. Thanks for coming through."

"My pleasure. Where you headed?"

"Not sure right now."

Rock looks at his watch. "You ate yet?"

"No."

"Why don't you roll with me then?"

"Where you going?"

Rock flashes a sly grin. "If you don't have anywhere to go, does it matter?"

"Well . . . yeah, it does."

"Alright, I'm heading to the Realness. Me and a few brothers get together every Wednesday at the meeting place, break bread, and break down truth."

Andre recalls Fredrick's offer for him to attend.

No way I want him to know the straits I'm in.

"That's alright. Thanks, though." Andre heads toward the fountain entrance.

"Dre."

He turns around.

"Pride."

"Pride?"

"It'll have you trying to hustle up somewhere to go just so you can hide."

"Hide from what?"

"The truth. Come on, man. You eat hot wings, right?"

A tear runs down Andre's cheek, and he's glad the darkness conceals it from Rock's view.

18

Andre never knew that chicken could taste so good. Fiery wing sauce collects at the corners of his mouth, and he feels like an animal—chawing, swallowing, only to tear more meat from the bone in hungry glurps. He looks up from his plate and notices Rock smiling.

"Haven't eaten all day," Andre says, a large ball of chicken lodged in his jaw.

"I ain't mad," Rock says. "Go 'head and get your grub on, brother."

Andre sees Fredrick stroll in. The moment he spots Andre, he does an about-face and heads for the steam table in the back of the room stocked with wings and baked beans. Two other men enter and grab plates.

Rock looks at his watch. "After you guys get your gut fuel, we'll go 'head and get started."

The five men gather at a table in the center of the room. Fredrick and Andre avoid looking at each other while Rock makes the introductions.

"Fredrick, you already know my brother Andre. Mark and Strange-O, this is Andre. Andre, Strange-O and Mark."

Strange-O pokes his hand out first. "That's my old emcee name, but I prefer it to my real one. My mother smote me

150

with one of them old-school COGIC names, Obadiah. But I love her anyway and it's a pleasure to meet you."

Mark pumps Andre's hand next. "What up, Dre? You mind if I call you that?"

"Nah, it's good," Andre says.

"Alright," Rock chimes in as he looks at Andre. "We usually open with prayer. You're welcome to participate if you want."

Andre has never really prayed. Sure, he's spouted things, usually in anger, to that impersonal force that seems to hover over all of human existence, but prayer? Never that.

He's not sure how to respond, and it must have been evident because Rock says, "Don't sweat it."

Andre steps to the side as the four men join hands and bow their heads. Rock closes his eyes, takes a deep breath, and relaxes. After another beat he begins.

"Father, we thank you that you're God and we're not. And we accept that you're sovereign over all peoples and activities in the earth. We thank you that you've given us eyes to see and hearts to believe that you are in fact God. And we acknowledge that you're good . . ."

Anger purls around Andre's stomach. Then he remembers.

Andre Bolden Sr. was an actuary for Farm Bureau Insurance Company in tiny Hertford, North Carolina. He also served as the treasurer of the tiny country church the family belonged to. Andre's mother, Margretta, was a schoolteacher who taught six days a week—five at Hertford Grammar School and one at Sunday school at the Bagley Swamp Baptist Church. They were by-the-Book Southern folk.

Rock's prayer drones on. "And we thank you that you're holy and righteous, which gives you the right to judge sin . . ."

Andre cuts out onto the street and looks up at the night sky. A dirty fury grips his head like interlocking pliers. "Good? Prove it then!"

In his periphery, Andre sees people on the sidewalk alter their path and veer away from him, but he's not moved. His gaze is fixed firmly on the dark expanse that surrounds the earth. His unanswered recriminations diffuse into the night.

"Yo, Dre." Rock pokes his meaty dome out of the meeting place. "Why'd you bounce?"

Andre turns his back on him. "I'm not going back in there, man."

"Hang on a second."

Rock disappears into the building and returns with a chair in each hand. He's followed by Mark, Strange-O, and finally Fredrick. The men encamp around Andre and take a seat. Reluctantly, Andre sits.

Several people pass by with strange looks.

What are these fools doing out here in the freezing cold on a Wednesday night?

Rock, Strange-O, and Mark are focused on the meeting, but Fredrick seems nakedly self-aware as he spies each person that passes to see if he's being seen.

"So Dre," Rock says. "We're bringing the Realness to you. What's on your mind? The floor—well, the sidewalk—is yours."

"I don't have anything to say," Andre answers.

"Why'd you roll out, fam?" Strange-O asks.

Andre sours and shoots him a prickly glare. "I'm not down for twenty questions, alright? Now I'll sit here and listen until I get cold, but that's it. Matter fact, let's go back inside because I'm cold right now."

Rock cracks and then Strange-O. Andre does his best to appear too serious to participate in silly snickering, but after Mark breaks up, yuks push past Andre's lips. Fredrick is the last to join in the laughter.

"Yo," Mark says as he laughs and points at Andre, "you were looking mad serious until your nose exposed you!" He sings, "Rudolph the red-nosed black dude!"

Rock slaps Andre on the back, still laughing. "And you're carrying your own chair inside, Rudolph, 'cuz it's nippy-bob out here!"

Fredrick extends his hand to Andre, who studies it before he finally takes it. "I'm sorry if I offended you," Fredrick says.

Andre shakes his hand even though he still doesn't trust him. He is still a dude and he is sniffing around his ex-girl.

After everyone has filtered out of the meeting place, Rock pulls Andre aside. "You need a place to stay tonight?"

Andre contemplates whether he should retreat from his earlier candor, because technically he doesn't need a place to stay. He's a lease holder on an apartment—he's just not able to get in it. Plus he's sure that if he really pressed Sandra, she wouldn't have him on the street.

Rock stares Andre dead in the eye and waits for an answer. "It's not rocket science, Dre. Earlier you said you didn't have anywhere to go."

Andre tangles with his ego. "Yeah, I need a place to stay," he admits, despite an aversion to further emotional exhibitionism.

"Done." Rock slaps him on the back and heads for the door.

A canary yellow 1955 Studebaker Champion coupe skirts the curb. Rock subtly flosses behind the wheel of the glimmering, vintage vehicle sitting on triple-gold Daytons. To Andre, the scene is an exercise in cognitive dissonance—a midthirties, rugged brother outfitted in Carhartt from head to toe behind the wheel of a brightly colored antique ride with hip-hop rolling from the speakers.

Andre smiles without even realizing it. He's made aware that his choppers are on flash once he slips into the well-oiled, white leather seats.

"What's up with all the teeth?" Rock promptly asks.

"You, man. I've never seen a brother your age in a classic car, especially a yellow one. You can afford something like this on a preacher's pay?"

"Brother, I ain't no preacher. I just try to live my life by the Scriptures with God's help. The offering we take up keeps the lights on, oil in the furnace, and helps us feed and clothe some of the people around here. And pay?" Rock shakes his head. "I don't do this for money."

"Then how can you afford a whip like this?"

"For my paying job, I'm a bouncer. At Club New York."

"A bouncer? At Club New York?"

"Yeah."

"Isn't that like . . . contradictory?"

"To what?"

"The whole preacher or living by the Scriptures thing you just said."

"You'd be surprised how open people are to Jesus after they fall on their face drunk and split their head open in VIP."

Andre snickers.

"I'm serious," Rock says.

"You talk about God at the club?"

"As God is my witness, I never once brought it up on my own. Opportunities just pop up. Plus it's the only job I could get where it didn't matter that I had a record. And half of New Jersey Truth I met up in there. Fredrick, Strange-O. All of those cats."

"And a lot of stars come through there too."

"Yeah, but what's a star? At the end of the day they're people just like everybody else."

"I hear that," Andre says.

He notices a Snoopy air freshener dangling from Rock's rearview mirror. The smug, vanilla-scented beagle transports Andre to the tidy brick house at the end of North Covent Garden Road in Hertford.

Andre's father always hung a new Snoopy air freshener on his rearview mirror after he waxed the car. The smell was so wonderfully dizzying.

What I wouldn't give for a hug from Pops.

Which was always followed by a firm kiss on the top of Andre's knuckle head.

"You okay?" Rock asks.

"That air freshener just takes me back. My pops used the same kind."

"You serious? Mine did too. Your pops still alive?"

"No. Died in a car wreck."

"Mine died in Vietnam." Rock extends his hand and gives Andre five. "Big ups for making it through the tough-life matrix. Not having a pops puts you at a competitive disadvantage in life, especially in the department of manhood."

Before Andre can respond, Rock cruises to a stop in front of the Greenville police precinct. "You can drop off firearms here, no questions asked. Just go to the front desk—"

"I'm familiar with the program," Andre says.

He sits for several moments and stares out at the empty street before he opens the door. Once he's inside the station, Andre searches for Jackson and Carollo.

A pale-faced officer swallowed up in his uniform sits—or rather is keeled over—at the front desk. He looks over fifty, but his manner makes him seem twice that. He smacks hard on gum, and his emerald green eyes pierce Andre as he approaches.

Andre holds out both hands. "I'm going into my waist to pull out a weapon. I'm just here to turn it in."

The officer sits up straight and places his hand on his service revolver. The fiery excitement that zings through his pupils makes Andre fear that he's being set up.

"Go ahead. I'm watchin'," the officer says. He speeds his chewing, which makes his gaunt face look like a rolling bag of bones.

Andre slowly removes the weapon and plunks it on the desk. The officer's chomping slows to a normal pace and his posture shrinks as he sinks back into his uniform.

"Is that it?" Andre asks.

"That's it."

Andre hurries out of the station as quickly as he can without compromising his cool.

Rock lives in Bayonne on the second floor of a midrise apartment building a block from the water. Andre steps into the smartly decorated living room, looks around, and says, "Bayonne on the bay, huh?"

"You start a gang and drama has a way of finding you," Rock says. "Even years later when you're trying to keep your nose clean. There's the couch, the bathroom's down the hall, and my room is off-limits. I don't have to worry about you tossing yourself off the balcony, do I?"

Andre looks as deadly serious as he can. "No."

"Cool. Good night."

Andre removes his shoes, turns off the light, and gets comfortable on his second couch in as many nights. Twinkling lights dazzle the surface of New York Bay, or is it Newark Bay or Kill Van Kull? Andre doesn't care. He folds his arms across his chest, and as he surrenders to burnout, he thinks, *Maybe tomorrow will be better.*

19

Andre's cell phone startles him awake. The display says *NYC MTA*.

"This is Andre."

"Andre Bolden? This is Human Resources at the Metropolitan Transportation Authority. Can you come in for an interview tomorrow morning?"

Andre pumps his fist. "What time should I be there?"

"Ten a.m., 347 Madison Avenue. Between 44th and 45th. Report to the fifth-floor boardroom."

"Thank you. I really apprecia—"

The person hangs up, but it's no matter.

Andre springs from the couch. "Yes!"

He bops to a silent beat, glides into a Stanky Legg, and then slams into a poker-faced Rock.

"Oh. My fault," Andre says.

"This your morning ritual or something?"

"No, that was the MTA. They called me for an interview."

"Looking to switch jobs?"

"I got let go from New Jersey Transit awhile ago."

"What happened?"

"Long story."

"Well, congratulations on the interview. I hope it works out for you. What's your plan now?"

"Get this job, get back into my apartment, and get things working in my favor again."

"You have a place to stay tonight?"

"Not really."

"Well, you can stay here another night," Rock says as he sweeps his hand through the room. "As you can see, I don't have a lot of space or I would let you stay longer."

"I really appreciate it," Andre says. "Can I use your bathroom? You know, to take a shower?"

"Go 'head. There's towels and washcloths in the closet."

A musty funk lights up the bathroom when Andre peels off his clothes. He turns on the shower and quakes at the thought of how rank the tang would be if it were summer. After he hand-washes his underwear with Pine Sol from under the sink, he wrings them out and spreads them on the edge of the tub. Biting hot water and Strawberry Botanicals body soap wash away seventy-two hours of feculent life.

Once out, Andre brushes his teeth with a finger and re-dresses minus the drawers, which he stuffs in his pocket.

Rock is at a small table guzzling down a bowl of Lucky Charms when Andre comes out of the bathroom.

"Want some breakfast?"

"Sure."

Andre feels awkward eating cereal at someone's table with wet underwear in his back pocket. When he finishes and stands, there's a wet splotch on the seat.

Rock notices Andre studying the chair. "You pee on yourself or something?"

Andre is stumped.

If I tell him, it's embarrassing. If I don't, it's nasty.

"Sorry, man. I got a wet spot in your chair."

Rock circles the table. "How'd you do that?"

The blotch is the size of a grown man's hand, and Andre is not sure how he can lie his way out of this one in a way that's convincing.

"I'm just going to be straight with you. I washed my underwear in your sink. I was planning on finding a Laundromat in the neighborhood to dry them out."

Rock's cereal spoon is in one hand and he scratches his head with his other, his eyes locked on the spot. "I can't say I've ever had this happen before." He looks up at Andre. "I have a washer and dryer in here, you know."

"Oh. Didn't know that. Mind if I use the dryer?"

"No problem," Rock says. "Just make sure you spray it with Lysol when you're done."

Another awkward moment.

Rock erupts. "Just kidding!" He slaps Andre on the back with the spoonless hand.

* * *

Little Dre has a firm grip on Andre's top lip with one hand and tears at Andre's eyelid with the other.

"Little man, Daddy's not going to drop you!"

From the moment Andre hoisted Little Dre onto his neck, it's been a father-son battle royal.

"When I rode on your grandpop's shoulders, I felt like I was on top of the world."

Oblivious to nostalgia, Little Dre slips one leg off of Andre's neck and starts to slide down his arm. However, he doesn't release Andre's eyelid or lip.

"Owwww, Dre!" Andre stops, bends in the direction that his lip and eye are pulled, and lowers his shoulder so that Little Dre can glide the rest of the way down. Junior Dre doesn't release his death grip until both feet are planted on the ground. Then he takes off running, giggling like there's no tomorrow.

As Andre watches him run, he vows that no matter how bad things get, he will never make another attempt on his life.

Little Dre spins around and says, "'Mon, Dah-dee, 'mon."

Andre smiles and takes off after him. Dre screams as Andre scoops him into his arms. "I got you!"

Little Dre laughs and kicks until Andre puts him down so that he can take off again.

Hakeem smiles when he sees Andre and Little Dre barreling toward him. Andre overtakes Dre just before he reaches the bench where Hakeem sits.

"So this is you and Sandra's little man, huh?" Hakeem sticks his hand out and Little Dre promptly slaps him five. "Handsome little guy," he says. "So how've you been, Dre? Everything going alright?"

"It's been real," Andre answers. "Hold on a second." He escorts Little Dre to the sandbox and carefully sorts through the granules before he allows him in. Satisfied that the sandbox is safe, Andre settles on the bench beside Hakeem. "Shame you can't let your kid play without checking first."

"I wouldn't have even thought to do anything like that."

"When you have kids you will. I've found broken glass, used condoms, and even a nickel bag of weed."

"In Bayonne Park?"

"Not here, but every place is the same. You can't trust anything when it comes to your kids."

The two of them observe Little Dre's carefree frolic.

"So tell me," Hakeem says, "how come you're not willing to come by the office anymore?"

"Because the guys that sell drugs across the street from you are OGC."

"I know that. But what does that have to do with you?"

"Somebody in OGC has it in for me. I'm just not sure who."

"I haven't seen anyone over there in a couple of weeks. But how'd you get tangled up with OGC?"

Andre shakes his head. Hakeem stays put.

"I saw my cousin get killed. And OGC is responsible."

"But how do you *know* they're responsible?" Hakeem presses.

"I just know, alright?"

Little Dre looks up from the sandbox, wipes snot from his nose with mitted hand, waves, and smiles. Andre smiles and waves back.

"I'm going to have to work this out on my own, Keem."

"I don't think that's the wisest way to handle it."

"Of course you'd say that. You're a shrink. Besides, my insurance is gone. I can't pay you anymore anyway."

"We can worry about payment later. I've observed enough to give you a diagnosis. But it'll require another session, preferably indoors, so we can discuss it."

"I don't know where we'd do that because coming to your office is out."

"I do make house calls."

"If I had a house, you could call it."

"You're without a place again?"

"I still have my place," Andre says. "My landlord just won't let me back in it until I pay back rent."

Andre hangs on to see if Hakeem thinks of something he hasn't already. When it's apparent he doesn't, Andre stands and says, "Alright, I'll catch up with you later."

Andre gazes up the steep stoop. He hoists Little Dre into his arms, collapses the stroller, straps it onto his shoulder, and mounts the steps. The moment he depresses the buzzer, the door flies open.

Ms. Rutigliano's eyes sear him like a blast of scalding steam. She notices Little Dre and cools. "This your son? He's gotten so big. He's adorable."

Little Dre reaches for Ms. Rutigliano.

"Awww, how cute. Come on in, it's cold out there."

Andre steps into the parlor and marvels at Ms. Rutigliano's instant temperature shift. She takes Little Dre into her arms, removes his hat, and unbuttons his coat.

"I didn't plan on staying long, Ms. Rutigliano," Andre says. "I just wanted to appeal to your sense of compassion and ask if I could get one suitcase out of the apartment."

Ms. Rutigliano is bouncing Little Dre in her arms and he's loving every minute of it.

"You think you're the first tenant that's tried to beat me? You get stuff out and you'll never pay me. A Texas-sized no, Andre, and that's my final answer."

"I've had on these same clothes for three days."

Ms. Rutigliano stops bouncing the baby and gives Andre a once-over. "You still look clean." She heads toward the back of the house with Little Dre in tow. "I just baked some coconut brownie avalanche cookies. He'll love 'em. Loads of chocolate, coconut pieces, and caramel swirl. We'll be right back."

Dusty old bat. She's like a female Mr. Hyde.

Ms. Rutigliano returns with a ziplock bag stocked to the creases. Little Dre toddles beside her with a mouthful of cookies. She hands Andre the bag and proceeds to rebundle Little Dre.

"Cookies you can have, but suitcases?" She wags her bony finger in Andre's face. "Tough chance." She opens the front door and hustles them out.

Little Dre waves and beams a chocolate-covered smile.

"Bye, sweets."

Slam!

Rahjaan squints at himself in the side-view mirror of a parked car, fascinated by the fleshy feeling on the tip of his tongue as he obsessively jams it in the hole vacated by his front tooth. Without warning, a black Crown Victoria bears down on him so swiftly that he has no chance to peel off and run.

Detective Jackson hops out. "Where've you been?" he asks.

"Um . . . I been around, but . . . I don't think I wanna play anymore," Rahjaan answers.

"And when did you decide that?"

"I mean, it's not like I'm gonna make the NBA or anything."

"Rahjaan, this is not about you making the NBA. It's about you staying off the streets so you can make it to eighteen and still have the right to vote." Jackson looks at his watch. "Practice starts in fifteen minutes."

"So you putting out APBs on people when they miss a few practices?"

"People? You're the only one not showing up." Jackson looks at his face. "And what happened to your tooth?"

"Um . . . lost it in a fight."

"What did I tell you about that?" Jackson asks. "You keep that hot head and you're going to lose more than a tooth. I've seen it happen a million times."

"It wasn't my fault, Detective Jack, and I don't have my jersey anyway. You the one that said nobody can be on the court in street clothes."

"The only person who controls your fists is you, Rahjaan."

Jackson pulls a jersey from the backseat that has "Det. Jack's Rim Rattlers" emblazoned on the front. He flips the jersey around and displays the back. "What does that say?"

Rahjaan sucks his teeth. "'Forgot mine.'"

"Right. And the number zero because that's what excuses are worth." He tosses Rahjaan the jersey. "Make sure I get it back after practice. Hop in. I'll give you a lift."

"You know I ain't riding in the car with no DT."

"The windows are tinted."

"But the streets ain't."

"Okay. But if you're not in the gym and ready to play in ten minutes, I'm coming to get you."

"Detective Jack, I gotchu. Be easy."

20

Andre recites the lyrics to the Grandmaster Flash classic "New York, New York" as he approaches 347 Madison Avenue. He hasn't been to the "big city of dreams" in at least a year. Andre is dazzled by the high volume of traffic pushing through the streets. His palms itch to grip and to spin the steering wheel of a bus again. A couple of 2011s go by, followed by an '09 and two '08s. Andre grins.

No geriatric busses.

"Later for New Jersey Transit," he says. He cheeses all the way to the fifth floor of 347.

When Andre steps off the elevator, he actually *feels* like a bus driver. Ever since he became an operator, he regarded driving as something he did, not who he was. But when he sees black-and-white pictures of enviro-killing dinosaurs alongside color portraits of clean-air hybrids, he rolls back his shoulders and stands tall.

A chunky but friendly receptionist directs Andre to the conference room. Ten imposing leather chairs surround a strong mahogany table with brass brads tacked around the circumference. Not sure which seat to take, Andre selects one in the middle. The top of the table is so glossy that Andre can see his reflection. He smiles at himself, winks, and does a swagger nod.

That's right, I'm UP IN here!

He checks out his "new" suit and recalls how Rock came through this morning. He gave Andre a ride to the Salvation Army thrift store on King and purchased a Brooks Brothers suit in surprisingly good condition for only twenty dollars. The waist is a little big, but nothing that Andre can't easily gather together with his belt and conceal with the suit jacket. He just has to remember not to open the jacket—for anything.

A short, slender, fiftysomething Asian man enters the boardroom and quietly closes the door behind him. He spots Andre yawing at himself in the mirrored tabletop.

"What are you, your own personal nutcase or something?" the man asks.

Andre stands at attention and extends his hand. "Andre Bolden. Part-time comedian, full-time bus operator."

The man shakes Andre's hand and peers deeply into his eyes. "You are a nut job, aren't you?"

"You caught me in a private moment. I'm sure you've done funny stuff when no one was looking, right?"

The man's face is grave-chamber serious. "I don't do funny."

Pause.

"Well, thanks for bringing me in for an interview," Andre says brightly.

The man sits and opens a manila folder. Andre also takes a seat. "Almost three years with New Jersey Transit. Why are you looking to leave?"

"Well, the New York City MTA is the high-water mark for public transportation. I learned the ropes at New Jersey Transit so I could—"

"Jump ship," the man interrupts. "We get a lot of you's in here. Disloyal, but I gotta admit most of you's are good drivers. I haven't called the two references on your application. But I did notice that your immediate supervisor from NJT isn't on here. I take that to mean he doesn't know you're looking?"

Hadn't thought of that, but it sounds good. Now I don't have to lie.

"Exactly," Andre says, unaware that he just lied.

"So you need to know that this is just the first step in the interview process. I'm the guy that meets the flesh and blood off the streets to make sure that nut jobs that entertain themselves in tabletops don't get hired."

The man holds a steady gaze on Andre, and after several uncomfortable moments, Andre smiles. "Don't take that to mean anything. I'm just a happy guy."

Another lie.

The man continues to boil Andre in a callous stare. "I don't know about you, Bolden. You know how many people wanna drive for the MTA?"

"Hundreds?"

"Thousands. We *are* public transportation. And you're crazy. So maybe we should just say goodbye." He stands and extends his hand to shake.

"Listen, Mr. . . . ?" Andre says.

"Chin."

"Mr. Chin. I *need* this job. And I guarantee you I'll be an asset to the MTA. I approach my employment the same way I approached my assignments when I played college football—with discipline, tenacity, and precision." Andre takes it upon himself to quickly thumb through Chin's folder, slide out four photocopies, and hold them up. "I didn't get driver of the month four times in thirty-two months for nothing."

167

Mr. Chin sits back down and smiles. "Congratulations. You made it to the next round. I like to simulate the pressure you'll experience driving the streets of New York. That way I know how you'll react in high-stress situations."

Andre is unable to smile because the cold fingers of angst are still gripped around his neck.

Mr. Chin slaps him on the back. "Lighten up. You did fine." He throws his head back and laughs so hard tears run down his cheeks. "'I don't do funny'! That was classic!"

Andre is not amused. His heart beats so fast that his rib cage strains to keep the fumbling muscle in its cavity. He counterfeits a smile and says, "Funny."

"Next you'll meet with Dan 'the Dragon Man' Houzchict," Chin says, pronouncing the name *house chick*. He winks at Andre. "He's a little man, but a tough guy with a big heart." He escorts Andre out the door and turns deadly serious. "I don't like surprises. So is there anything you need me to know before you go? Because trust me, I'm going to find out anyway. My job is to crawl up in your rear chambers with a pickax to see what I can find. You know why?"

Horrified, Andre wobbles his head no.

"Because the MTA is looking for lifers, not fly-by-nights."

Andre is surprised at the pressure he feels as he looks into Chin's coal-black eyes. An unsettling conviction upsets his peace. *Is he just jerking my chain again?*

And then the beastly question. It scratches at Andre's conscience with dirty nails. *Have you ever been convicted of a crime?*

Andre shakes loose from conviction's clutches and utters a resolute, "The application speaks for itself."

"Great. You and the Dragon Man are on for Tuesday at two."

Andre is pilloried by guilt on the three-block walk to Grand

Central Station. Seated on the subway platform, he massages his temples and watches three rats play leapfrog on the tracks. In the past, Andre's lies were never tailed by remorse; instead they brought inner comfort because in his mind they protected him.

Down the darkened subway tunnel, twin white lights creep along the surface of the rails and then crawl along the grimy tile walls. The train appears next. Andre latches on to the headlights and stands. Guilt goads him closer to the edge, and by now the train is near enough that he can see the conductor. They lock eyes as the train speeds into the station, and rather than jockey for position to board, Andre bolts up the stairs and back onto the crowded street. He wades through traffic and contrition, convinced that he's being driven by something outside of himself. Yet he obeys his conscience and returns to 347.

The chunky but friendly receptionist smiles and says, "Forget your umbrella?"

Andre cockles his brow and points out the window. "There's no rain in the forecast."

"I know. Just kidding."

Andre shakes his head in frustration. "Just one big comedy troupe in here, huh?"

"I guess so. What can I do for you? Didn't expect you back so soon."

Chin appears out of nowhere. "Andre, what's going on?"

Andre looks at the receptionist, who looks directly at him and smiles.

"Do you have an office we can go to?" he asks Chin.

"Sure," he says.

Andre follows him down a long corridor to a closet-sized office and takes a seat. He starts to sweat so he unbuttons his suit jacket, and folds of bonus pants material flop out.

Chin smiles and points. "Suit's a little big, huh? Talk to me."

Andre looks down at his pants and fleetly rebuttons his jacket. "On the question that asks if you've ever been convicted of a crime, I put no, but that's not completely true."

Chin's eyebrows inch up his forehead a hair. "I have to say, Andre. You're the first person to ever admit to anything like this. How'd you get wound up in the justice system? You don't seem like the type."

"I'm not. I made a really big mistake when I was in college. It was seven years ago and something I'll regret for the rest of my life."

Chin grabs Andre's application and a pen. "So what happened?"

Andre is tempted to reconsider, but it's too late because he's seated in front of a man who holds the balance of his fate in his mucky little hands.

"A neighborhood friend asked me to drop off a cooler full of exotic fish at Newark Airport. But there was more in the bags than just fish. My creative writing professor and football coach testified to my character and work ethic. The two things that will make me successful here at the MTA."

"Drugs?"

"Yeah . . . drugs." Andre resents that Chin pares down the worst decision of his life into a single word.

"You know what, Andre? I'm glad you told me this. And I like you. So let me see what I can do." Chin stretches his arm across the desk. "We'll call you."

"But what about Tuesday at two with Houzchict?"

"We'll call you."

"Mr. Chin, my conscience brought me back here. I was about to get on the train but came back because I wasn't comfortable being dishonest."

"I believe you, Andre. So let me see what I can do. And like I said, we'll call you."

21

Montclair Mercedes sits on Prospect Avenue, which separates the lush greens of the Montclair Golf Club from the rustic beauty of the Eagle Rock Reservation Conservancy. Dewey Horton built this dealership from scratch, and in the thirty years he's been in business, he's had the pleasure of serving one president, three governors, countless freeholders, several New York Giants, two Grammy Award–winning rappers, and Bruce Springsteen. Mr. Horton wisely leveraged the dealership's prime location and high-end clientele to open six other dealerships in northern New Jersey.

Despite his success, Mr. Horton dabbles in insecurity when he attends Wharton alumni events. After all, who gets an Ivy League MBA to sell cars?

Mr. Horton was pleased when Sandra decided to follow in her father's footsteps and choose St. Peter's for her undergraduate studies. He fully expected Sandra to go to graduate school, and she didn't have to go to Penn or major in business—she could choose any discipline that would give her a leg up to accomplish more than he did.

Mr. Horton removes his black square glasses, rubs his eyes, and winces at the thought of his Baby Love as a single mother in one of the worst neighborhoods in New Jersey. It tears him up in ways that are beyond the bounds of explanation. There's not a day that goes by that he doesn't wonder if pulling the plug on Sandra's tuition was the best way to handle her indiscretion.

He looks out onto the lot stocked with the finest automobiles that money can buy and replaces thoughts of Sandra with more comfortable ruminations on sales. *No ups in two hours. But it'll pick up. It always does.*

Mr. Horton's secretary Myrna peeks into the office. "There's a gentleman here to see you named Andre Bolden."

Mr. Horton furrows his brow. "Andre Bolden?"

"That's what he said."

"Give me a minute."

Myrna leaves and Mr. Horton peers out of the window he had built to allow him to monitor activity on the sales floor. From this perch he's seen everything from marital slugfests to a push-up contest between James Gandolfini and Rex Ryan. Today, however, it's the characterless father of his grandson in a funereal Brooks Brothers suit.

He straightens his tie and buzzes Myrna. "Send him in."

Andre paces in, looking sheepish, and extends his hand across the desk. Mr. Horton can't bring himself to stand and makes no effort to smile or retrieve Andre's hand.

"Sit down," Mr. Horton says, more poisonous than he intended.

Andre smiles uncomfortably. "Thank you."

Mr. Horton gives Andre a long, thorny stare, but Andre seems determined to meet his gaze no matter how hot his displeasure.

"What are you doing here?" Mr. Horton asks finally, removing his glasses and leaning across the desk. He sees a touch of fear in Andre's eyes.

"Were you struggling to come up with words when you were tricking the wits of my daughter?"

Andre swallows. "Mr. Horton, I'm really sorry about everything that's happened up until this point."

"And what is an apology supposed to do?"

"Hopefully? Start a conversation."

Mr. Horton sits back in his chair, puzzled. "So what do you have to say for yourself?"

Andre takes a moment to answer. "First I'd like to say that I really do love your daughter—"

Mr. Horton springs up with finger extended and mouth agape before he catches himself. He clasps his fingers together, lowers his chin, and covers his mouth with the locked knuckles of both fists.

"And I want to get back together with her," Andre continues.

Mr. Horton's eyes poof like a mushroom cloud. "You mean marry her?"

"Yes, sir. That's what I mean."

An excruciatingly long beat punctuated by a torturous silence.

"Andre, what are your spiritual underpinnings?"

"Spiritual underpinnings?"

"What God do you serve? Do you serve God at all?"

"With all due respect, Mr. Horton, I don't see what that has to do with Sandra and me getting back together."

This young man doesn't have a clue.

Nevertheless, Mr. Horton is intentional in his calm. "Being a husband is about more than paychecks and chest hair. A man is supposed to be the spiritual head of his household. That means you're the leader when it comes to matters of God and the spirit. And if you forsake that responsibility, it's impossible for you to adequately lead your wife and children."

Andre seems to be listening, but he looks lost.

"You've never heard any of this before, have you?"

"No, I haven't."

"So what does marriage mean to you?"

"Basically, a man and a woman committing themselves to each other for life, and in me and Sandra's case, raising Little Dre and, hopefully, having a couple more Little Dres."

"And in your world, God has no part in that?"

"Sandra is getting back into the God thing and that's cool, but for me, God is more a concept than anything."

Mr. Horton goes silent.

"You're into God, Mr. Horton, but look at you. You have reasons to believe. But God ain't concerned about me. My life is messed up right now."

Andre shakes his head and appears to be scuffling with his emotions. "I didn't come here to talk about this, Mr. Horton. I came to apologize, and to let you know that I want to do right by your daughter . . . and to ask you for a job."

Okay, now I get it.

"Andre, I'm going to be straight with you. I don't like you very much. And after all that you've done, I can't believe that you have the brass to come in here and ask me for a job."

Andre parks his eyes on the floor. "So no matter what I do, the relationship between us won't change?" He looks up.

Mr. Horton is flush with frustration. On the one hand, he thinks it best if Sandra, Andre, and Little Dre work it out, but on the other hand, a spiritless man is a recipe for disaster in any marriage to his daughter.

Andre stands. "Take care, Mr. Horton." He jets out of the office without attempting to shake.

Mr. Horton picks up the phone and watches Andre scurry across the lot.

Sandra is surprised to see her father's number blink on her cell phone. She steps away from the maître d' desk and answers quickly. "Daddy, are you okay?"

"*I'm* okay, I'm just wondering what's not working in the head of your ex . . . boyfriend, or whatever you call the father of my grandson."

"What are you talking about, Daddy?"

"He just came here in a suit and asked me for a job. Cloaking the whole mess in an apology and some business about wanting to get married."

"To who?"

"Aretha Franklin, Sandra. Who do you think?"

Sandra shakes her head. *I know it must've killed Andre to do that.*

"I'm telling you, I was mad enough to curse!" Mr. Horton says.

Sandra chuckles. When she was growing up, Mr. Horton would sometimes tell her what he was like before he got "saved," but those stories clashed with the only version of her father that she ever knew—Dr. Hardness, tough, clean.

"You're *laughing*?"

"I'm sorry, Daddy. The idea of you cursing someone out, especially Andre, is funny to me."

"Baby Love, I don't think this is funny, particularly since Andre wants to marry you. Did you know that he's a borderline atheist?"

"Daddy, you're overreacting. And Andre and I aren't even together, so you don't have to worry about me marrying him."

"So what are you going to do?"

"About what?"

"Your situation. Your life. Something's got to give, Baby Love. And I'm here to help you. So if you want to go back to school, I'll cover it. I'll even pay your rent while you go."

Sandra twists one of her braids and looks across the empty restaurant. "It's getting busy here, Daddy. I'm going to have to talk to you later."

It's 11:27 p.m. and Andre has been tucked away in the Pavonia/Newport train station for the last two hours. He found a *New York Times* on a bench and read through every story in just under an hour. Not willing to be alone with his thoughts, Andre starts through the *Times* a second time.

After every other sentence, he looks up to see if anyone is watching him. Thus far he's invisible, yet he feels as if everyone knows that he's been in the same spot while no less than fifteen trains rumbled by.

His stomach loudly grouses about its hollow state, and he remembers the bowl of cereal that he had at Rock's this morning. The thought of magically delicious frosted oats and sweet, colorful marshmallows casts a spell on Andre that dazzles his digestive juices.

He flips open his phone and dials Sandra, only to realize that he's underground without a signal.

A homeless man trudges over and parks next to him.

Four empty benches and he chooses this one.

A wild odor whiffs from the homeless man's filthy body. He looks at his watch. "The sun comes up in another eight hours. How many more times in that time are you going to read that same *Times*?"

Andre eyes the man. He is white with a fantastically wrinkled face, a messy red beard, and matching, bushy eyebrows that he raises when Andre's gaze doesn't abate. He extends his hand and Andre reluctantly shakes.

"When I first came underground, I wore a suit too. I was vice president of global transaction services at Investment Banking Systems. You heard of them?"

Andre nods his head as the man hastily rubs his.

"In 2005 I'm in Frankfurt Airport, and . . . somehow my thoughts start going faster than I could manage. One thing led to another . . . and that's basically how I wound up down here. But it's not as bad as you think. Responsibility's not all it's cracked up to be."

He looks at Andre. "You're wondering how I knew you were homeless? It's pretty obvious." He points to a woman in a business suit on the opposite platform. "She's homeless too. Know how I know? She had on the same suit yesterday and she hung out down here for three hours before she finally got on a train. I'm sure she slept in a car because it's safer than sleeping in the station, especially for a pretty woman like her. Probably still has a job but can't make her mortgage. What's your story?"

Andre stands as the next train pulls into the station. "I don't have a story and I'm not homeless." Andre steps onto the train, and when the doors close the old man jams his thumbs in his ears, wiggles his fingers, and wags his tongue. Then he points at Andre and snickers. He's missing the same three teeth that Auntie Cheeks was without.

Andre stands in front of 64 Martin Luther King Drive. It's 3:47 a.m. He pushes open the door on rusty hinges and climbs the rickety stairs to the second floor. Bobby "Blue" Bland's "I've Been Wrong So Long" wails through the crack under Mr. Burrell's door.

Andre does his signature knock. Sandra doesn't answer so he whips out his cell phone. A text message buzzes through. *Your bill is 60 days past due. To avoid an interruption in your service—*

Andre deletes it.

The sound of four locks being released fills the dark hallway. Sandra opens the door. Her hair is disheveled and she appears to be absorbed in fatigue.

"*What* are you doing here, Andre?"

"I woke up on the train so I decided to come over here. I'd like to come in."

Sandra closes her eyes and pushes open the door.

Andre lowers his hackles because he expected a fight. He had rehearsed every point and rebuttal on his walk from the train station. He sits on the couch, removes his shoes, and loosens his tie.

"What do you think you're doing?" Sandra asks.

"I told you I was sleeping on the train. Why should I do that when you have a place?"

"I've already told you that we're not married, so we're not going to act like a married couple."

"Married couples aren't the only people who spend the night together, Sandra! Stop killing me with the morality play."

Sandra reopens the front door and leans against it. "Good night, Andre."

"So what happens if I refuse to leave?"

Sandra yawns and covers her mouth, looking too tired to fight.

"Sandra, *please.*"

"Andre, *please.* Respect my house and what I'm trying to do here."

Sandra leaves the door ajar and drags herself to the bedroom. She returns with her purse. "Here's fifty dollars. It's all I have. That should get you a few nights at one of the SROs around here."

Andre takes the money. "So you'd rather me shack with dope fiends and hookers instead of here with you?"

"I'm just trying to help."

"What do I have to do to make things right between us?"
She sighs.

"I don't have anything, Sandra. And what I want more
than anything is you."

"I'm not having this conversation at four o'clock in the
morning."

Andre starts to leave but turns. "I don't care if you want
to hear it or not, but I love you, Sandra. And I'm not afraid
to say it anymore."

"Stop doing this to yourself, Andre."

"I'm only acknowledging the truth."

22

Once upon a time, the White Horse Hotel was a playground for the nouveau riche who made their fortune running the Pennsylvania Railroad. Before tunnels were built to Manhattan, the railroad dead-ended in Jersey City. But that was a hundred years ago. Today the hotel is a scum magnet that attracts human waste from Hoboken, Union City, Kearny, Bayonne, and East Newark. Andre jams the buzzer, wondering how he became one of them.

A spindly old white man in his midseventies peeks through the glass door that leads to the street. When Andre spots him, he buzzes with refreshed insistence. The old man shuffles to the door, jangles through his pocket, and pulls out a key ring loaded with openers.

"Hang on, man. What's your problem out there?" After considerable effort, the old man selects the correct key and swings open the door.

"My problem is that it's been a long day," Andre says.

"Mime's been long too, but I don't come to your place and knock the snot out of your means of entry!"

Andre follows the man to the front desk and is hit square in the face with a stench strong of urine, sex, and hard times. The old man is obviously immune to the funk.

"How long you're for?" the man asks.

"I have fifty dollars."

The old man's eyes light up. "Big splender, are you? Suit too. Your girlfriend click you out or something?"

"Something like that," Andre says.

"Well, at $7.19 a night that would get you . . ." The old man taps out the math on an antiquated adding machine as he tugs at the one shock of white hair that remains on his cucumber-shaped head. "Six point nine nights." He grins wide. "Swap me a nice tip and I'll give you a whole seven."

Andre frowns. "How do you calculate nine-tenths of a night?"

The old man frowns back. "You the police, are you?"

"Police? Please."

"Then how come you don't know about ninth of nights, seventh of nights, or any mathematical inclimate of fifteen minutes for a room?"

"Look, man. I just want to get a shower and some sleep."

"Shower's a dollar a night extra."

Andre does the math in his head. "So that's 6.1 nights if I want a shower?"

"Minimum stay is a fort of a night. Fifteen-minute inclimates. You can't rent a room for less time than that."

Andre slides his rumpled dollars across the counter. "Just give me the room with the shower."

The ring of the adding machine sounds off again.

"What the heck, I'll give you the seventh day since I'm an Adventist."

Andre stares at him blankly.

"You know. Like, Seventh-Day Adventist?"

"It's too early in the morning for a sermon."

"Thirty seconds. I promise. Then I'll give you this." He dangles Andre's key and smiles.

Andre sighs. *Everybody's got a gimmick.* "Twenty-nine, twenty-eight, twenty-seven—"

"Okay, here grows." The old man's twiggy arms and weathered lips flap furiously. "God wants human beans to see a clear picture of his character in the deepest pot of our hearts. And he showed his character when he made human beans and gave us the choice to love him or to hate him. He also showed his character with the death of the Christ on the cross to pay the punishment for our sins. But the biggest show is Christ's empty grave-cave, which proves he's alive! Living to fill us with his love! Hallelujah!" The old man nods and gives Andre a "so whaddya think?" goofy-toothed grin.

Andre nabs the key. "If you're so filled with God's love, then why are you working in a place like this?"

The old man's smile vanishes. "I live here. What's your excuse?"

Andre swallows a crusty piece of humble pie. "Guess we're in the same boat then. At least for the next seven days. Sorry for acting like that outside."

"No problem, buddy. Good night." The old man ambles off into an office behind the front desk.

Andre's room has more in common with a crawl space than any kind of accommodation for a man of his size and expectation. The sound of rough sex peals through the wall from the room next door. Andre drops on the frumpy bed and covers his ears, but that only muffles the shrieks and rattling mattress springs. Andre stands and pounds the wall until his fist throbs. "Shut up! Shut up! Shut up! Shut up! Shut up! Shut up! Shut up!"

Andre feels his husky voice reverberate around the room before he realizes that all is still. His chest heaves as he breathes heavily, uncontrollably, through clenched teeth. He balls his fingers into fists, digs his nails into his palms, and squeezes his eyes shut tight as an antidote to the pressure that grows in his head. He feels delirious, crazy, dangerous, but he can't stop where his head takes him.

He grabs the raggedy nightstand by the bed and raises it above his head as he faces the window. He sees his reflection in the glass and doesn't recognize the man glaring back at him.

The reflection in the window starts to cry. The man's face twists into a monument of hurt, pain, and childhood disappointments come of age. Now he sobs savagely, but it's okay because it's not him. It's someone Andre doesn't know. Someone Andre doesn't want to be. Someone Andre hates.

His phone buzzes, and after the second vibration tickles his thigh, Andre replaces the nightstand on the floor and retrieves the phone from his pocket. *Sandra* blinks on the display.

"Hello?"

"Why do you sound like that, Andre?"

"Like what?"

"I don't know. Trembly."

"I'm cool."

"Well, I'm worried about you."

Andre sees a quiver of a smile in the window but chooses silence because he wants to see just how great Sandra's concern is for him. She finishes with, "I woke up a few minutes ago and I just felt like you were in trouble. Where are you?"

"The White Horse."

"You know someone was murdered there last year, right?"

"Yeah, I heard about it."

Quiet on Sandra's end, followed by a sigh. "Andre, I'm going to tell you something, but I don't want you to take it the wrong way."

"Go ahead," he says.

"I still have love for you, okay? But it's not the way you want me to have it. You're the father of my son, so I don't

183

want anything to happen to you. And I don't have a problem with you. I forgave you a long time ago. But right now we're two different people with different wants and needs in life."

Andre can't help it. He's taking it the wrong way. Excitement rises in his lower parts.

"One last thing, Andre. You asked what you would have to do to make it right between us."

Andre's spirit lifts from the filthy floor to the peeling ceiling. Now his silence is motivated by disbelief.

"You there?" she asks.

"Yeah, I'm here."

"Since you were honest with your feelings, I figured I could be honest with mine." Sandra pauses for a beat. "The only way we could begin to even *think* about being together again is if I'm able to respect you with the level of respect I have for my father. Actually, even more than him because if you're my husband, you have to occupy the highest position of respect in my life."

"That's not fair, Sandra. Your dad is paid."

"This isn't about money. But you do have to be a *real* man of God. Because if you're not, then we'll be unequally yoked."

"What do you mean, 'unequally yoked'?"

"Together, but pulling each other in opposite directions. Look, I'm trying to live my life for God. So if you're living your life for yourself, or even for me and Little Dre, we'll always be moving in different directions. And eventually the family will be torn apart."

"Sandra, you're starting to sound like some kind of religious fanatic—"

"See? You're criticizing me. We can't be together like that. If you can't accept me for who I am, even if it's different from how I used to be, then you're fooling yourself if you think you really love me."

Andre is quieted.

"Can you read something for me?" she asks.

"Read what?"

"Is there an Old Testament there?"

"The only thing here is misery and me."

"Okay, Mr. Misery and Me," Sandra says sarcastically.

Andre opens the drawer to the nightstand that he was about to toss through the window and finds a tattered Testament inside.

"What do you want me to read?" Andre asks.

"Turn to Lamentations chapter 3."

Andre locates the table of contents and flips to the book. "Which verse?" he asks.

"All of them."

"It's sixty-six verses here."

"Just read," Sandra says.

Andre sighs and begins.

> I have suffered much
> because God was angry.
> He chased me into a dark place,
> where no light could enter.
> I am the only one he punishes
> over and over again,
> without ever stopping.

Andre stops. "Is this some kind of joke?"

"Go to verse 19," Sandra says.

> Just thinking of my troubles
> and my lonely wandering
> makes me miserable.
> That's all I ever think about,
> and I am depressed.

Andre fixes on *depressed.*
Okay, I admit it. I'm depressed.
His admission forms a large lump in his throat, and when he swallows, his eyes swell with optic rain. "I'm not reading any more of this," Andre asserts.
"Why not?"
"For what? To see how much God has ruined my life?"
"Of course not, Andre. That doesn't make any sense and you know it. Go to verse 37."

> No one can do anything
> without the Lord's approval.

Andre recalls Rock's several statements on sovereignty as his eyes drop to the next line.

> Good and bad each happen
> at the command
> of God Most High.
> We're still alive!

A thin silence.
Sandra breaks it. "You're almost to the end. Go to verse 60."
Andre is not sure why, but he does.

> You know every plot
> they have made against me.

Andre pictures the weaselly eyes of the gunman floating around in the darkness of his black hoodie.

> Get angry and go after them
> until not a trace is left
> under the heavens.

23

Clops is slouched in a seat in the waiting room at Greenville Hospital. He clips his fingernails between peeks at a television slung high in one corner. Rahjaan bursts through the doors of the hospital's dental clinic and flashes his top choppers.

"Looks good, right?"

Clops inspects Rahjaan's smile. "Yeah, that is a good job."

The dentist stands behind Rahjaan and beams brightly.

"Did you throw in like a free cleaning or something?" Clops asks.

"Well . . . yes, I did do a cleaning. But I didn't throw it in, it's standard."

"Hold up. You telling me that after I spend four g's on a tooth I don't get anything? No free toothbrushes, nothing?"

The mousy, bespectacled dentist turns crimson, but he doesn't seem in the least bit intimidated by Clops's aggressive posture. "What you paid for, sir, was a new tooth. The same service done elsewhere would've cost you a whole lot more. All the services we offer here are heavily subsidized by Medica—"

"Don't patronize me, man." Clops's eyes narrow. "Even

the Chinese restaurant gives you a free can of Nestea when you spend more than twenty bucks."

Apparently not sure how to respond, the dentist turns on his heels and disappears into the clinic. Clops taps Rahjaan's chest. "Let's bounce before I flip in here. They don't even know who they dealing with."

Hakeem climbs the decrepit steps deep in the bowels of the White Horse. He reaches the fourth floor and knocks on door number three. Andre greets him with a shamefaced grin. "Beats sleeping on the train."

Hakeem gives him five. "You don't have to explain anything to me. You're surviving, and that's laudable."

Both men cop a squat on the nasty bed.

"I would offer you something, but there's no refrigeration here," Andre says.

"Don't worry about it. I'm here to see how you're doing. I'm glad you called."

"I had quite an experience last night," Andre says. "I almost lost it completely and then Sandra called."

Hakeem smiles big.

"What are you smiling at?"

"It's the first time you called her Sandra instead of your girl."

"It is what it is. But she did tell me what I had to do to get her back."

"Oh yeah, what's that?"

"Earn her respect and go to church."

"That's what she said?"

"Basically."

"What were her exact words?"

"She said she had to respect me more than any other man she knows, and that I had to be a *real* man of God."

"The respect part I get, but you equate being a real man of God with going to church?"

"That's what makes you a Christian, right? And sitting in a church for a couple of hours a week is a sacrifice I'm willing to make to get her back. It's the 'getting a good job' part that's going to be more difficult. But once I do that, you'll be getting an invitation from us on high-end card stock embossed with all six of our names." Andre smiles and etches the names on invisible parchment suspended in air. "'Andre Jerome Bolden and Sandra Elyse Horton request your presence as they weave their lives together in ever-binding matrimonial bliss.'"

"Cute," Hakeem says. "But that's a pretty heavy set of demands she laid on you, given the history of your relationship. So I think you're going to have to do a little more than get a good job and go to church, brother."

Andre stares at Hakeem as if he's raining complex drops on his simplicity parade. "I'm just happy she's coming around. She's been an ice block for the last six months."

"Fair enough, but what I really want to discuss is your diagnosis."

Andre stands and immediately begins to drag his nails across his head. "I don't know if I'm up to hearing that right now."

"A diagnosis is simply a solution to a problematic situation."

Andre entwines his fingers atop his head and considers. "Alright, hit me."

Hakeem smiles. "You make it sound like I'm about to put you out of your misery or something. I have an idea." He removes a small notebook from his pocket. "I'll write it on this sheet of paper and give you a pencil in case you want to write something in response. How's that sound?"

"Alright, cool," Andre says. "Hit me."

Hakeem jots down four words, folds the paper, and passes it to Andre, who takes a deep breath and opens it.

"Are you serious?"

Hakeem nods and Andre cracks a smile. "I thought post-traumatic stress disorder was for people who were in Iraq or Afghanistan, even Vietnam."

"In my opinion, it's one of the most common but undiagnosed issues in the African American community," Hakeem says. "It happens when a person experiences or witnesses significant trauma."

It seems Andre has already retreated into himself. "This started with the accident."

"To an extent, yes. But there's two distinct stages in the development of PTSD. An initial trauma that may or may not lead to anything diagnosable is followed by a second traumatic incident that triggers full-blown PTSD. In your case there were multiple triggers: your relocation to New Jersey while you were still grieving your parents' death, and then the death of your grandmother. After that, you were abandoned by your aunt. That's four significant traumas. A lot for a young mind to handle."

Andre stares at the floor.

"Do you need a minute or would you like for me to continue?"

Andre looks up. "I'm good. Go ahead."

"The first night I saw you on the bus, I suspected PTSD. You demonstrated hyperarousal, which means you startle easily, and that's also a symptom. Have you ever found yourself feeling emotionally distant, or have you ever had trouble being affectionate?"

It was the spring semester of Sandra's sophomore year, and she and Andre had just had sex for the first time.

Looking uncertain, Sandra wrapped herself in the bedsheet. "You were just all over me and now you can't even lay here?"

"That cuddling stuff just ain't me."

Sandra drew in her breath sharply, shook her head, and said, "I won't be doing this again."

"Why not?" Andre asked.

Sandra didn't answer.

"We just took our relationship to the next level," Andre said. "We can't go back on that now."

"Why not?"

"Well. I'm a man, so—"

Sandra threw off the pure white bedsheet marred by crimson teardrops and marched to the bathroom. Andre marveled at her sumptuous curves and the fact that no matter what happened between them—he forever owned the irrevocable tokens of her virtue.

Sandra slammed the door. After several moments she reemerged wearing Andre's bathrobe and got in his face. "If you can't stay with me if we're not having sex, then you don't love me."

Andre didn't answer. It was a year into their relationship and he had never told her he did. He couldn't bring himself to, because throughout his life, everything he had loved had left. So he never allowed himself to love, or at least to admit it. That way he could protect the object of his love—and himself.

Not long after that argument, Mr. Horton discovered Sandra and Andre's arrangement. Sandra hadn't returned Mr. Horton's calls for almost two weeks, and what started out as worry had sharpened into suspicion. So he decided to drop by his alma mater unannounced.

Mr. Horton's heart was in a sling as he parked his spotless 1993 Dodge Dynasty in front of Gannon Hall. He felt squeamish because he knew that when daddy's little girl became secretive about her social life and stopped returning his calls, those were telltale signs that another man was controlling the reins of her heart.

Mr. Horton had himself wrested daughters from their fathers' affections, but now he found himself on the receiving end of the same tragic irony. He knew this day would come; he had only hoped that it would happen at an altar in a beautiful church after he had invested thirty thousand dollars—a princely sum given his tight fist—on Sandra's special day.

Mr. Horton reminisced about the first time he laid eyes on Sandra. She was pink, wrinkled, and crying hysterically the moment she was thrust from the dark womb into the harsh light of the boorish world. She stopped howling the instant Mr. Horton cooed, "Hey, Baby Love."

Sandra hadn't yet opened her eyes, but she scrunched up her face and turned to the voice she recognized, because Mr. Horton had read to her every night in Wilda's belly.

Sandra didn't see her father when she traipsed out of Gannon Hall loaded down with books, but when he said, "Baby Love," she froze. She slid into the car, not sure if her manufactured smile masked her fear—a fright so palpable that she was certain she would wet her pants.

"Baby Love, I've been trying to reach you."

"I've been busy with school and stuff, Daddy."

"What kind of stuff?"

"You know tests, projects. Stuff like that."

Mr. Horton seemed to be trying to find a collected response to Sandra's hedging. "Are you and Andre living together?"

"I don't *live* with him. It's more that . . . I spend a lot of time there."

Sandra never intended to move in with Andre, it just kind

of happened. The closer they became, the more time she spent at his apartment. Eventually her overnight bag became a suitcase, weekends turned into weeks, and visits to the Laundromat in the basement of Andre's building replaced the need to return clothes to her dorm room.

"Then why did the dorm director tell me that your room has been empty for the last two months?" Mr. Horton asked.

Sandra didn't have anything to say.

"Are you two having sex?"

Sandra looked away. Shame and embarrassment stained her conscience.

"You were raised to respect yourself by respecting your body, so how could you disrespect yourself like that?"

I am NOT having this conversation with him.

Sandra looked up to see her father's eyes mist over as he shook his head. He pulled Sandra into a hug. "Baby Love, there's a reason God intended for a man and a woman to enjoy sex within the context of marriage. In exchange for your intimacy, a husband gives you his name and his life. That protects you. Otherwise, the best you can expect is heartbreak or, God forbid, an illegitimate pregnancy."

Sandra's own tears began to form. "I'm sorry, Daddy."

She didn't know what else to say because her perfect image in his eyes was now ruined. Yet she had no intention of leaving Andre because she had committed her body to the relationship, so now she had to make it work.

24

Day 5.5 at the White Horse. Andre and Hakeem sit in a ratty common room populated with down-and-outs, over-the-hill hookers, dirty suburban stoners, and a smooth Indonesian dude who runs some sort of shady operation out of the hotel.

Hakeem looks around. "Why can't we talk in your room like last time?"

"Because that room is not healthy. And these people have their own stuff going on, so they're not thinking about us."

Hakeem gives the colorful cast another once-over, appearing uncomfortable with the idea of an open-air session. "Okay, so here's how I'd like to approach your treatment. I'd like to work through the accident first—"

Andre tenses.

"Did you notice that?" Hakeem asks.

"Notice what?"

"It's almost like you flinched when I mentioned the accident."

"Didn't notice," Andre says, now diffident.

"But that's fine," Hakeem assures him. "See? We're already on the road to recovery."

Andre feels like a stranger at his own therapy session, poked around by Hakeem's prodding about things he can't see.

"Here's what's happening, Dre. The trauma of losing your parents has you in an emotional holding pattern. Like a boxer waiting for the next blow, you brace yourself at the mere mention of the accident as if you expect the pain to blindside you like a rabbit punch. That's why we need to work through the accident first. Because the trauma you experienced created a fearful, somewhat intractable personality that wasn't able to easily cope with the difficult circumstances that came later in your life."

Andre extends his hand. "You just nailed my story, Keem. Really." Hakeem shakes it, but Andre sustains his grasp and looks him in the eye. "I really appreciate you doing this. And as soon as I get another gig, I'll be able to take care of your pockets again."

Andre's cell phone buzzes. The display says *NYC MTA*.

"Speaking of gigs, let me take this. Hello?"

"Andre, Mr. Chin from the MTA."

"Yes, sir, Mr. Chin. How are you?"

"I'm fine. Look, I was so impressed with your honesty that I felt I needed to call you to personally tell you that we won't be considering your application for the bus operator position."

"Oh." Andre sinks his head into his hand. "Is there any advice you can give me that would make my candidacy successful in the future?"

"Sure . . . Lie."

Andre waits to see if this is another of Chin's zingers.

"Okay, that's all, Andre."

"Thanks for your time, Mr. Chin. And please keep me in mind for future openings."

Cast down, Andre looks up.

"Bad news?" Hakeem asks.

"Story of my life. Bad News Bolden. That name pretty much sums up my world. Bad news becomes me."

Hakeem slides his rusted folding chair close to the flimsy card table. "Consider our session officially over. Now I can talk to you like we're just 'boys. Is that cool?"

"Go ahead."

"A wise man once said that suffering produces perseverance; perseverance, character; and character, hope."

"Since when did spouting masochism make one wise?" Andre asks. "And the sacraments of a bitter existence? Who deemed that a vaunted prize?" Andre scribbles the thought in his notebook and recites aloud the rest of what gluts his mind. "Nihilistic philosophy only births more pain. It's fruitless to espouse folly, repackage it as wisdom, and spew it in a wise man's name." Andre pencils that in too.

"That was off the top?" Hakeem asks.

"The gift has been known to rear its head when things get ugly."

"Check out this verse," Hakeem says. "'Every good and perfect gift is from above, coming down from the Father of the heavenly lights, who does not change like shifting shadows.'"

"That's you?" Andre asks.

"No, that's from a brother named James the Just."

"James the Just. Hot name," Andre says. "'Father of the heavenly lights.' Sounds like some old New Age ish."

"Actually, it's from the Bible."

Andre smirks. "The Bible? Your name is Hakeem Shabazz and you rock a Sunni-Muslim–inspired Philly beard."

"This beard is Coptic, fam."

"Coptic?"

"Means Egyptian. The Coptic faith started in Africa ten years after the crucifixion."

"The crucifixion of who? Jesus?"

"Yeah."

"So you're a Christian?"

"Orthodox. Night and day from the stuff you see practiced in America."

"What's the difference?"

Hakeem rubs his Coptic-style beard and considers. "Protestantism is from Europe and didn't show up until the sixteenth century. Coptic originated in Africa early in the first century, so culturally it's a no-brainer which one is more relevant to me as a person of African descent."

"So Hakeem Shabazz is a Coptic name?"

"Actually, no," Hakeem replies. "My mother and father were in the Nation of Islam when they met, but they converted two years before I was born."

"Converted from the Nation of Islam to Christianity?"

"It's more common than you think. My dad was from down South so he was raised Protestant. This was back in the sixties. But when he moved up here to go to medical school, he was attracted to the social justice and message of empowerment that was coming out of the Nation at the time. So he joined and changed his name from Arthur Howard to Na'im Shabazz."

"But what led him to convert back?"

"According to him, Islam made him disciplined but couldn't stop him from sinning."

Through his window, Andre watches the jagged outline of buildings transform into indefinable black figurations as the sun sets on his last day at the White Horse.

All at once, shimmering, silver light splashes through the window and dances crosswise above the sill. Andre is gripped with a euphoric fear that enchants his every sense. He angles his head abruptly to discover the source of the light.

The moon.

Andre is two quarks from being crushed. All the God talk

has caused his heart to lust for the fantastical—indisputable evidence that would, once for all, put his doubts to rest.

But what if I am alone in a godless universe with no meaning other than what I ascribe to it?

Something about that doesn't make sense, and it's powerfully unsettling at the same time.

Andre's old friend despair hikes up the back of his neck, scampers across the surface of his bald head, filters through his eyelashes, and complicates his ability to see.

Andre drops on the bed and dials Sandra.

"Hey, Dre. Everything alright?"

"No."

"What's wrong?"

"I'm really not getting life right now. I just don't understand it."

"You're not thinking of doing anything crazy, are you?"

"No, nothing like that."

His phone beeps. "Hold on, that's Rock. Hello?"

"My brother."

"What's going on, man?"

"Heading over to the Realness. I can shoot through and scoop you if you want to roll."

"Well . . . okay, why not? You know where the White Horse is?"

"You forget who you talking to?"

"Right," Andre says, smiling. He clicks back over. "Hey, I have to meet Rock downstairs."

25

The usual suspects are at the meeting place—Rock, Strange-O, Mark, and Fredrick. Although Andre would never admit it, he's starting to feel that the Realness quartet is okay. Of course, he would never let his guard down completely, especially with Fredrick.

He thinks of Hakeem and wonders how he would fit into this setting. Andre figures he could invite him, but quickly checks himself, for to invite Hakeem would mean two things: that he's coming back and that he sees value in what takes place here.

Andre buries the thought and digs into steaming hot wings and green leaf salad peppered with shiny grape tomatoes.

Fredrick grabs a plate. "What's happening, Andre? How's things?"

Suspect, Andre says, "Everything's alright."

"Well . . . if you're open to it, I wanted to offer my help."

Andre speculates on what Sandra could have told him, and his heart hardens toward her. He's tempted to get her on the phone this second. "Help me how?" he asks.

"I have an extra bedroom in my apartment, and if you need it, you're welcome to it."

Need and ego rattle between Andre's ears like sabers, and the clash has him at odds with his own speech.

Fredrick gives Andre and his manhood space to breathe. "You don't have to let me know right now. It's just an offer."

"I'll think about it," Andre says.

"Cool."

Fredrick turns to leave and Andre says, "Fredrick."

He turns around.

"Thanks."

The five men gather at the table in the center of the room. "So what's real tonight, fellas?" Rock says.

Andre speaks up immediately. "I'm assuming you guys are all Protestant, right?"

The quartet looks around at each other and nods.

"Protestantism is European and began in the sixteenth century," Andre states confidently. "Coptic is from Africa and started in the first century. So wouldn't it make more sense for you to be Coptic instead of Protestant since you're all black?"

Strange-O says, "I'm not black. I'm like KRS-One—brown, from the Boogie Down."

The table gives Strange-O the evil eye, but he responds with, "Don't front. Y'all know y'all went crazy when that song came out just like I did."

"That's not the point," Fredrick injects. "Andre asked a serious question and you bring up Boogie Down Productions."

Strange-O slaps Fredrick on the back and grins. "You know that was funny! My timing was impeccable!"

"Anyway," Fredrick says, directing his attention back to Andre, "I only know a little bit about Coptic, but I was never that interested because it seemed too much like Catholicism with all the candles and icons."

"Actually, the Coptic Church preceded the Catholic Church by a couple hundred years," Rock interjects. "And here's an interesting black fact for you—Egypt used to be a Christian nation."

"Word?" Mark chimes in. "Egypt was Christian? Isn't Egypt the largest Muslim country in the world right now?"

"That would be Indonesia," Rock says, "but Egypt was Christian three hundred years before Muhammad was born, and Ethiopia was Christian a hundred years before his first crusade."

"How do you know all this stuff?" Andre asks.

"I was locked up in Sing Sing, and they had a degree program that was offered through New York Theological Seminary. My focus was religion in history."

Andre tries not to look impressed. "How'd you wind up in prison in New York? Aren't you from Jersey?"

Rock smiles. "Another example of God's sovereignty, brother. The JCPD couldn't get me on anything, so I got cocky and decided to expand my operation into Harlem and black Brooklyn. And that's when I got caught. But if I would've gone to prison in Jersey, I wouldn't have a degree because Jersey doesn't offer degree programs in prison, thanks to Bill Clinton."

When the meeting comes to a close, Fredrick gives Andre a pound and says, "Take care, man."

As Fredrick heads for the door, Andre ponders his looming checkout from the White Horse, and the thought of sleeping on the train makes him blench.

"Fredrick."

"What's up?"

"I think I'd like to take you up on your offer."

"No problem. I only ask that you participate in a jobs initiative that I do at the Salvation Army."

Andre feels baited and switched upon. "So this is a package deal."

"I just want to try to help you get a gig, man. You still interested?"

Andre recognizes that Frederick's offer is infinitely better than the iron horse or the White Horse no matter how he dissects it. "Yeah, I'm interested."

"Alright, I'll pull my car around," Fredrick says.

Andre waits on the curb in front of the meeting place. Fredrick cruises up in a black BMW 650i convertible, and instantly Andre is salty. He thinks back to his senior year in high school.

Andre and Roderick Teal were the best receivers in the city. They had the same number of touchdowns, but Andre had ten more catches. However, Roderick was five inches taller and twenty pounds heavier, and his school won the New Jersey State Championship that year. Roderick went on to star at Virginia Tech and signed a four-year, twenty-eight-million-dollar deal with the Detroit Lions, eighteen million guaranteed.

Andre considers that even if he rode the bench in the NFL, he could have afforded a car like Fredrick's.

"Hop in, it's open," Fredrick says.

Andre sinks into the plush leather interior and marvels at the dashboard that emits more snazzy brilliance than a Christmas tree. "Nice ride," he says. He remembers hearing somewhere that the best way to combat jealousy is to compliment the object of your envy.

"Thanks. It's a lease," Fredrick says. "Good for the summer, but when it snows? Forget about it."

Andre huffs in his head. *Probably has no idea what it's like to freeze to death at a bus stop or walk when you don't have the fare.*

"I grew up riding the bus," Fredrick continues. "But most of the time, my family used Tom and Jérry."

"Tom and Jerry?"

Fredrick looks at Andre. "Our own two feet."

They crack up and the mood in the car lightens slightly. Andre settles into his seat as Fredrick zips toward downtown. He passes the Goldman Sachs tower and slows at 77 Hudson Street, a glimmering condominium whose upper floors vanish into the night sky. Andre knows the building well because Sandra's restaurant, Torch & Basil, is on the ground floor.

Frederick disappears into an underground parking garage that's like a clandestine car show. There are Benzes, Escalades, Bentleys, and an occasional Prius for the environmentally friendly.

Andre takes in Fredrick's comfortable cool as they enter the building's extravagant lobby. He feels like a kid tooling around in an older brother's brave new world.

The man at the concierge desk is white and at least ten years older than Fredrick. "Good evening, Mr. Boyd," he says.

"Rich, how are you, man? Cold out there, isn't it?"

"Indeed it is. You two gentlemen have a good night."

Andre imagines how uncomfortable he would feel if he was there by himself. When he steps into Fredrick's apartment, he is greeted by an unfettered panorama of the Manhattan skyline. The view through the floor-to-ceiling glass windows is breathtaking.

"Welcome," Fredrick says. "I'll give you a quick tour, and then please make yourself at home."

"This place is off the meter," Andre says.

Fredrick grins. "Thanks. Your room is down here."

Fredrick leads Andre down the hallway and points out the kitchen with Italian cabinetry, white quartz countertops, and stainless-steel Viking appliances. Next is the bathroom, which is equally indulgent. It has a chiseled marble feature wall, double trough sink with signature faucets, and a limestone floor.

Andre has never been in a space so magnificent. He struggles to understand how Fredrick can afford something so lavish. He's not a professional ball player and he certainly doesn't look like he's slinging. And even if he is, none of the dealers Andre knew had apartments like this, even kingpins who held down several neighborhoods.

"I don't mean to pry, Fredrick. But what do you do?"

"I manage a hedge fund." They stop in front of a room at the end of the hall. "To be honest with you, Dre, it's not a day that goes by that I don't marvel at my life."

"If I lived here, I'd marvel too."

"I don't just mean the house. I went to Alfred E. Smith High School in the South Bronx and majored in automotive technology. I figured I'd learn about cars and then open a shop, maybe a few. I'd always been good with numbers. Most of my classmates just wanted a job fixing cars, so I was considered the ambitious one. But then I took the SAT."

"What was your score?"

"Fifteen twelve." Fredrick shakes his head. "I always knew I was smart, I just never knew I was that smart. But enough about me. Here's your room."

Andre steps in and is met with staggering views of the Statue of Liberty and the glistening lights of the Verrazano Bridge. Emotion tugs at the corners of Andre's eyes, and his heart lightens at the notion of easement.

"Fredrick, why are you doing this?"

Fredrick rubs his chin and considers. "I just felt it would be selfish for me to be in this apartment by myself while you're out there scrambling for a place to live."

Andre points his fist to Fredrick and gives him a pound. "I appreciate it."

"It's the least I can do," Fredrick says. "And since we're roommates, we should probably chase the eight-hundred-pound gorilla out of the room."

"What do you mean?" Andre says, playing ape.

"Can I be candid?"

"Go ahead."

"There's no denying Sandra's beautiful, but ex-man drama is precisely why I've always steered clear of women with children."

Andre is not sure if he should be offended or refreshed, but before he can muster a response, Fredrick finishes.

"And I know it's none of my business, but I'd like to see the two of you get back together. You have that handsome little boy and it's obvious he loves you. We need more nuclear families, because nowadays anything goes."

26

Andre wakes up to sailboats—four of them, small and white—thirty-seven stories below, inching up New York harbor. Rivulets of water drizzle down the edges of the large-scale bedroom window. It hasn't snowed in a week. A winter thaw has gripped the city.

Andre moves closer to the window, and the sun warms his cheeks. A handwritten note is on the chest of drawers.

> If you can make it, I'll be at the Salvation Army tonight at 6:30. Come thru and let's see what we can make happen on the employment front.
>
> Fredrick

Andre creases the note, slips it into his pocket, and takes a turn through the sizable apartment. Everything looks barely used.

Probably had a gorgeous honey decorate his spot.

Andre grins.

Probably several.

Andre imagines the quality and quantity of women that someone like Fredrick must traffic in. He's paid, and he lives in a bachelor pad that's flier than any Andre has seen, even in music videos.

He stops in front of a window that looks west. He locates Booker T. The lime green fire escapes radiate like toxic waste. Due south and farther west is Greenville, a black smudge rubbed on the horizon.

The Salvation Army is housed in a beige, characterless building surrounded by a black wrought-iron gate. Several people mill about outside. Andre stakes a place on the fence and dials Sandra.

"Hello?"

"I thought you didn't answer when you were at work."

"Normally I don't. But when I saw it was you, I picked up. Is everything okay?"

Andre smiles at Sandra's concern. "I'm cool. I'm at this job thing that Fredrick does at the Salvation Army."

"Fredrick from New Jersey Truth?"

"Yeah."

"How'd you two wind up hooking up?"

Andre plays along. "I'm actually going to be staying with him for a little bit. At least until I get my pockets right. Then I can take care of what I owe Ms. Rutigliano and get back into my place."

"Wait a minute. You're *staying* with Fredrick? How'd that happen?"

"Come on, Sandra. You're telling me you had nothing to do with it?"

"With what?"

"You didn't tell him anything about my situation?"

"Why would I discuss your personal business with Fredrick?"

"Right," Andre says, guilty that he suspected her of foul play.

Just then, Fredrick hurries up the walkway. "Sorry I'm late, everybody." He sees Andre. "What's up, Dre? Thanks for coming out."

Andre acknowledges Fredrick's greeting with a nod and says to Sandra, "Let me run."

Fredrick unlocks the building, and the group of ten or so people follow him into a computer lab. The room fills quickly as several more people stream in. The yammer in the room is not unlike a high school lunchroom even though the people here range in age from early twenties to midfifties.

"May I have everyone's attention, please?" Fredrick asks.

A group of men in the back bushwhack each other with overblown sports banter.

"I need all eyes up here," Fredrick says more forcefully. The room quiets. "Who's here for the first time?"

Andre raises his hand along with two others.

"Okay, those with passwords log in to your job sites. I'll get to you after I get the new people up and running."

Fredrick sits beside Andre. "Everything go okay at the house today?"

"Yeah, your place is on point."

"Thanks, and I notified the front desk that you'd be staying with me, so you shouldn't have any problems getting in the building. So let's get started. First I do an assessment of your education, experience, skills, and interests." Fredrick logs in to the computer in front of Andre and creates an account for him. "Don't be offended by the first couple of questions. This is a basic form that I created because we get all kinds in here, from people who finished eighth grade to Wall Street types who were downsized. Let's start with your education. Did you finish high school?"

"Yes."

"Any honors or distinctions?"

208

"I graduated with honors, I was an all-district wide receiver, and I got a full athletic scholarship to St. Peter's College."

"St. Peter's? They're one of the sponsors of this program."

"Really? Small world," Andre says.

"It is. Did you get your degree?"

"Completed three years."

"Any plans to go back?"

"I don't think that's possible."

"Why do you say that?"

"Because I didn't just stop. I was expelled."

"Oh, okay. Disciplinary or academic?"

"Disciplinary."

"What was your GPA?"

"It *was* 3.02, before I got kicked out. But because of every-thing that went down, I wasn't able to officially withdraw. So I failed all of my classes that last semester and my GPA tanked."

Fredrick stops typing. "You were an honor student and they still kicked you out? Did you file an appeal?"

"Well. No. Because felonies and appeals go together like blacks and Republicans."

Fredrick laughs. "Got it. So you have a record now, I'm assuming?"

"Basically."

Fredrick thinks for a moment. "What was your major?"

"Journalism."

"Okay," Fredrick says. "In a perfect world, with unlimited resources and no obstacles, what would you be doing and where would you be doing it?"

Without hesitation, Andre says, "I'd be a starting wide receiver for the Pittsburgh Steelers."

"Steelers? What about the Jets or the Giants?"

"What about 'em?" Andre asks.

"Okay. Moving on. Why'd you pick journalism as your major?"

"Because when I started college, I hadn't completely given up on playing pro ball. My thinking was that I could cover the NFL after my playing days were over."

"Sounds like a good plan. Now all we have to do is figure out how to get you back on track to reaching your goals. Of course, barring a miracle, playing in the NFL isn't going to happen, but covering it doesn't seem too far-fetched."

Andre is overcome with an odd sensation that he hasn't felt in a long time. Hope.

As the session draws to a close, Fredrick sidles up to Andre and says, "I'm heading back to the house after we wrap up. You can catch a ride if you want."

Andre assesses the likelihood of running into OGC on this side of Bergen and determines that it's not likely. OGC never operates beyond the bounds of the illest Greenville blocks.

"Thanks for the offer, but I'll walk."

"Alright, cool," Fredrick replies.

The street is empty. Andre feels free because he can walk without his hands in his pockets for the first time in months. He is refreshed to blow breath that he cannot see.

Light slashes between Andre's feet and glistens on the wet sidewalk. Andre turns just as a darkened car eases into the street behind him. He spins around, quickens his pace, and wonders if he's being paranoid. Behind him, the vehicle guns its engine, and the acrid smell of exhaust smolders in his nose.

Andre takes off and burns up the sidewalk with blazing speed. He flashes back to Dante and imagines himself and his cousin being shot in the back on the same street less than three miles apart.

He blows around the corner. Tires screech. The car is gaining on him.

Andre anticipates gun bursts and wonders what it's going to feel like to be shot through with gilded metal, copper alloy, and lead. Then he stumbles upon a startling realization.

I don't want to die.

The car pulls up beside Andre and the driver's window eases down.

Andre decides that if he's going to get shot, he's not going to make it easy, so he breaks, spins 180 degrees, and dashes in the other direction. The car reverses, backs up onto the sidewalk, and blocks his way of escape.

"Andre! Stop! What are you running from?" Mr. Horton asks.

Andre keels over with his hands on his knees and heaves like a winded buck.

"Get in the car. Let's talk."

Andre climbs in, but keeps his chagrin-tinged gaze glued to the street.

"What's going on?" Mr. Horton asks.

Andre rubs his head with both hands. He's not sure what he should say to Mr. Horton, if anything. "What are you doing out here?" Andre asks.

"Sandra told me you were at the Salvation Army, and I wanted to talk to you. But son, what made you take off like that?"

Andre leans his head against the car window.

"Okay, then," Mr. Horton continues. "Let me tell you why I'm here. And that's assuming you're even remotely interested in what I have to say."

Andre meets his eyes. "Go ahead."

"I've learned in my sixty years that on every issue, a person is either a part of the problem or a part of the solution. And

I realized that when it came to you and Sandra, a lot of times I've been a part of the problem. So first I have to apologize for treating you the way I did when you came by the dealership with nothing but an olive branch and a need. I felt some conviction after you left, but I was able to dial up enough anger to block it out, because as far as I was concerned you didn't deserve my forgiveness."

"It's alright," Andre says, humbled by Mr. Horton's humility. "You don't have to apologize."

"You don't understand," Mr. Horton counters tartly. "An apology is as much for the offender as for the person offended."

"Okay," Andre says. He's not sure exactly what Mr. Horton means but is content to let it ride for the sake of peace.

Mr. Horton offers Andre his hand. "I'm here to offer you a job if you're interested."

"Are you serious?"

"Very serious."

Andre shakes his hand heartily. "I'll wash cars, keep the lot clean, it doesn't matter."

"The father of my grandson is not sweeping any lot of mine. Are you interested in selling cars?"

Andre is stumped. He has always been good at writing, but selling is a different matter altogether. "At this point, Mr. Horton, I'm willing to try anything."

"You won't start on the Mercedes lot. First you have to prove yourself at my Toyota dealership here in Jersey City selling used cars. Your pay will be a draw against future commissions, and don't expect any special treatment."

"I'd prefer it that way. And thanks. I really appreciate you giving me an opportunity."

27

Andre does his signature knock on Sandra's front door and she answers with a quizzical nod. "Did my dad get in contact with you?"

"Yes, he did."

Sandra steps aside and allows Andre in. "What for?" she asks.

"Why?"

"Because I want to know, that's why."

"Is Little Dre asleep?"

"Yes, now what did he say?"

"Nothing you'd be concerned about."

Sandra can't see Andre's grin as he walks toward the bedroom and lowers his voice to a whisper. "Can I go in and see him?"

"Not until you tell me what he said," Sandra whispers back.

Andre faces her. "I'll tell you what he said if you give me a kiss."

Sandra punches him in his chest and whispers sharply, "You know I'm not kissing you!"

Andre steals one.

Sandra covers her mouth. "I can't believe you!"

"Yes you can." Andre kisses her again. Sandra swings for

his head, but Andre makes her miss as he slips into the bedroom and lifts the sleeping Little Dre from the crib.

"I love you, little man," he whispers.

Sandra rises up behind him and thwacks him twice—a punch for each peck.

"Ouch!" Andre whispers tersely. He lays Little Dre down and regathers the comforter around his shoulders.

Back in the living room, Andre takes a seat on the couch and acts as if he doesn't notice Sandra staring down his throat. She removes one of her cute little flats and launches it across the room. It tumbles across the top of Andre's head.

"What are you doing?" he asks.

"That's for kissing me." She readies her second shoe for launch. "If you keep stalling, this one's next."

Andre plants himself next to Sandra on the love seat. She bounces up and takes his place on the couch.

"You don't need to sit next to me to tell me what my dad said. And you better not kiss me again, Dre. I'm not playing."

"I'm sorry," he says. "Not for kissing you because that was nice. It made me think about—"

"Stop it or I'm going to ask you to leave," Sandra snaps. "You're getting a little carried away and it's making me uncomfortable. Seriously."

"I wasn't going to say anything foul. I was just going to say that it made me think about the first time we kissed. You remember that?"

"Of course, but we're not talking about that."

"That's because you don't remember," Andre teases.

"Anyway, Andre. What did my dad want to talk to you about?"

"You tell me where our first kiss was and I'll let you know."

"Great Adventure on the Medusa. Now what did he say?"

Andre's face brightens. "You had just gone natural and

had your hair braided for the first time. I told you that your hair looked just like Medusa's."

"Andre!"

"Okay, okay. Dr. Hardness offered me a job."

Sandra screams and claps her hands like the cheerleader she once was. "Are you going to take it?"

"Of course I'm going to take it. I don't know anything about selling, but anything beats unemployment."

"Andre, you're a natural salesman. All dogs are. You listen to what a woman says, determines her likes and wants, and then use it to sell her on yourself. If you treat car buyers the way you treat women, my dad will love you."

The life bleeds out of Andre's face and Sandra goes silent. "Dre, I wasn't saying that to be . . . I mean . . ."

Andre stands. "It's cool," he says and slips out the door. He leans against the hallway wall, studies the ceiling, and recounts that night.

Andre was nervous that evening. He pulled up to Sandra's job at the Newport Center Mall in the sporty white Honda Civic that her dad had given her the summer after her freshman year. From the way Sandra stood in front of Macy's, with her pretty mouth poked out and her arms folded across her chest, Andre knew she had already heard.

A couple of hours earlier he was at a stoplight with another woman in Sandra's car when her best friend, Liette, pulled up. Andre knew he was caught, so he acted like he didn't see Liette even though she practically fell out of her car, flailing her arms to get his attention. The light turned green and Andre zipped off.

On a normal night when Andre picked Sandra up, she got in the car, laid a kiss on him, and let him drive to their apartment. That night, however, she stormed the driver's side and snatched open the door.

"Get out!"

Andre had learned a long time ago that the best way to ease out of getting caught was to remain calm.

"What's going on?" he asked innocently and stepped out of the car. He attempted to touch Sandra's cheek with his pucker, but she ducked and sneered.

"I can't believe you had some woman in my car!"

He feigned incredulity. "Who, Tangi? She's a friend from high school. I just gave her a ride home from the bus stop."

"I don't care if it was Mother Teresa. You don't have another woman in my car!"

Sandra sped off, melting two black slabs in the lot.

When Andre got to their apartment, he unlocked both bottom locks, but the two double bolts remained. They could only be opened from inside and Sandra kept them secure.

Andre slammed the door three times with the meaty part of his fist. "Sandra! Open the door!"

"Go stay with that scamp you had in my car!"

"You better let me in! I'm not playing!"

Andre noticed how genuinely indignant he looked in the door mirror. He grinned at his performance. An old lady waddled down the stairs and rolled her eyes at him. When she disappeared from sight, Andre continued. "I'm calling the police because you're in my house!"

"Call them! I'll be right here!"

"Okay! The next time I see a friend stranded on the side of the road, I'll just leave her there. You happy now?"

Sandra kicked her side of the door so hard it dented. "See? I caught you! How can someone be stranded at a bus stop?"

Andre realized the inconsistency in his stories and toned

216

down the rhetoric. "You're acting real insecure right now, Sandra. You need to work on that because it's not cute."

"Both of y'all need to work on shutting up!" someone shouted from the apartment next door, and then turned their stereo up loud enough to wobble the walls.

Sandra couldn't prove that anything was amiss, but she still didn't let Andre in. From then on, Andre could expect to be locked out if Sandra heard anything about him and another woman, even if it wasn't true. Sandra's bougie friends, the "meddling detectives" as he called them, seemed to be stashed everywhere.

The initial intrigue that Andre had had for Sandra's highfalutin world had long since devolved into insecurity. At times he and Sandra seemed to operate in separate universes. Not to mention Sandra and her uppity friends had interests in places and things that Andre had neither heard of nor seen.

As he approaches 77 Hudson Street, Andre finally accepts that he justified his faithless ways because he convinced himself that Sandra was ashamed of him—even though she never said or did anything to indicate that was true. Andre was projecting and he knew it, because deep down he didn't think he was good enough for her, her parents, or her circle of friends.

Doesn't matter what I thought. Cheating on her was a cruel thing to do.

Rich, the concierge from last night, is at the desk when Andre enters the palatial foyer, and his eyes have been locked on Andre from the moment he appeared on the quarry stone entryway outside the building.

Andre nods and says, "Good evening," as he passes through the lobby.

"Can I help you with something, pal?"

"No. Thanks. I'm going to 3709."

"You a guest of somebody here?"

"Yes, Fredrick Boyd. He told me he notified the front desk that I would be staying with him."

Rich flips through a book on his desk, but Andre knows his type. Under the guise of following rules, they humiliate you, even when they know exactly who you are. To Andre, their actions are designed to let you know that you're not worthy to feel comfortable in "their" world, and you're better off if you don't forget it.

Rich's probing finger stops at a line in the ledger. "Okay. Andre Bolden. Is that you?"

"Yes, that's me."

"You have ID?"

Andre takes out his wallet and shakes his head. "You saw me walk in here with Fredrick less than twenty-four hours ago."

"Lotta people live in this building, pal, and I'm not good with faces."

"How do you get a job as a doorman if you can't remember who comes in and out of a building in the span of eighteen hours?"

"I'm a concierge. And no need for the attitude. I'm just doing my job. Have a good night, sir."

Upstairs, the apartment is still. Andre passes Fredrick's closed bedroom door and hears movement. He strains to hear if any sounds of passion emanate from within.

Every inch of Andre's body misses being with a woman. He realizes that it's been sixteen months since he and Sandra were last together. And it's not that Andre couldn't have easily found another woman in that time. He just wasn't up to expending the emotional energy required to get on the field and play the game.

He lies in bed and visualizes Sandra's perfect body. Andre's resolve to get her back is enlarged by his excitement at knowing that she has only been with him. And he wants to keep it that way.

He imagines burying his face in her coconut-scented hair and kissing the back of her graceful neck as she reaches around and grazes his bald head with French-manicured nails. How he desires to place all of her hair to one side and plant sweet kisses on her shoulder as he massages her arms with his rough hands. Then he'd gently run his thumb along her collarbone and down to her sprightly—

A knock at the door.

"Come in," Andre says.

"Got a taste for anything?" Fredrick asks. "I'm about to order something."

"Anyone else joining us?" Andre asks, flashing a wily grin.

"You thought I was in there with a woman?"

"Of course," Andre says, still smiling.

"I won't be getting down like that again until I'm married."

"You serious?"

Fredrick grins. "Loins been on lock for almost three years."

Andre laughs at the comedy of Fredrick's statement even as he struggles to wrap his mind around the concept. "How does a hot-blooded man go three years without plowing in someone's fertile fields?" he asks.

"Honestly, if you would have asked me that three years ago, I would've said it was impossible. And don't get me wrong, I'm human, so I think about it, but I don't dwell on it because my commitment is to doing things God's way."

Andre smirks. "You expect me to believe that if a fine honey approaches you, you're going to say, 'Nah, boo, I ain't having sex. God ain't into that because we're not married'?"

"I don't say those exact words, but that scenario has happened. And it would've been easy to just knock it out and keep it moving, but I'd feel convicted afterward. Trust me, I've done it."

"Was she fine?"

"Of course she was fine," Fredrick says. "That's the only way I get down."

They slap five.

"So we agree on that," Andre says.

Fredrick continues. "When I first got serious, I figured if I just stopped 'wilding out' and settled down with one girl, everything would be cool. So I hooked up with this news anchor—" He pauses to think. "As a matter of fact, I met her at Club New York the same night I met Rock."

"What channel is she on?" Andre asks, intrigued.

Fredrick waves off the question. "Not important. But here's what is. We planned to have a very active night together. But I had to put her in a cab before we even got started good because I felt guilty. And *believe me*, that had never happened before."

28

Torch & Basil is squeezed to the beams, and Mr. Trizonis's face is composed of the spooky dauntlessness that the nightly dinner rush brings. Sandra groans aloud because he's headed straight for her.

"Sandra, I need you to work through your break. We have an extra-special guest in the private dining room. A big tipper and you don't have to split it with the waitstaff. I'll take care of them myself."

In Trizonis's world, an "extra-special guest" is typically a snide celebrity with bizarre requests not on the menu, an über-rich and crotchety old pervert, or a powerful boss from New Jersey's notoriously dirty political machinery.

Before Sandra can make a stink, Trizonis is back on the dining room floor, glad-handing his well-heeled guests as if his life depends on it—probably because it does.

In addition to the penthouse atop 77 Hudson Street (which, Sandra found out from Fredrick, Trizonis financed by rolling it into the restaurant's mortgage, which, depending on how honest your accountant is, is patently illegal), Trizonis also owns a Mediterranean villa in East Hampton with 0.1 miles of private beach on Long Island Sound.

The refrain that he uses to crack the whip on the restaurant staff is that after Hudson and Suffolk county taxes, two mortgages, and full tuition to Vassar and Mount Holyoke for his twin daughters, he lives "a pauper's life."

Yeah, right, Sandra thinks.

She takes her time getting to the private dining room stashed in the back of the restaurant off the kitchen. Trizonis designed it so that the rich and famous could whisk in discreetly to escape the roving eye of paparazzi and diners drunk on stardom's merry wine.

Sandra composes herself and calls upon her homecoming queen persona. The chasm between her fanciful high school existence and her present makes her past feel like a life lived by someone else.

That's when the scent hits her. Sharry Baby Hawaiian Orchids—Sandra's favorite flower, but one that she has never received. Without warning, her eyes get misty. The candied fragrance draws out Sandra's longing to be sought after by a man who is trustable, secure. And her carefully constructed, feminist shield is powerless against this sensory assault that stirs up fairy-tale-laced romantic desires—desires that she has buried since Andre summarily wounded her trust.

Sandra suppresses a sigh when she hears a Baroque piano solo drift from the room that is as beautiful as she would like her life to be.

Inside the private dining room, all eight tables are covered with Sharry Baby orchids, and in a far corner, illumined by the flicker of a lone lavender candle, is a familiar face. He rises and offers his hand.

"I'm Andre Bolden, and I'd like to get to know you better."

Sandra raises both hands to her mouth but moves to cover her eyes when her tears sparkle. Andre wraps his arms around her and says, "Sahn, I'm willing to do whatever's necessary to recapture your heart."

Sandra is speechless, overwhelmed by the sweetness of the moment. She allows herself to rest amidst Andre's sturdy arms and looks up at him. "Whatever's necessary?"

"Yes."

"Even go with me to New Jersey Truth?"

"I should've known you'd go there."

Sandra smiles. "Doing whatever is your idea, not mine."

"Okay, we can play by your rules. But just know that I'm pursuing you. And this time I'm going to do it right."

Applause erupts behind them. Sandra spins to see the entire restaurant staff, led by Trizonis, clapping. Mortified, she buries her face in Andre's chest.

"So can I call you?" he asks in her ear.

"You already blow up my phone whenever you get ready, Andre."

"We're starting over from scratch, remember?"

"Okay. It's 201—"

"I'm a writer so I'm not good with numbers. Could you jot it down for me?"

One of the waitresses gives Sandra her order pad and pen. Sandra scribbles her number and stuffs it in Andre's hand.

"Enjoy your favorite flower," he says. "And I hope to enjoy mine one day again real soon." He extends his hand to shake.

"Corny but cute, Dre."

"Are you going to leave me hanging?"

Sandra punches him in the arm and shakes.

Clops stands in front of his cook spot on the corner of Warner and Rutgers. The tumbledown structure has been reduced to ashes.

"My first piece of property and they burn it to the ground," he says disgustedly. He angrily kicks scorched wood off the sidewalk and back onto his lot.

The beast. I bet the fire department didn't investigate this suspicious fire.

He sneers.

That's because they all in the same gang.

Clop feels powerless until what Rock used to preach pops in his head.

"Being a man means never being a punk."

Young Claymont would always nod, his eyes wide with wonder.

"And if you gotta knock somebody out to let 'em know that, you do it. You understand?"

Rock's pre-prison maxims fired up blasts of moxie in Claymont's juvenile genes—Uncle Rock was the definition of manhood, and what he said was how life was defined.

"You do what you gotta do to protect your enterprise," Rock would say.

In the present, Clops realizes that his hands are freezing. He jams them in the pockets of his North Face and starts up the block.

Do what you gotta do to protect your enterprise.

Selling cars is harder than Andre thought. He's been thrust into a world of concepts and terminology that may as well be a foreign language. After two weeks he hasn't sold a single vehicle. Never comfortable with debt, Andre felt a tinge of guilt when he picked up his thousand-dollar paycheck for the first half of the month, despite the blue goose egg that was scrawled beside his name on the white sales board in dry erase marker.

Michael Frostburg, Andre's sales manager, summons him

into his office and drops an ink pen on his desk. "Sell me this pen."

Andre recalls what Sandra said about him being a natural salesman and starts blathering. "This is what you want because it looks good. And even better, you'll look good using it. What kind of pen are you using now?"

"A Bic."

"Great pen, but you look like—" Andre glances at the pen on Frostburg's desk. "A Bexley type. Which gives you top-of-the-line quality, but they're more reasonably priced than the other top-shelf brands. And once you use a Bexley, you won't want to use anything else because—"

"When are you going to ask me for my business?"

"I was getting to that."

"You didn't get to it fast enough. Now I've given you a thousand dollars of my money and you haven't given me any sales. I want my money back, Bolden. So you owe me big. A thousand dollars is a lot of paper."

Frostburg looks out onto the lot at a young white couple who just climbed out of a dented Ford Taurus. They team-strap a baby into a stroller. "See that couple right there?" he says. "Get out there and sell them a car!"

As Andre approaches the couple, he thinks about Frostburg's words. *I should've let him know that the person who signs the checks around here is my almost-father-in-law, so he hasn't GIVEN me anything.*

The couple hears Andre approach. The husband faces him, cringing in horror. "We're just looking, okay?"

Andre holds his hands up. "It's okay. I'm here to help. Let me know if you have any questions."

Frostburg stands in front of the door with arms folded when Andre attempts to reenter the dealership. "What do you think you're doing?" he asks.

"They said they're just looking."

"You're gonna let them get away with that? They're 'just looking' because you haven't sold them anything yet! Now get back over there and don't let 'em leave until you sell 'em a car!"

Andre reverses and tries to remember the lines that he learned in training, like, "The only pressure on this lot is in the tires," or "The toughest sell is convincing yourself that you actually *deserve* that new car."

The husband spins around, red-faced, and says, "You don't get it, do you? We're only looking, and we'd like to do it in private. In family peace."

"I just thought you'd like to know that we're giving away free cars today."

"Free cars?"

Andre pulls a Matchbox-sized Toyota from his pocket and places it in the man's hand.

"Good one," the husband says and relaxes a touch. "So tell me, and *be honest*. How much below sticker can I get this?"

Andre circles the shiny white Camry that the husband has his eyes on. "That all depends," he says and gives the couple's car a once-over. "Ninety-five, right?"

"Yeah."

"I could probably get you two hundred for that on trade-in, so you can knock that off the price. How much do you want to put down?"

The husband looks at the wife. The wife looks at him and says, "Two thousand?"

"Up to?" Andre offers, recalling this tactic from one of the training videos.

She shrugs. "Twenty-five hundred, I guess?"

Andre takes out a four square, a piece of paper divided into quadrants, and begins to scribble numbers all over it. This is serious. This is war.

He looks up at the couple and says in a way that makes it seem like an afterthought, "Financing with us?"

"Through our own bank," the husband replies. "We're already approved."

Andre frowns. "What rate did they give you?"

"Four percent."

Andre was taught to say that he could beat any percentage rate even if he didn't know if the dealership's finance department was able to. Frostburg emphasized this by saying, "You have to keep the sale open long enough to close it."

"I'm sure we can do three and a half here," Andre says. "That could save you forty, fifty bucks a month on your payment, easy."

The couple's eyes brighten.

Andre turns on his heels and says assertively, "Follow me."

The couple and their stroller dutifully follow Andre into the dealership for his first sale.

***

A gaggle of ogling coed grills are reflected in the shiny rims of Fredrick's 650i as he rolls through St. Peter's campus.

He parks, hustles into Dineen Hall, and pokes his head into a well-appointed office. "What's happening, Father T?"

"Fredrick, what's going on, pal of mine?" Father Turchini is squeezed into a black shirt and priest's collar, but his presentation is more hip than venerable. He's a large, graying, Bronx Italian who, according to his own personal lore, used to promote hip-hop parties on Arthur Avenue in the late seventies before the genre "ever crossed the Hudson, let alone the continent."

"I met someone who was a student here seven or eight years ago," Fredrick says. "He was on athletic scholarship but was dismissed for disciplinary reasons—"

"Andre Bolden?"

227

"How'd you guess?"

"You can't forget Bolden. We haven't had an athlete like him here since. And I gotta tell you, that was one of the most difficult decisions I ever made in my life. I often wonder what happened to him. How is he?"

"He's actually staying with me for a while until he gets back on his feet."

Turchini looks concerned. "Is he alright?"

"He was driving a bus for New Jersey Transit, and doing quite well there, until his boss found out he had a felony."

Turchini sighs. "Still following him."

"What if he wanted to come back?" Fredrick asks.

"What are you, acting as his personal proxy or something?"

"He doesn't even know I'm doing this. I'm just trying to help out in any way I can. He has a little baby with a wonderful young lady he's trying to make things right with."

"Please don't tell me you're talking about Sandra Horton."

"You know her too?"

Shaking his head, Turchini says, "Of course. Her father is one of our esteemed alumni. Owns a bunch of car dealerships around North Jersey. So Andre and Sandra had a baby?"

"He's a little over a year old."

"I guess Mr. Horton saw that coming." Turchini looks genuinely hurt. "The whole thing is really sad. Two bright students, one an exceptional athlete, the other from a prosperous family, neither of them graduate, and then they have a baby out of wedlock."

Turchini pauses and stares out the window. "That's the kind of thing that makes me glad I'm in the priesthood. I don't envy any parent who was in Mr. Horton's situation. I mean, do you keep paying tens of thousands of dollars of your hard-earned money on tuition for a child who's living a lifestyle that you don't agree with, or do you just pull the rug out from under their future? Tough call either way."

29

Andre steps into Vittas Haberdashery with his black Brooks Brothers suit draped across his arm. The dapper salesman who served Clops approaches him.

"Sir, how can I help you?"

"I'd like to get this tailored."

"I'm sorry, we only service the suits that we sell."

"Oh," Andre says as he admires the sharply styled mannequins. "I've walked by this store my whole life, and I always said that the moment I had a reason to come in here, I would." He focuses on the salesman again. "I thought this was the time, but I guess it's not." Andre turns to leave.

"Let me see what you have there," the salesman says. He looks at Andre and then the suit. "Forty-two Long."

Andre smiles. "You're exactly right. I just need the waist taken in."

"You probably need the breast taken in also. You have to ensure that your lapels lay properly because the face of a suit is like the face of a beautiful woman, the first and most enduring part that you see." He removes the measuring tape from his neck and measures Andre's chest and waist.

"When will this be ready?" Andre asks.

"For you? Tomorrow morning. It's my pleasure to serve

229

a member of the community who recognizes the value and longevity of our brand."

⊞

Andre knocks on Sandra's door clad in his freshly tailored Brooks Brothers suit. He has a blue iris and pink tulip bouquet. Sandra opens the door and her eyes widen.

"Dre, you look very nice!"

Andre is swept up in a thrall of flattery and embarrassment. He gives Sandra the flowers to shift her attention away from him.

Little Dre clops across the floor in tiny Buster Brown dress shoes and leaps into Andre's arms. The junior Dre wears pinstriped pants, matching vest, a crisply ironed white dress shirt, and a burgundy bow tie. His formerly tangled 'fro is parted in the middle and laid to the side.

"We better go," Sandra says. "We don't want to miss the bus."

Outside, Andre hails a cab. Sandra playfully rolls her eyes. "Excuse *me*, Mr. Big Spending on a cab."

"I've sold a few cars. And I'm going to get myself one after I'm back in my place. Then I can drive you two around and you won't have to catch the bus anymore."

Andre collapses Little Dre's stroller and places it in the trunk of the cab. He slides into the backseat, nabs Little Dre from Sandra, and plops him on his lap.

"Ocean and Danforth," he directs the cabbie.

Sandra turns to him. "So, Mr. Big Spending, are we catching a cab home too?"

Andre smiles and kisses Little Dre on the cheek. "Don't worry about it. Just sit back and enjoy the ride."

The cab double-parks in front of New Jersey Truth. Andre tells the driver, "Pull up so that my girl—so that my son and my—could you pop the trunk, please?"

Andre grabs the stroller and opens the door for Sandra and Little Dre. He feels warm and tingly as he holds Sandra's hand and leads her between the dirty bumpers of two parked cars. He shakes out the stroller and straps Little Dre inside.

Two bodies materialize. Andre locks onto Clops's beady eyes, and every stretch of his being chills to the bone. He sees Rahjaan and the glint of burnished steel. Rahjaan's eyes get big when he sees Andre. He pauses for a breath but closes his eyes and squeezes anyway.

A hot metal storm erupts, and spent shells ping and dance across the sidewalk.

Andre shields Sandra and fire slices through him. He twists his body in an attempt to cover Little Dre but stumbles as the stroller rolls toward the street.

Screeching tires clash with the sound of repeated gun bursts.

Sandra's shrill scream turns into a sickening moan.

Andre grabs Clops's shooting arm and in exchange gets several dizzying kicks to the head. He crashes headlong to the pavement.

Little Dre rolls into traffic. Big Will slams on brakes an instant before the stroller passes in front of his bus. The stroller rams the curb and flips over.

As the block is tossed into panic, Clops and Rahjaan vanish.

Andre blinks several times as a brilliant blue sky blows in. Suddenly he's aware that he's on his back staring up at it.

Then he remembers.

Sandra!! Dre!!

His mind shouts, *Get up!* but his body doesn't respond. Andre turns and sees Sandra's smoke-colored knee boots. Pain explodes through him when he flops onto his belly. He deposits a ragged trail of blood on the sidewalk as he feebly drags alongside Sandra's motionless form—pawing, grabbing at her in search of holes, injuries.

Nothing.

The closer he gets to her head, the more frenzy grips his own.

He caresses Sandra's face in both hands and sees a small trickle of blood draining from her ear.

Andre's head lightens and his sight goes white.

The block is an amassment of chaos and caterwauls as people cower on the ground and sprint about helter-skelter.

Big Will throws his bus into park and jumps off when he spots Andre bleeding on top of Sandra. A rueful bawl escapes his throat. He looks up at the handful of people with cell phones pressed to their ears, but emergency vehicles are nowhere in sight.

"I'm not waiting!" he shouts at no one in particular. He peels Andre off of Sandra and stretches him across two seats of the bus, then he gently lifts Sandra from the concrete. She hangs limp in his arms. He lays her on the floor in the aisle of the bus.

Rock races out of New Jersey Truth just as the bus disappears into traffic. A sobbing woman collapses into Rock's arms and says, "Your nephew."

"My nephew what?" Rock asks. He notes the smudged blood all over the sidewalk.

The woman searches to see who's listening and softly says, "He shot up Sandra and her boyfriend."

The resounding drumbeat in Rock's chest causes his eyes to dart about wildly. "Where are they?"

"A bus driver put them on his bus." She points across the street. "The baby's over there."

A cloud of witnesses are gathered around the stroller. Rock dodges oncoming traffic and pushes through the crowd.

Little Dre is still strapped inside and bursts into tears when he sees Rock, who lifts him from the stroller and pats him gently on the back. "It's going to be alright, little man."

Then reality stomps all over Rock's instinct to comfort.

I don't even know if they're alive.

Rock begins the work of establishing in his mind that the lady must be mistaken.

What connection would Claymont have to Sandra and Andre?

Nevertheless, Rock's insides are ablaze as he crosses the street and slips into the meeting place just as Detectives Jackson and Carollo show up.

Inside, Rock attempts to transfer Little Dre to Grammy Lee, but he screams. Rock takes him to the rostrum, and he calms as soon as he's under the hot stage lights. Rock addresses the people who remain.

"Our sister Sandra Horton was injured in the incident out front."

A heavy gasp pierces the ceiling.

"And Andre, her—Little Dre's father was injured too."

Little Dre blinks into the blinding light and his big eyes swell with tears. Rock holds him tight and a tear runs down his own cheek.

"I don't have any more information other than they're on their way to the hospital. But we're gonna ask God to intervene in this situation because he can. Now for those of you who want to leave, I understand. But I want to personally ask all of you to stay until we finish praying. Then we'll be dismissed."

No one leaves their seat, so Rock bows his head. "Great One. Nothing ever occurs to you because you know the end from the beginning. And since you're not bound by time or space, you knew that this would happen before you formed the universe with the words of your mouth. We present Sandra and Andre to you. And we ask that you protect them from injuries seen and unseen. We pray that the medical staff that tends to them would see them as valuable and worthy of their respect. Give the doctors wisdom and direct their care.

"And finally, we pray for this little man here. We ask that you shield him from any lingering emotional scars and the bitterness that can come from them. Use this incident to show him that you are sovereign over injury and evil. We humbly make these requests in the name of the Messiah. So be it."

When Rock attempts to pass Little Dre to Grammy again, he clings tighter. "Little man, I need you to stay with Grammy Lee. She's my mommy. And she loves babies, especially little boys. She raised two of them herself. And I'm not gonna be long. I'll be back. I promise."

Little Dre looks at the two men at the back of the room and reaches for Grammy without shedding another tear.

Rock approaches Jackson and Carollo.

"Nice prayer, Reverend," Jackson says.

"I'm not a reverend—"

"Lighten up, Rocky," Carollo says. "We're just glad to see you out of prison and doing something positive with your life instead of running from us."

Rock fills his barrel chest, holds his sigh, and folds his arms.

"We're hoping that someone in your church—" Jackson begins.

"A church isn't a place, Detective. It's a body of believers in the Messiah who follow his teachings—"

"Knock off the semantics," Carollo interrupts. "We have a job to do."

"And you don't have to raise your voice at me to do it," Rock counters. "Now, I've spoken to you with nothing but respect even though you greeted me with an insult."

Carollo stares at Rock with lifeless eyes and Rock glares back.

Jackson leans between them. "We wanna see if any parts of the body gathered here will answer a few questions for us, Rocky. Okay?"

Rock looks from Carollo to Jackson and returns to the microphone. "Family, Detectives Jackson and Carollo from the JCPD are here. And they'd like to ask some questions. So if any of you were outside when the incident took place, please come forward."

No one moves.

Rock approaches Jackson and Carollo. "I'll ask again when you're not here because if the wrong person sees you talking to the police, it can get you in trouble."

"You're the leader here, Rocky. What do you know?" Jackson asks. "You had to see or hear something."

Rock carefully considers. "I've only spoken to one person. So if I get credible information, I'll contact you."

Carollo buts in. "But what do you know now?"

"I already told you. I don't *know* anything. And I'm not sharing hearsay with two DTs eager to make a collar. You guys ain't exactly the Boy Scouts."

▮▮▮

Big Will careens to a stop in front of the emergency room at Christ Hospital. A young man in scrubs is smoking in front of the building. Will grabs him and says, "I need help!"

"I'm only a lab tech—"

235

Will shoves him aside.

Everyone notices the six-foot-three, 230-pound black man in the blood-covered bus uniform when he enters triage.

"I have two seriously injured people on my bus!"

The nurse at the desk snatches up the phone, and as soon as she hangs up, two men burst through the door with gurneys.

Sandra and Andre are strapped onto stretchers and rushed inside.

30

Rock stops in front of a derelict apartment building on the corner of Chapel and Rutgers Avenues.

In the shadow-drenched hallway, Rock jams an elevator button that never lights, so he tackles the stairs.

When he reaches the fourth floor, his blood is so hot that his palms sweat. He knocks on the first door beyond the elevator, and one of Shaminique's eyes appears in a crack held at length by a security chain.

"He ain't here," she says.

"You don't even know what I'm here for."

Shaminique rolls her eyes. "You obviously don't understand, Rock. Ain't nobody scared of you no more. So you can't just show up at people's house like you used to and expect them to do what you say. I told you Cyclops ain't here!"

Shaminique slams the door, but Rock lowers his shoulder and lunges forward before she can get it completely shut. She tumbles back onto the living room floor.

Rock's broad shoulders clog the threshold of the apartment.

Clops steps out of the bedroom at the back of the house. "What you doing here, Unc?"

No words. Rock rushes him and lifts him off his feet. Clops

stiffens his legs to regain his footing and plants blow after blow on the back of Rock's head, which does nothing to loosen his iron grip. Rock wedges his forehead into Clops's chest and rams him into the wall. The force of the impact enables Rock to tip Clops off his feet and ram him into the floor.

Shaminique grabs a knife from the kitchen and screams, "Get off him, Rock! Don't think I won't cut you! Get off him!"

Rock rises and squares his back to the front door.

Clops scrambles to his feet. "Put that knife down, Shaminique! I can handle mine!"

She keeps the dagger pointed at Rock.

"I said put it down!"

Shaminique places the knife on the kitchen counter well within her reach.

Clops turns his attention to Rock and throws his fists up. Rock charges him again. A loud *pap-pap* bounces off the walls as Clops catches Rock solidly on each side of his jaw. But Rock doesn't flinch. He goes low and grabs Clops around the waist, slams him to the floor, wrestles his way on top of him, and hammers him hard, twice to the face.

Shaminique charges Rock, slicing wildly through the air. He shields his face with a sofa pillow an instant before she fillets it.

Rock jerks Shaminique to the floor, twists the knife from her hand, and stands. A trickle of blood streams from the corner of his mouth. He points the knife at Clops.

"Word's already on the street that you did it."

"I've been here since last night, so I don't know what you talking about." Clops nudges Shaminique. "Right?"

She stares at him, looking bewildered, her confidence in him now shaken.

"If either of them die, I'm coming after you," Rock says.

He points the knife at Shaminique. "And harboring a fugitive is gonna get you a bid too. You better ask yourself if it's worth it."

▄▍▄

Andre's closed eyelids render him trapped inside a loathsome darkness. He slithers along the edges of lucidity, convinced that he's still somehow in the land of the living.

From the bottom of this place, Andre screams, *I'm alive!* but only reaps an earful of the emotionless bleep of machine. He senses distant pains rippling across nerve endings drunk off of stiff shots of fentanyl and hydromorphone.

Suddenly, bursts of orange slice across the black veils that mask Andre's sight. Then he remembers that he has eyes and that he can open them. He beholds three teenagers on the cleft of a craggy, graffiti-marred palisade across from the hospital. They reflect sunlight into Andre's face with hand mirrors.

The teens notice Andre noticing them and immediately engage in the sophisticated hand ritual that identifies them as OGC. Finished throwing up gang signs, one teen presses his thumb and pointer finger together and zips his lips.

A second teen points at Andre, cocks his thumb, and fires an imaginary shot. "POW!"

The three teens crack up like broken glass and evaporate.

Andre blinks.

Was that real?

A regal Iranian doctor enters the room, and Andre's insides melt because he's now aware that he's conscious, and convinced that the gangster phantasm was true.

Everything rushes back at him. Sandra, Little Dre, gunshots, screams—the pain.

Andre attempts to sit up, but the lines and tubes running

everywhere leave him tethered to the bed. He gags on a catheter shoved down his throat.

The doctor touches his hand. "Please relax. I am Dr. Hammurabi, and it is good to see you waking. You are very blessed, my friend."

Andre chokes on the tube as he attempts to cough up a host of questions.

"You were hit four times," Hammurabi says as he points to Andre's right pectoral muscle, left thigh, left forearm, and right calf. "Pain will be your companion, but tragedy is not likely to visit you. You have all soft tissue wounds, my friend."

Hammurabi's smile makes Andre nauseous. Despite the discomfort of the hose in his throat, Andre gurgles and half-spits what sounds like, "My wife and son . . ."

Hammurabi deciphers Andre's frothy bleat and frowns. "Your wife didn't make it."

Andre shuts his eyes so tight his face hurts.

"I'm sorry," Hammurabi says softly.

Andre's eyes snap open, and he's attacked by pain so severe that tears drain his eye sockets. He looks out of the hospital window, and the three teens are back on the palisade stage with a fourth OGC. They point Andre out as if he's on display in a meat case. He can hear them yell faintly, "Snitch on a crime, you get clapped in a ditch 'cuz you dime!"

The teens scatter when Hammurabi enters. Andre is struck by the irony of gang members fleeing when a white coat enters the room—as if in the midst of vice and violence, they retain the qualities of schoolboys who play "knock on the door and run."

"Yes, yes, my friend," Dr. Hammurabi says. "You are waking again. This is good news because I have reduced your dosages. You seemed to start hallucinating in the middle of our last conversation." He places his stethoscope on Andre's chest. "You must relax. Your heart rate is greatly increased."

Andre stares at him and chokes out, "Sandra."

"Yes, she is a couple of rooms down. But I cannot tell you more because you are not married. There's someone here to see you."

Mr. Horton looks like a fraction of himself when he enters the room. He squeezes Hammurabi's shoulder as he departs.

It's as if Mr. Horton anticipates Andre's question. "Little Andre is fine. But Sandra . . . not so much."

It's a peculiar sight for Andre to see Dr. Hardness creased with emotion.

"Her brain is swelling," Mr. Horton says. "They're pumping her full of steroids, but it's not working. It's all kinds of pressure in her head."

Andre swallows, and the catheter moves up and down in his throat. Acute pain returns, particularly in his chest, and inspires tears.

"It's okay," Mr. Horton says. "We're going to pray."

Andre doesn't hear the prayer because his mind detonates with questions that have no ready answers. He is taunted by an abiding desire to scream—at God, and call him evil, because once again he has allowed something terrible to happen to someone he loves.

31

Were it not for the gauze that crowns Sandra's head, there would be no indication that she cracked her skull when her head smacked the pavement amidst the hail of bullets. Her face is peaceful, like a baby doll's whose eyes automatically close when you lay her down. Mrs. Horton brushes her hair until it's night-on-the-town together. She applies Berry Burst moisturizer to Sandra's lips and dabs the corners of her mouth to remove any excess. She takes a seat and holds Sandra's hand.

"Little Andre asked about you today. I told him that when you woke up, he would be the first to know. Of course that wasn't good enough for him. He brought me his shoes and said, 'Ma-ma going.' He'll be so happy to see you. So you can't give up in there, you hear me?"

Mrs. Horton looks at Sandra, half expecting her to answer.

The corners of Mrs. Horton's mouth quivers, and she hurries out of the room. She hides her face behind a two-handed mask of brown fingers.

Rock takes a deep breath. Despite witnessing scores of fights, shootings, beatings, and more, hospitals make him uncomfortable. To him, they're like prisons with needles instead of handcuffs, a place where young and old pass away into eternity.

Andre is propped up in bed, minus the catheter. As soon as he sees Rock, he closes his eyes.

"Dre, what's up?"

Andre turns to the wall. The only movement is his Adam's apple as it floats up and down as he swallows.

Rock resists the temptation to wage a war of attrition by taking a seat and waiting for Andre to open his eyes. Instead he says, "You know how to find me."

Once Andre is certain that Rock is gone, he opens his eyes.

Rock is still smarting over Andre's diss when Grammy Lee answers the door.

"How's Sandra and Andre?" she asks.

"Neither one of them are talking."

"Did Andre take a turn for the worse or something?"

"No. He's choosing not to talk. Could be depressed, probably angry. Maybe both. I don't know."

"How's Sandra?"

"Still hasn't woke up. But her mother's there every day. Keeps her hair done, eyebrows arched. She looks like Sleeping Beauty. And her mom talks to her like she can hear her."

"She can," Grammy says. "There's countless examples of people remembering conversations they heard when they were unconscious. Any new information from the police?"

Should I tell her?

"No."

"I don't know what's happened to Greenville," Grammy says. "When your father and I moved here, this was a place for blacks to move up in the world, own a home, raise a family." She shakes her head. "But all of that's dead now . . ." She reminisces aloud about the days before guns, gangs, and Greenville became an unholy trinity.

"Relax, Momma. I'll get you some water."

Grammy sits in her favorite chair and Rock drapes a blanket over her feet.

In the kitchen, Rock bypasses the faucet and peers under the sink.

Still there.

The hole that he cut out of the wall fifteen years ago.

Claymont was eight when he caught Rock hunched under the sink stuffing the hole with sacks of cannabis, dirty money, and a gun.

"Whatchu doing, Unc?" young Claymont asked, ever eager to find ways to bond with his high-strung uncle.

"Why don't you try doing what I'm doing?" Rock asked.

"What's that?"

"Minding my own business. And I better not ever see you under here. You understand me?"

"Yes," Claymont said.

"Yes, what?" Rock demanded.

"Yes, sir."

"Now get out of here."

Rock slips on one of Grammy's dishwashing gloves, gropes around the hole, and removes a .40 caliber Glock pistol with olive drab frame.

A wave of guilt batters him. He's reminded of his sister's expectation that he would teach Claymont to be a man. And that's what he did, according to what he knew at the time.

Before prison, Rock thought that being a man meant being the hardest head on the block. And if he had to knock somebody's block off to maintain his ascendancy, he did.

In Greenville, Rock's path was not unique. If you didn't play ball, go to college, or tote a gun for the government, you hustled, applying your ambition and native talents to a career in the streets. After all, it was America where you bought low, sold high, built your brand, and dominated the competition. And that's exactly what Rock did.

Now, fifteen years after he marshaled his wildest friends into an organized unit, OGC controls the majority of crack sales in New Jersey's second-largest city and has a reputation as one of the more ruthless gangs in the state.

Rock stares at the crude OGC tattoo on the web between his right thumb and pointer finger.

"Rocky, did you forget about me?"

"No, ma'am."

He places the gun in the hole and fills her cup.

Andre now has a room without a palisade-stage view of the street. Jackson enters, clutching a Sweet Sunshine Get Well Soon bouquet. Carollo trails him with a giant smiley face balloon that he ties to the foot of Andre's bed with a measure of good riddance.

"Andre, how are you?" Jackson asks as Carollo takes a seat.

Andre stares at him blankly.

"Come on, Andre. We're here to help you find the guy you saw come after you and your girlfriend."

Andre chooses silence all the more.

Carollo whacks the arm of his chair. "You know something? It's your tax dollars what pays us to keep your neighborhood safe. I live in Garfield, so who shoots who in your hood doesn't affect me. I do this to help you."

"Help me?" Andre springs up, grimaces, and growls, "Are you going to be around when they retaliate?"

245

"So you're saying it was more than one shooter?" Jackson asks, ever angling for information and an edge.

"I'm not saying anything. I've already been threatened since I've been in here. But you didn't know that, did you?"

Jackson and Carollo are silent.

"That's because you can't protect me! If you could, this wouldn't have happened in the first place!"

Jackson throws his hands up. "We didn't come here to antagonize you."

"But you did."

"Okay. Sorry. Is that what you want to hear, Andre?" Jackson nudges his partner.

"Sorry," Carollo says reluctantly.

"I just want to know what you saw," Jackson continues.

Andre stares at him longingly.

He looks like me, but he's on the other side.

Andre turns his back on Jackson, and the burn brought on by all the sudden movement twists his face into a scowl.

Jackson licks his thumb and snaps a business card from his breast pocket. He places it on the nightstand, and on his way out stops in the doorway. "Funny thing happened on the way to the ballistics lab. The bullets they pulled out of you were from the same gun that was used on the guy you hit with your bus. So you think real hard about that, Andre. And then you call me when you're ready to tell me what you know."

Andre harbors an image of himself buried to his neck as a storm tide rolls in. The first wave bubbles across the floor of his nasal cavity and drowns his sinuses. He disgorges a noseful of water and recaptures his wind when the water retreats. But the next wave . . .

Andre shakes the image and angers at the thought of the beady-eyed gunman and his young flunky.

They got me with small arms, but I'm gonna come back at them with something bigger.

He presses the call button and a nurse appears.

"I'd like more pain medication, and then I'd like to go by ICU."

The nurse transports Andre to the other side of the hospital in a wheelchair.

He has her stop at the entrance to Sandra's room because Mrs. Horton and some women he doesn't recognize are huddled around Sandra.

Why do they have to have their hands all over her?

Mrs. Horton looks up and waves Andre into the room. After the ladies say, "Amen," they surround Andre and, without his permission, lay their hands on him too.

The strident petitions of religious women fill the room. Andre is suspicious of what he feels rising inside of him. It swells with each woman's cry out to God on his behalf.

Andre's head and shoulders drop, despite his commitment to resist the wail that toils in his belly.

The prayers don't stop.

It seems to Andre that these women call out every problem he has with their Creator.

"Take away the pain and disappointment that caused him to distrust you!" one cries.

"Show him that you're real and that you're concerned about his life!" another shouts.

"Remove the confusion and grant him the grace to see that you're sovereign!" a third calls out.

"Repair the breach in our family and make him a part of it," Mrs. Horton adds softly.

The women's words travel throughout Andre's body, and the pain that he felt after rising up against Carollo dwindles to a dull ache.

Finally, the wail ekes out of Andre's throat as an anemic groan.

"Amen!" the women say in unison.

"Amen," Andre whispers soft enough that only he can hear.

One by one the women touch Andre and depart until only Mrs. Horton remains. "I'm going to leave you two alone," she says.

The quiet that settles in the room spooks Andre as he watches Sandra's chest rise and fall. He uses his right arm to grab the side of the bed, and bolts of pain shoot through his wounded right pectoral muscle. When he pulls himself up, he shifts his weight to his left foot, and agony vibrates through his injured left thigh. Andre disregards the pain in his damaged left forearm and struggles up from the wheelchair. He grits his teeth, tilts over, and gives Sandra a painfully sweet kiss.

32

Physically and emotionally drained, Andre slumps in his wheelchair on the journey back to his room. Mr. Horton and Detective Jackson are huddled outside his door. They notice Andre rolling up.

"I have reason to believe that Andre is withholding information that can help us in this investigation," Jackson says.

"What information is that?" Mr. Horton asks.

Jackson's eyes glimmer. "Andre and I have a little history that keeps him from being as forthcoming with me as I'd like him to be. Why don't you ask him?"

Mr. Horton's face frosts over. "I think I will."

Andre ignores Jackson but acknowledges Mr. Horton by limply raising his finger as he's wheeled into the room. Two male nurses hoist him into bed amidst more misery.

Mr. Horton rises and extends his hand to Jackson. "I'll be in touch."

"Great," Jackson says. "And you can trust me on this. We're going to find out who's responsible."

Mr. Horton takes a seat beside Andre's bed. Andre closes his eyes and slowly releases air through his lips in the hope that the stabbing spasms will subside with it.

"Andre," Mr. Horton says.

Andre opens his eyes.

"Do you know who did this to you and Sandra?"

Andre briefly closes them again. "OGC."

Mr. Horton is blown back into his seat. "You're in a gang?"

"No, I'm not in a gang," Andre retorts.

"Then what are you talking about, it's OGC?"

Andre monitors the door, glances out the window, and lowers his voice. "I saw my cousin get killed when I was still driving for New Jersey Transit. And the shooter saw me."

"You saw your cousin get killed, and you didn't say anything to the police?"

"I didn't know him, Mr. Horton. I found out all of this after the fact. And I didn't see who did it. He saw me."

Mr. Horton manipulates his temples with jittery fingers. "Do the police know this is gang related?"

"I don't deal with the police."

Mr. Horton bounces up and broods over Andre with clenched fists. "My daughter is in there fighting for her life, and you—what if they send somebody in here to finish the job?"

Despite the evening chill, Rock is huddled on the balcony of his apartment with a conflicted conscience. The view of New York Bay usually comforts him, but tonight the cold, dark waters exacerbate his sinking sensation.

Rock thought that all of his fiery rage had been "buried with Christ" when he was submerged in the prison pool by the chaplain at Sing Sing. Rather than a dove descending on his shoulders as the voice of God proclaimed, "This is my son in whom I am well pleased," converted jailbirds crowed, "Yo, son! The heavens rejoice when thugs embrace God's decrees!"

Despite that moment of spiritual exhilaration more than a

decade ago, the venom that fuels Rock's present anger toward his own flesh and blood is unlike any he's felt since his days of running the streets.

Thoughts of Carollo seep in.

When Carollo was still a beat cop, he got his rocks off by whacking Rock in places where the bruises wouldn't show.

"You a punk," Rock seethed after that first beating. His lower back, buttocks, and thighs were on fire.

A month earlier, Carollo had led a JCPD raid on Rock's apartment that turned up nothing.

"Where's the smoking gun?" Rock mocked as Carollo exited the house. "Violating a black man's Fourth Amendment rights."

A red-faced Carollo responded, "Expect to get hammered when I see you on the street. And I promise you, I'm going to keep doing it until I find something on you or you take up another profession."

Cuffed in the backseat of Carollo's cruiser four weeks later, Rock remembered the threat but jawed anyway. "I bet that's why you became a cop, so you could get a badge and a gun and run around the hood like you hard." Through the rearview mirror, Rock saw that he had found Carollo's soft spot, so he dug deeper. "If you was a real man, you'd take these cuffs off so we could go one-on-one. But punks with badges don't do that. They cuff people before they swing on 'em. And I promise you, if I ever see *you* on the street and you off duty, you can expect—"

Carollo slammed on brakes, opened the back door, and battered Rock speechless. Of course Rock didn't file a complaint because internal affairs would have lovingly cast lots for the opportunity to burn a complaint offered up by OGC Rocky Jenkins.

Rock's cell phone rings.

"It's Dre."

"So now you're calling me?"

"Sorry," Andre says. "But I need to talk now. It's pretty important."

This is the part of servant leadership that Rock hates—used up when people need you, conveniently dismissed when they don't.

And I'm supposed to just take it? Like I don't have any self-respect?

"I'll try and stop by tomorrow," Rock says.

He hangs up and tosses his phone on the table.

Mr. and Mrs. Horton step out of their stately Italianate Victorian. The north sides of the mature oaks that surround the house are plastered with ice sheets that blew in with the storm that galloped through the Watchung Mountains at daybreak.

"Dewey, I'm not riding in that Dodge," Mrs. Horton proclaims. "We can either drive two cars or you can ride with me."

"We're not driving two cars, and I'm not riding with you, Wilda."

"Just drive my car," she says.

"I like my car better. It knows me. And do we have to go through this every time we ride somewhere together?"

"Your car is seventeen years old and ugly," she says.

"Vanity, Wilda. That's all that is. I sell it every day."

Mrs. Horton tosses her keys through the air and Mr. Horton catches them. "Spare me the faux asceticism and drive the car, man," she says.

Mr. Horton climbs behind the wheel of the Mercedes and fumbles around for the keyhole.

Mrs. Horton shrieks.

"What?"

She points through the windshield.

OGC is spray-painted across the front of the house in large black letters.

The young Montclair police officer marvels at the elaborate cherry-paneled foyer. "Nice place you got here."

"Thank you," Mr. Horton says.

"Michael Strahan lived in this neighborhood, right?"

"Two streets over."

"So'd you ever see him? You know, like driving around or anything?"

"Officer"—Mr. Horton looks at his badge—"Sandifer. I'm really not interested in discussing anything other than my house being vandalized."

"Sorry, Mr. Horton. I'm just a big-time Giants fan, you know?"

No answer.

"Okay, so let's get down to business," Sandifer says, his game face on now. "What connection do you have to the gang?"

"None whatsoever," Mr. Horton answers, taken aback.

"I mean, is there any reason OGC would want to vandalize your property?"

"Yes. My daughter and her . . . friend were the victims of a gang-related shooting two weeks ago. And according to her friend, the shooting happened because he witnessed the murder of one of his family members a few months back."

"I see," Sandifer says as he scribbles notes.

"As soon as I found out about that, I reported it to the detective in Jersey City who's handling the investigation.

I wanted to get police protection in the hospital for my daughter."

"Sorry to hear about your daughter. How's she doing?"

"Not good. In a coma since it happened."

"What about her friend?"

"He got shot up pretty bad too, but none of his injuries were life threatening."

Officer Sandifer gnaws on the eraser of his pencil. "I don't recall ever hearing of an incident in Montclair involving OGC. They don't tend to travel. Your daughter's friend, is he talking?"

"No."

"Not surprised. And I'll let you in on a dirty little secret since we're talking JCPD and not us. Municipal police departments don't always do the best job protecting witnesses. What they usually offer in exchange for testimony is a cheap motel until trial and a seat on a Greyhound when it's over."

"I'm not sure I'm following you," Mr. Horton says.

"Okay, picture this." Sandifer puts his hands up with his thumbs forming the bottom of a frame. "A ranch house in the painted hills of Arizona, a new identity, and mint juleps?"

"Okay."

"Hollywood, my friend. Only happens in the movies. Local police departments just aren't equipped for that kind of thing. We barely got enough cops on the street with all the budget cuts. Look, a handshake and a thank-you from the DA is free. After that, it's up to the person who testifies to start a new life."

Mr. Horton frowns. "So a person is supposed to leave their job, their family, basically everything they know after they testify?"

"They don't *have* to do that, but what would you do?"

Mr. Horton is silent. The upper and lower arc of the spray-painted O is visible through the window in the foyer. He thinks about Sandra, Andre, Little Dre, Wilda, himself.

"How do you get people to do that?" Mr. Horton asks.

"Some are willing to take the risk in the interest of justice, but more and more people are choosing not to. And it's not just in bad neighborhoods. In a lot of places the DA won't even pursue charges if they only have one witness and no forensics evidence to back it up. Think about it. You spend months preparing a case, get to trial, and your one witness gets spooked or bumped off, and then *poof*." Sandifer wiggles his fingers for effect. "There goes your case and many thousands of taxpayer dollars. Wanna hear a sad story that happened right here in Jersey?"

"Go ahead," Mr. Horton says, warming to the cold-blooded reality of what he's now entrenched in.

"A grandmother sees her granddaughter get shot through the face," Sandifer says. "The little girl was riding her bike and gets caught in the crossfire between rival gangs. The grandmother doesn't testify because she lives in the same projects where the gang operates."

"So what happened with the case?"

Sandifer closes his notebook. "Nothing. Grandma figured she'd rather her and her family live than be killed if she testified. That's the kind of pressure she was getting. Seventy-five years old. It's a shame." He stands and extends his hand. "You take it easy, Mr. Horton. I'm gonna compare notes with the JCPD. And my sergeant told me to tell you that he added a few extra patrols on your street overnight for the next couple of weeks. He said you sold him a car ten years ago and it still runs great."

33

Andre is hunched over in his wheelchair, savaged by his inability to turn back the clock and angle his body in such a way as to break Sandra's fall. He buries his face in her palm. "I wish we could switch places."

Andre's recollection of the wrongs he did to Sandra sets upon him like a whirlwind, and suddenly her hand is soaked with his tears.

Her hand moves. Then her entire body convulses and her chin thrusts upward. Every machine in the room goes berserk. A horde of nurses crashes the door.

"She's having a seizure," one says.

Another nurse spins Andre out of the way and collapses the sides of the bed. They spirit Sandra from the room and leave Andre suspended between echoes of hysteria and Sandra's dangling IV.

Andre covers his head as anguish boils over his body. He looks to the ceiling.

Take me, man. I can go.

Mr. and Mrs. Horton enter the room.

"Where's Sandra?"

Andre shakes his head. "Seizure."

Mr. Horton smacks the door and blows out of the room. Mrs. Horton follows.

Andre awakes still parked in the space where Sandra's bed once was. The sun has set and long shadows slice the room into silver and dark swatches. A candy striper passes and doubles back.

"Mr. Bolden, you've been in here all this time?"

Andre nods.

"I'll take you back to your room."

Andre sees Mr. and Mrs. Horton walking slowly down the hall.

"How is she?" Andre asks.

They look at him blankly.

"I'm really sorry," Andre says.

Mr. and Mrs. Horton move on.

Back in his room, Andre stares at the ceiling for hours, or so it seems, even though it could have been only minutes. Time won't release him except to bully him with regret.

Feeling trapped, Andre converses with God. Or is it himself? He doesn't know because it's all in his head.

You should've just killed me with my folks.

Give me a reason.

One good reason why I'm here?

Pause.

Nothing.

But it doesn't matter because I'm going to solve this as soon as I get out of here.

Andre feels a presence in the room. He looks up and it's Little Dre who stretches out to him.

"He wanted to see you," Mrs. Horton says.

"'Ey, Dah-dah," Little Dre says as he hugs his father tight

around the neck. It feels so good that Andre ignores the misery chorus that roars through his members when he reciprocates Little Dre's embrace.

"Daddy missed you so much."

"Where Ma-ma?"

"She's sleeping in another room."

"Andre, I want to ask you something," Mrs. Horton says, assessing him sharply with her eyes.

"Okay."

"I want to let Little Andre see Sandra."

Andre swallows a lump of solid fear.

Mrs. Horton grabs his hand and looks him in the eye. "I want to do it because I believe God is going to raise her up, Andre. Can you believe that with me?"

Andre nods his head.

"Then we're agreed," Mrs. Horton says.

She rolls Andre down the hall. He holds Little Dre, who looks up at him and makes funny faces, unaware of what he's about to encounter. Andre fights back tears as he makes faces back at him, determined to keep his promise to Mrs. Horton.

Little Dre's playfulness halts when he sees Sandra lying in bed, not moving. He reaches for her. "Ma-ma."

Mrs. Horton takes him from Andre's arms and walks him to the bed. "She's going to get up, baby."

Little Dre looks at Mrs. Horton and then back to Sandra. He reaches for his mommy again. Mrs. Horton sits him between Sandra's arm and breast. He pats Sandra's chest and smiles. "Ma-ma." He steals a kiss and quickly reaches for his father.

Mrs. Horton shuttles him back to Andre. Once he's in Andre's lap, he buries his face in Andre's chest, but doesn't cry.

Rock pops his head in Andre's room. "My brother."

Andre plays it cool so as not to reveal his disappointment at how long it took Rock to finally show up.

Rock grabs a seat. An awkward silence.

"So why did you want to see me?" Rock asks.

Andre feels his way back to the sense of guilty responsibility that hemmed him in after Mr. Horton blitzed his convictions.

"I saw who shot me and Sandra," Andre says.

Since the shooting, Rock has wrestled with the realization that he is one with the cruelty that is at the core of Andre and Sandra's bind—and Andre's words make it worse. He thinks of a disturbing proverb. *A thief's partner is his own worst enemy. He will be punished if he tells the truth in court, and God will curse him if he doesn't.*

"And it's the same person who murdered my cousin," Andre finishes.

Rock's stomach takes a bilious turn toward queasy.

"Did you hear about the guy who got shot down the block from the police station on Bergen a few months ago?" Andre asks.

"Yeah."

"Well, I saw it happen. And the guy doing the shooting saw me see him. It was the same guy, man. But this time he had a young dude with him that slings on Communipaw. This is OGC, Rock. And they were coming to murk me to make sure I don't say anything."

Rock unconsciously crosses his pointer finger over his thumb to cover his OGC tattoo and settles it in his mind. "I'm bowing out of servant leadership, Dre."

"You're quitting?" Andre asks.

"Not quitting. Just not qualified. Too much darkness in my closet."

There's a hearty ruckus outside of Andre's room, followed by men's voices. In tramps Strange-O, Mark, and Fredrick.

"Hot wings, baby!" Strange-O says as he pokes a Styrofoam container emitting hot-sauce-scented steam under Andre's nose.

"And check the radish roses!" Mark chimes in. "I carved 'em myself!" He proudly displays a green leaf salad with a smattering of the red and white flowered fruit.

Fredrick has a bottle of sparkling cider in each hand. "What's real tonight, fellas?"

Rock tries to mask his embarrassment. He forgot it was Wednesday.

Strange-O elbows him. "Where you been at, man? Nobody's been able to get up with you."

"Sorry, brothers. It's been a lot going on," Rock says.

"Like what?" Mark asks.

Every eye in the room rests on Rock. He tidily diverts. "This ain't about me. What matters is that we're all here with Dre for the Realness." He raises a rugged hand to clap Andre across the shoulder but catches himself when Andre flinches.

Strange-O turns to Andre. "So are you eating under your own power yet, or do you have some sexy nurse force-feeding you blended soul food through a straw?"

For the first time in two weeks, Andre smiles without a teardrop accompaniment. "I've only had hospital food since I've been here," he says.

"Well, we got plenty for you tonight," Mark replies, smacking his lips.

Strange-O clutches the nurse call control like a mic and blows through it to test. "One, two, one, two. This is Strange to the O. We need some paper plates up in this piece. Over and out."

Andre and the Realness quartet crack up at Strange-O's clueless degree of certainty.

A nurse appears at the door. "What did you say?"

Strange-O smiles. "How you doing, Florence Nightingale? We're having a party in here for my man, and we need some paper plates in order to serve this chicken up right. Bring 'em fast enough and it might be a few wings in it for you too."

"First of all, we're a hospital, not Chicken Delight," the nurse says. "And second, it's too many of you here at one time. Who let all of you in?"

Hakeem pokes his head in. "Got room for one more?"

"Nurse Williams, these are my best friends," Andre says.

"I'll let it slide this time, but keep it down in here." She turns to leave and says over her shoulder, "And I'm coming back for my wings too."

"See? Chicken works like a charm," Strange-O says.

Andre breaks in and says, "Fellas, this is Hakeem Shabaaz. Hakeem, these are my brothers from the Realness, Rock, Strange-O, Mark, and Fredrick."

"I've been calling every day," Hakeem says to Andre. "What was up with the visitors ban?"

"Yeah, what was up with that?" Fredrick repeats.

Andre examines every eye in the room. "Honestly? After everything that went down, I wasn't up to hearing anybody talking about God was in control. I mean, Sandra's still in a coma. And one doctor said that the longer she's in it, the less likely it is that she'll ever come out."

Every vestige of joviality flees the room.

Mark stops chewing. "So why don't you mind us being here now?"

Andre peers at the darkness lurking outside of his window. "The isolation was killing me."

Strange-O places the container on the table. "Dre, you really know how to ruin four dozen wings, man."

No one laughs at Strange-O's attempt to lighten the mood.

"Dre, I'm 'a keep it real one hundred with you," Rock finally says. "And you can get mad at me if you want. But you ain't serving God, man. He would rather afflict you in this life than judge you in the next. Whether you believe that or not is on you." Rock moves toward the door. "I'm tired of tap-dancing around people that's offended by what's real."

After Rock bolts, the room is so quiet that you could hear a dead man breathe.

Rock is in Sandra's room with his head hung low.

"Everything okay, Pastor Jenkins?"

He looks up at the nurse in the doorway.

"*Please*. I'm not a pastor. My name is Rock. And things are about as well as you can expect, given the circumstances."

After the nurse leaves, Rock closes his eyes tight.

Something's gotta give or I'm gonna crack.

34

Two nurses turn Sandra in her bed. One bends and straightens both of her legs. The other does the same with her arms. Mrs. Horton watches them as Mr. Horton barks into his cell phone, "That's exactly what I *don't* want to happen!"

He hangs up and turns to Mrs. Horton. "They're saying the only way they can find out who spray-painted the house is if they come back and they catch them in the act. What kind of foolishness is that?"

"What did you think they'd say, Dewey? You expect them to find DNA in the spray paint?"

"I don't think I asked you for your crime-scene analysis."

"Well, if you're talking to yourself, next time keep it to yourself."

The nurses continue with Sandra's physical therapy as they glance uncomfortably at Mr. and Mrs. Horton.

Mr. Horton grunts and marches out.

Mrs. Horton plants her forehead in the palms of her hands.

* * *

Shaminique's building is enveloped in darkness because the streetlight that divided it from the sable-vested night was intentionally shot out by OGC soldiers.

Rock's canary-yellow 1955 Studebaker Champion coupe is just around the corner, out of sight.

Mr. Horton passes through the hospital parking garage and freezes. Three young men dressed in black surround his car and stare directly at him. One is seated on the trunk, a second leans against the driver's side door, and a third is camped out on the hood with his heels parked on the bumper.

Mr. Horton cycles through his options as he fingers the cell phone in his pocket. *Never been afraid of my own people, and I'm not going to start now.*

"What's happening, old man?" the one seated on the hood asks.

"You're sitting on my car," Mr. Horton says calmly.

"I know that."

"Can you excuse me so I can get going?"

The young man stands, but the one who's leaning against the driver's side door doesn't budge. He's an imposing figure whose face is masked with malicious intent.

"I'd like for you to move too, young brother," Mr. Horton says.

"We ain't related, so you better act like you scared."

"Why should I act like I'm scared?"

The young man gets in his face. "'Cuz I'm a killer, that's why."

"How long have you been a killer, son?"

The man places something cold and solid on Mr. Horton's temple. "I'm asking the questions. So you ain't got nothing to say."

"I just want to get in my car and get going," Mr. Horton says without flinching. "And you're better than what you're doing right now, son, and you know it."

The young man gnaws his bottom lip and his nostrils flare with each contemplative chomp. Mr. Horton is close enough that he can see something stir in the young man's eyes, beyond the angry visage.

Mr. Horton appeals to the humanity deep inside the eyes of a fiend. "I can help you turn your life around. But you have to want it for yourself."

The young man lowers his weapon. "You lucky, old man." He turns to leave. "And by the way, you got a nice house."

Andre is in the harrows of a deep sleep, and an uncertain din swirls about him.

Converte nos, Deus salutaris noster, et averte iram tuam a nobis.

He feels a presence surrounding him, and he intuits that the sound is distinct from the presence. In his desperation to understand, Andre is overpowered by a caustic peace.

Deus tu conversus vivificabis nos.

Andre retreats into himself, but the darkness he finds there is more upsetting than the presence that now envelops him so tightly that he's powerless to flee. A hand grabs his shoulder.

Andre's eyes snap open, and he is shocked to see Father Turchini kneeling beside him with his head bowed.

"Father T. What are you doing?"

Turchini removes his hand from Andre's shoulder and opens his eyes. A huge grin spreads across his face. "What do you think I'm doing? I'm a priest, for crying out loud."

Andre is not sure what to make of the man who banished him from St. Peter's. "How'd you know I was here?" he asks.

"What, are you kidding? It's all over the news. Hi ya doing?"

"Day to day," Andre says. "You've put on a little weight since the last time I saw you."

"Try twenty pounds. I've been moonlighting as a short-order cook at a Jamaican restaurant across the street from my apartment."

"No kidding?"

"Totally kidding. Just getting old, Bolden. North of fifty and these things happen. But I'll tell you something. That restaurant has brown stewed chicken to die for."

Andre is revisited by the shuddersome experience he just had in his sleep. "Father T?"

"Yeah, what's up?"

Andre attempts to collect his thoughts. "I was halfway asleep, but I felt like something was in the room. Then I woke up and saw you there."

"Felt something in the room? Can you be a little more specific?"

Andre shakes his head. "It was almost like . . . I don't know . . . I was completely surrounded, you know what I mean?"

"Not sure. Did this presence inspire fear?"

Andre thinks for a moment. "No, I actually felt a weird sense of peace, but even that was uncomfortable. And I heard your voice but couldn't make out anything you were saying."

"That part's easy. I was reciting Psalm 85 in Latin."

"Why Latin?"

Turchini shrugs. "Just the way I was taught. And I have good news. I've cleared it with the Board of Regents, and we want to restore the balance of your scholarship so you can finish your degree."

Rather than rejoice, Andre thinks of Sandra in her condition, and his eyes burn. "Thanks, Father T."

"It's my pleasure." Father T smiles and shakes his head. "Bad News Bolden. It's good to see you again, pal of mine. And call me. The administration's ready to make you a Peacock again."

Andre's heart is in half as he slowly drags toward Sandra's room with a hospital-issued aluminum cane. The white rubber stopper sticks to the floor and helps him to balance each step. The anticipation of release is dulled by the reality that he'll leave Sandra behind.

She's propped up in bed, but her chin has slid down her chest. Andre grabs her hand and battles the impulse to shift her into a more comfortable position.

"Sahn, I'm going home. I didn't want to leave you, but they told me I have to go because the rest of my recovery can be done at home. But I'll be here to visit you every day." Andre kisses her cheek. "If I didn't think you'd punch me in the face when you woke up, I'd kiss those lips." He touches her chin. "Maybe that'll wake you up."

Andre closes his eyes and gently kisses her lips, but she doesn't move. He kisses her once more and lays his head on her chest. A tear rolls down his cheek. "I'm so sorry. If I would've known this was going to happen, I never would've gone with you."

He wipes a glob of snot from his nose and holds up his cane. "They gave me this. If you could see me walking with it, you'd crack up. I move like a crusty old man, but the doctors say I'm lucky."

Andre recounts the guys he knows who are confined to wheelchairs, who wear colostomy bags, or who died from gunshot wounds. He comes up with four permanently injured and five permanently dead.

He thinks of Freaky Ty, who was ambushed in his front yard at his nineteenth birthday party while his whole family watched. He was hit eight times but, miraculously, fully recovered. Nevertheless, the bulbous, brown keloids distributed across his chest and back remain.

Of the fifteen people who saw the drama unfold with their eyes wide shut, none saw a thing.

Andre swallows hard. Fear trickles through his pulse as he visualizes the faces of the shooters. The beady-eyed gunman looked frightening and the younger one looked frightened, but the result of their ballistic fury was the same: Sahn in a coma and he with a cane.

Andre grabs Sandra's hand with a surety. "I'm going to do it, Sahn. And whatever happens, happens."

Sandra squeezes Andre's hand ever so slightly.

"Did you just do that?" Andre hoists himself up from the chair and stumbles to the nurses' station. "She just moved! She squeezed my hand!"

The nurse looks up. "Probably reflex. She'd have to do it on command for it to be considered anything other than the body's normal functions."

"Can you at least come look?" Andre implores.

She follows Andre as he limps back to the room and grabs Sandra's hand. "Sahn, squeeze my hand."

Nothing.

"Come on, baby. Squeeze it."

She lies motionless.

Andre drops his head. The nurse shakes hers piteously. "It's okay, Mr. Bolden. These kinds of things happen all the time. But Sandra is still very, very sick."

35

Andre slips out of the hospital only after the bus materializes from the bleak, black night. Big Will lowers the steps so that Andre doesn't have to struggle to climb them. Once Andre is seated, Will kills the lights inside the bus and sets his route display setting to GARAGE.

He maneuvers onto Bergen Avenue. Fortunately, there are no squad cars parked in front of the police station, so he's able to comfortably clear the curb without blackening it with tire rubber. The lighted O on the sign affixed to the brick police fortress captures Andre's attention as it flickers its last and goes dark.

Jackson boards the bus.

Clops and two of his lieutenants emerge from the drab shadows of Shaminique's building. The muscular first lieutenant slides into the driver's seat of a Durango parked at the curb. The skinny second lieutenant climbs into the backseat on the passenger side. Clops scans the block before he opens the front passenger door.

Rock snatches him from behind and twists his arm behind his back. The two lieutenants draw their heat, but not before

Rock places a heater on Clops's temple. "Back up or get his brains on your face."

"Stand down," Clops orders them.

Rock heaves and half drags Clops to his car and mashes him onto the hood. He secures his hands in plasticuffs and thrusts him into the front seat.

The lieutenants in the SUV tail Rock with no headlights as Rock keeps the Airsoft Tec 9 replica handgun angled at Clops's head for effect.

Clops misshapes his face and sucks his teeth. "Fake gun for the soft one. I should've known you weren't packing no real heat."

Rock thunks him in the temple with the weighted butt of the prop gun. "Shut up!"

Clops shuts his left eye and winces. He attempts to wring his wrists free, but the zap straps cut into his skin. "I'm 'a kill you, man!"

Rock throttles him with the gun again, and through the rearview mirror he sees the SUV zoom up beside him. The gangster on the passenger side hangs out of the Durango with a short-barreled, pump-action shotty.

Rock jams his harmless gun deep into Clops's temple and shouts through the glass, "It ain't nothing for me to squeeze! Try me!"

The driver drops back into following position, still without headlights, as Rock accelerates and speeds onto the highway.

"Look at me, Claymont," Rock demands.

Clops ignores his command.

"Don't look at me then," Rock says. "But I know everything. The murder on Bergen, the shooting in front of my place. And I'm gonna put you on blast 'cuz you a black cancer. You preying on your own people."

Clops is not moved. "Uncle or not. You snitch on a crime? You get clapped in a ditch 'cuz you dime."

"I made that up, Claymont, so you can't scare me with it. I'm just letting you know what I'm gonna do so you can do what you gotta do."

Clops hawks and spits a wad of phlegm onto the windshield. It slides down the glass and separates into the defroster vents. "I hope you're cool with your whole building getting sprayed up. Women, kids, it don't matter to me, man."

Rock skids to a stop on the shoulder of the highway. "You threatening my people?" He pulls his face so tight that his eyes nearly pop out of his head. He reaches across Clops, opens the door, and shoves him out. "Threaten me, but not my people! And if you come by New Jersey Truth, I'm 'a be waiting for you!"

Rock speeds off as the Durango licks the guardrail and swerves to avoid drilling the back of his coupe.

Rahjaan has his head jammed between his knees, and his skinny shoulders heave with each felt emotion. Miss Pincus rubs his neck and speaks into his ear. "I ain't raised you to be no criminal, Rahjaan. So if you got yourself into some mess, you need to admit to it, take the responsibilities like a man, and get on with your life."

Rahjaan's caramel-colored face is red from the strain of bucking tears. "I didn't know I was really gonna have to shoot nobody, Moms."

All of the color diffuses from Miss Pincus's face. "Oh, God. God, no. Not my baby." She buries Rahjaan's head in her saggy bosom and rocks him back and forth until her fire returns. "What happened, Rahjaan? And don't you lie to me!"

"I shot two people and a baby."

Miss Pincus erupts. "You the one shot those people in front of that church?" She pummels Rahjaan as he coils on

271

the couch and covers his head and face. She collars him and yanks him toward her. "You the one did it?"

Rahjaan drops his head, but Miss Pincus snatches his chin up. When he tries to hug her, she vaults from the couch, lights a cigarette, and takes a long drag as she paces around the living room.

"If you're old enough to shoot at families, you're old enough to go to—" Miss Pincus flops on the couch and stares at the ceiling. She blows a long stream of smoke through her nose. The fume curls around her head and mirrors thin air.

She throws her arm around Rahjaan's neck and gently draws her cheek back and forth across the top of his head. "Put your coat on. We gotta go see Detective Jack."

Grammy Lee stands on her porch and watches the JCPD march in and out of her sanctuary. She feels violated, embarrassed, betrayed, and she's having a hard time strangling her anger because Claymont knew the story of his grandfather well.

Rocky Jenkins Sr. was a sergeant in the 720th Military Police Battalion and died on Hill 665 in Khe Sanh, Vietnam, on Christmas Eve of 1973. He planned to join the JCPD upon his return to Greenville, but instead came home in a flag-draped coffin. He was buried with full military honors in Holy Name Cemetery on West Side Avenue.

Rocky's death paid off this house, and Claymont has the nerve to bring death in this house?

Jackson lassoes her attention by holding up a plastic zip-lock bag. A .40 caliber Glock pistol with olive drab frame is tucked inside.

"Doesn't look good for your grandson, Mrs. Jenkins."

Grammy Lee refuses to cry in front of a cop, even a black

one. "Okay, Detective. Now can all of you kindly leave my house?"

———

"Absolutely," Jackson says. He turns to the remaining police personnel and commands, "We're good here. This nice lady wants her house back." Jackson extends his hand to Grammy Lee and smiles. "You take care, Mrs. Jenkins."

He privately chides himself. *Greenville. You love me. You love me not.*

As it does every morning, the sun glances over the aged and battered roofs of Greenville. One, two, and then three JCPD black-and-whites quietly edge up Chapel Avenue as the first evidence of daylight kisses the street.

The same scene unfolds on Rutgers Avenue, except an anti-riot armored vehicle follows the three police cruisers.

The two brigades band together at the corner in front of Shaminique's building.

Four sharpshooters armed with .30 caliber sniper rifles spill out of the armored vehicle and scramble into the dark vestibule. Six uniformed officers trail them inside.

Moments later the sharpshooters emerge on the roof and take up positions at each corner. They aim their weapons over the roofline, making every route of escape a death trap.

Clops and Shaminique are out cold, wrapped tightly around each other. Clops's cell phone goes off. He groggily answers, "It's me."

"Claymont Jenkins?"

"Who this?"

"This is the Jersey City Police Department. Take a look. We have you surrounded, my friend."

273

Clops leaps out of bed in his boxers and grabs the two guns on the nightstand.

Shaminique is startled awake. "What's going on!" she screams.

Clops spreads the curtains with both barrels and mugs the window facing Rutgers.

"The beast," he spits. He ricochets into the living room and looks out onto Chapel.

More cops.

"If you want me, you're gonna have to come get me!" Clops growls, waving his pistols in the air.

Behind him, the front door explodes off the hinges, and through a cloud of smoke, six cops flood the room with their weapons drawn.

"Drop those guns and get on the floor!"

Clops places both barrels in the soft pocket under his chin. "And what if I don't?"

"I'm gonna paint this place with your brain guts! Now put the guns down and get on the floor!" the officer shouts.

Clops twists his face into a snarl. "I can paint it myself!"

All six cops have their service revolvers trained on the infamous Cyclops, the elusive, second-generation leader of OGC. A career-defining kill for whoever takes the first shot.

Clops glowers at the wall of officers.

I ain't going to jail.

He snatches the pistols from his chin, but before he can get off a shot, an explosion of city-issued .45 caliber slugs spin him full circle and blow through his chest, back, and lower jaw.

Crumpled in a honeycombed heap on the floor, Clops's blood-covered hands open and release his tools. Three cops rush him and handcuff his prostrated body even as his soul descends into eternity.

36

In anguish, Rock stares at the navigation lights on a boat easing across New York Bay. The brilliance of the lights waxes stronger in the waning luminance of the setting sun. How Rock wishes he was on board, no matter where the boat is going.

Claymont is gone.

The reality hurts worse than he can feel.

Rock recalls waking on what would be his last day of freedom. He spotted ten-year-old Claymont hiding in the closet, staring out at him with his big eyes and an even bigger smile. Had Rock known that would be the last time he would see Claymont for as many years as Claymont had been alive, he would've given him an uncustomary hug. Instead, he drove through the Holland Tunnel into Manhattan with forty-six pounds of marijuana stashed in the door panels of his 1960 Chrysler New Yorker convertible.

To Rock, Claymont's transformation from bug-eyed innocent to gun-toting Cyclops happened overnight.

Or did it?

Despite collect calls from prison in which Rock encouraged Claymont not to make the mistakes he did, his greatest influence on Claymont was the memories—Rock the rugged, hood capitalist who organized red-handed black and Latino adolescents into Original Gun Clappers.

Something whizzes by Rock's ear and cracks the sliding glass door behind his head. A violent beat erupts in Rock's chest, and before he can react, a second blitz zips in front of his nose and leaves a pockmark in the window. A third projectile rattles the balcony rails as Rock hits the deck and peers down two stories below.

A drunken lady cocks her gangly arm back and prepares to hurl another igneous missile. Rock rises up before she launches.

"'Ey, lady! What are you doing?"

"Who you yelling at?" Miss Pincus slurs, hands fixed on her knobby hips.

"You just broke my window!"

"You gonna get more than that broke come Sunday."

Rock quickly looks up and down the street to make sure he's not being set up. "Who told you that?"

"I ain't getting into all of that. But they coming and they ain't bringing no offerings." Miss Pincus wobbles as she turns to leave.

"Hold up!" Rock shouts.

He runs through the apartment and bounds down the stairs, but the staggering lady is nowhere in sight.

Although Andre is seated across from Hakeem at Fredrick's circular dining table, his focus is across the Hudson on the Empire State Building as it lights up red, white, and blue for the night.

"You ever had one of those dreams that's so real you can still feel the emotions it stirs up hours after you're awake?" Andre asks.

"Oh yeah," Hakeem says.

"The crazy thing about this dream is that I got upset with my grandmother and my aunt, even though I felt like it was wrong the way I talked to them. But what I got off my chest felt necessary."

"Care to share?"

In his dream, Andre was sandwiched between Grandma and Auntie Cheeks at Cochrane Stadium. They were at a St. Peter's College football game, watching Andre play.

The argument started when Grandma smiled at Andre after the three of them saw him score a touchdown. "I'm so proud of you," she said. "But I'm not surprised. God has always had his hand on you."

Andre took offense and responded with a tone that would have surely earned him a smack in real life. "How can you say that? My mom and dad are dead."

Grandma turned serious. "And my son and daughter-in-law are dead. You do realize that millions of people are permanently injured in car accidents every year, don't you? But you just caught a touchdown. Could you have done that if you were crippled?" Before Andre could answer, Grandma snapped, "No!"

"Well, why did you die then?" Andre asked.

"Because it was my time." She turned from Andre in a huff and focused on the game.

Then Auntie Cheeks felt the need to get her two cents in. "Don't you look at me like that, Andre. I already know what you thinking. What I told you was true. Did anything ever happen to you when you were in that house by yourself?"

Andre had to admit that it hadn't, but he lashed out at her anyway because now he was old enough to say the things that he felt but couldn't put into words when he was ten.

"Do you know how scared I was? All you cared about was getting high!"

Andre was mad that his voice trembled. He got madder still when he started to break down. But his words wounded Auntie Cheeks deeply.

"I had a problem, Andre. And I'm sorry. I froze to death. Is that good enough for you?"

Recalling the moment in the present, Andre is horrified that he felt no pity, whereas now he borders on tears. Nevertheless, in the dream Andre launched into another attack.

"I couldn't even enjoy my high school graduation because I had nowhere to go since *you* let the house fall down!"

Auntie Cheeks pushed back. "You a lie, Andre! You had that brand-new athletic dorm to yourself for half the summer before anybody moved in! And who's the one started you playing football anyway?"

"At that point I woke up," Andre says now.

Hakeem considers what he heard for several moments before he speaks. "So what do you think about what was said in the dream?" he asks.

"I would be denying reality if I bought into the fantasy that somehow my life has been blessed."

"Is that what your grandmother said?"

"Look, Keem. My life is what it is, so you're wasting your time if you're trying to get me to see it any other way."

"Understand that this is not about what I see. This is about you accepting the truth about yourself. How long were you in jail?"

"Three days."

"Seventy-two hours and you were caught trying to load ten thousand dollars' worth of cocaine on a plane at Newark Airport?"

"Yeah."

"What was your bond?"

"Five thousand."

Hakeem laughs out loud. "I'm sorry, Dre. But black dudes who get caught trying to load coke onto planes don't get bond, and even if they did, I'm sure it would be more than five thousand dollars in fines alone. It's no way your professors would've been able to come up with that kind of money."

"Maybe not."

"So what would've happened then?"

"I probably would've been in jail for a few months, awaiting trial."

Andre doesn't adjust his poker face, but he slowly raises the curtain on the prospect that things could have been worse. Even so, he can't release the "unique victim" status that, all of his life, has functioned as a sadistic measuring stick that he used to judge other people's suffering. And if his horror trumped theirs, he beat his chest.

"How did the judge rule when you went to trial?"

"It never went to trial. They cut me a deal. Suspended sentence in exchange for ten years' probation."

"Aren't there minimum sentencing requirements for a charge like that?"

"Three years, I think."

Hakeem doesn't interrupt Andre's recollection of his story. After several moments he says, "Listen, Dre. No one can deny that you've had tragic circumstances in your life. But either they've been accompanied by a string of extraordinary luck, or something else is going on. Even with Sandra."

Andre looks up, ready to pounce.

"She's still alive, Dre. And breathing on her own. The miracle is that things aren't worse. The three of you were ambushed at point-blank range. You sustained no life-threatening injuries, and Little Dre was untouched."

Water collects at the edge of Andre's eyelashes.

"Do you have any thoughts on that?" Hakeem asks.

One word pops into Andre's head that he wouldn't dare let pass his lips.

Fredrick arrives with a stack of takeout containers, and Andre is relieved because he's spared the indignity of having to answer. His heart sinks when he sees the name stamped on the containers—Torch & Basil.

She's in there and I'm out here.

Hakeem stands. "We'll pick up here next week."

"You might as well hang out," Fredrick says to Hakeem. "The guys you met at the hospital are coming through for the Realness. We're doing it here tonight since Andre is still on injured reserve."

"And what is it that you do at the Realness, exactly?" Hakeem asks.

"Nothing formal. Just four brothers chopping it up and breaking down truth. You can't get that on CNN, Fox News, or the *New York Times*."

"Okay, I'll hang out," Hakeem says.

Strange-O arrives first. "Yo, Fredrick, this building is bananas! You must be rolling in it, ain't you?"

Fredrick blushes. "God is good."

"He's good alright. I was walking through the lobby, and since I don't curse anymore, I said what the fish said when he hit the concrete wall."

Fredrick, Hakeem, and Andre look confused.

A grin spreads across Strange-O's face. "Dam!"

All three men shake their heads.

Mark shows up next.

"Fredrick, the food's getting cold, so we might as well eat while we're waiting for Rock," Andre says.

Mark grabs a plate and asks, "What's up with him lately? He's been acting strange for the last couple of weeks."

No one has an answer.

Fredrick opens several takeout containers. "We have a variety of things here. Grilled pork belly with chilled corn salad, jumbo lump crab cake with buttermilk sauce, and vegetarian risotto with pencil asparagus."

"This looks banging!" Mark says as he digs in.

Strange-O looks like he's seen a ghost. "Man, where the *wings* at?"

"I just got off work," Fredrick says. "The restaurant downstairs was the most convenient, and they don't serve hot wings."

Strange-O shakes his head and reluctantly serves a plate.

"This grilled pork belly is on point," Andre says.

"So is this veggie risotto," Hakeem chimes in. "My moms used to make something like this when I was a kid."

Strange-O moves the strange food around on his tongue as he looks around the table. "Y'all ain't gotta try to act all Food Network since we downtown. Chicken is a Realness tradition."

A knock.

Fredrick answers and Rock drags in. "What's real tonight, fellas?" he asks blandly and grabs a plate. "Sorry I'm late. I had to call everybody and cancel the meeting for this Sunday."

"Really? Why?" Fredrick asks.

Rock takes a bite of crab cake and says nonchalantly, "OGC put a hit on the building. And I'm not putting anybody in the middle of that."

Anger swells in Andre's stomach and extinguishes his appetite. He slams his fork on his plate. "This has got to stop. I'm not letting these dudes run me."

"Dre, you already shot up, so whatchu trying to say?" Mark asks.

"I'm saying I'm not going to spend the rest of life being intimidated by no gang."

Hakeem speaks up. "Why don't you just call the police?"

Rock looks at him. "We talking OGC, man. Police don't matter 'cuz they gonna keep coming. If not today, then a day when the police ain't around. So we either raise up now and establish that we ain't having it, or nothing's gonna change. Ever."

"And how are we supposed to stand up to OGC?" Strange-O asks.

"If you scared, just say so," Rock says. "No need trying to rationalize your fear."

"I didn't say I was scared!" Strange-O says.

"You don't have to. Your actions say it for you."

"Everybody's not an ex-con like you, Rock. So you can save the tough-guy act for somebody else."

"Strange, you don't want to take it there with me, alright?"

Mark intercedes. "Ain't no need of us turning on each other."

Strange-O ignores him and stands. "You puts no fear in my heart, Rock. Believe that."

Rock smiles. "You really outta hand, Strange. So you might as well go 'head and sit down. But I'm gonna be in front of New Jersey Truth at eleven o'clock sharp with or without you or anybody else."

"I'll be right there with you," Andre says and looks around the table.

Mark, Fredrick, Hakeem, and Strange-O appear to crawl deep inside themselves to count the cost of commitment.

"So they're going to come through blazing and we're going to do what?" Mark asks.

"Come on, man!" Andre shouts. "When are we going to stand up like men and take our hood back? They tried to take away the only two things in the world that matter to me. None of y'all even have kids, so what do you have to lose?"

"Our life," Mark says, "which happens to be your most valuable commodity."

Rock monitors the conversation with a resigned indifference. "If it's just me and Dre, then it's just me and Dre. And if you other guys find some heart, you know where we'll be."

37

Foot traffic on Ocean and Danforth is uncharacteristically light for a Sunday morning. Andre sits in front of New Jersey Truth in one of its folding chairs with the peacock blue cushion. He rests his weight and both hands on a hardwood, Masai-warrior walking stick.

Rock steps out of the meeting place, locks the door, and gives Andre a pound. "God is sovereign," he says softly, not to Andre as much as to himself, perhaps to shore up his own sagging confidence. He looks up and down the block and, not seeing any Realness faces, shakes his head almost imperceptibly.

Andre looks away from Rock and determines to encourage himself. Otherwise the scant distance between fortitude and fear that flutters in his chest would force him to fold. Oddly, fragments of a Kenny Rogers song spring to mind. "Hold 'em . . . walk away . . . run . . ."

Is God telling me to run?

"No," Andre says audibly as he struggles to his feet. He's standing for Sandra, for Little Dre, for Greenville, and for every person who has surrendered to thug-controlled streets.

When Strange-O bops around the corner, Andre and Rock

see him at the same time. Strange extends both fists and gives Andre and Rock a simultaneous pound.

"If they kill us, we shall but die," Strange-O cracks, incapable of seriousness even in the shadow of death.

"That's that 2 Kings 7:4," Rock says as he gives Strange-O a back-slapping hug. "And I got one for you. 'Do not fear those who kill the body but cannot kill the soul. But rather fear him who is able to destroy both soul and body in hell.'"

"That's that Matthew 10:28," Strange-O says, smiling. He and Rock give each other five and swing their grip back and forth before letting go with a snap.

Andre is envious. He feels shut out of their doctrinal code, which seems to give them extra backbone despite the anxiety that he knows they must feel as much as he does.

In the absence of a verse, Andre says, "Like men we'll face the murderous, cowardly pack, pressed to the wall, dying, but fighting back!"

"That's something you wrote?" Rock asks.

"Claude McKay," Andre says, proud that he can scoop Rock for a change. "That's from his poem 'If We Must Die.' He wrote it back in 1919 when we were getting lynched left and right."

For the first time since Andre has known Rock, he seems genuinely deflated. "Now here we are a hundred years later quoting it on the block, waiting for our own brothers to roll through with blasting orders," Rock says.

The three of them fall silent.

Psst!

Big Will gets off his bus and unties the tie from around his big, beefy neck. "I heard some chatter on my route so I'm here. Greenville in the building, baby." He doles out three firm handshakes.

A cab stops in front of the budding regiment and Hakeem

hops out. "What's real, fellas? Since you're not calling the cops, I figured you could use a Copt."

Andre leans on his walking stick and gives Hakeem a hearty hug. "Didn't expect you to come through!"

"I realized this is bigger than you and Rock. This is about the life of our community."

Fredrick's Beamer skirts the curb. Mark rides shotgun.

"Y'all late," Strange-O chides as he looks at his watch.

"But we're here," Fredrick bats back.

The atmosphere in front of New Jersey Truth borders on festive until a black Chevy Impala that groans under the weight of too many OGC eases onto Ocean.

Each man notices. They take up positions shoulder to shoulder in silence.

Andre's heart is flush with fear, but his face belies the fact. Hardness settles in around his temples, and a steely resolve takes up residence at the corners of his mouth. He attempts to swallow, but his throat is too dry to complete the process.

When the pitch-black windows of the Impala ease down and two men hang out, Andre slips his hand in his coat, pulls out, and aims at both gunmen.

One gangster points a TP9 Tactical Pistol with a thirty-round clip at the wall of seven men. A second gangster aims a micro Uzi submachine gun at them, a shade of fury splattered across his callow countenance.

Andre hits RECORD.

Watching the action unfold through the viewfinder of a high-definition palm cam arrests chunks of Andre's fear. It's like he's watching a movie—a personal snuff film that will feature his own demise.

The tension in the shooters' firing postures eases when they mark that Andre is recording them. Nevertheless, they keep their guns aimed.

They lock eyes with Rock—the founder, in the flesh. OGC hand signs go up out of respect.

Fredrick, Big Will, Hakeem, Mark, and Strange-O, all with arms tightly folded across their chests, melt the car with ice grills. Both shooters smirk and one of them shouts, "Y'all niggas ain't hard!"

They squeeze off, and a thunderhead of bullets clouds the sky.

The Impala hits the end of the block, and the howl of screeching tires is suspended above the street as the whip races around the corner.

When the smoke clears, the sidewalk is tossed with black bodies—like a grisly splatter painting on a concrete canvas. The New Jersey Truth sign is shredded to tatters from the curtain of gun bursts.

Andre hits STOP.

Slowly, each man swallows the tastes of life and checks their bodies for mortal injuries.

A blast of fear chills Andre's blood, but Rock is on fire. "That's what I'm talking about!" he barks, distributing stinging high fives to every raised hand. "No one can do anything without the Lord's approval!"

An image of the White Horse gallops across the blistered surface of Andre's memory, as Rock's words echo one of the verses Sandra had forced him to read.

Rock, Hakeem, Frederick, Big Will, Mark, and Strange-O explode into hysterics, but Andre remains pensive.

No one can do anything without the Lord's approval.

Andre succumbs to the thought.

And on the other side of town, Sandra opens her eyes.

Acknowledgments

To all the readers and supporters of *Unsigned Hype*, thank you. Your words of praise for that novel served as an encouragement as I labored through the writing of this manuscript. To Adrienne Ingrum and Andrea Doering—you both gave remarkable insight and guidance at crucial stages of the development of the story. To Jessica Miles—once again you pushed me and the story to the next level. To Nathan Henrion, Michele Misiak, Twila Bennett, Cheryl Van Andel, Deonne Beron, Rob Teigen, Claudia Marsh, and the rest of the team at Revell/Baker—it has truly been a pleasure working with you.

Thanks to Dr. Kevin Cokley, Stephanie Allain Bray, Victoria Christopher Murray, Lisa Cortes, and Terrie Williams, by way of Carol Mackey, for the snappy blurbs. Thanks to my cousin Dr. Ken Boyd for schooling me in the ways of dental implants, bridgework, and their attendant costs. Thanks to David G. Evans, Esq., and Martin Lynch, former president of the New Jersey Narcotics Enforcement Officers Association, for the information on sentencing in New Jersey. Thanks, Mac the doulos, for the verse that inspired OGC's snitching mantra.

Thank you, Thembisa Mshaka, Pete Rock, and Laura Carr, for the detective work.

To Stacy Hawkins Adams, Roburta Burroughs Massenat, Holly Flood, Je'Nein Ferrell, Tanya Steele, Toyi Ward, and Shawneda Marks—your comments on early drafts of the manuscript were exceedingly helpful. To Mom and Bump, the real-life Grammy Lee and Daverne, Chyance and Tasha, Eddie and Adrienne, Khary and Precious, Charlie and Janice, Danny and Anita, Wells and Holly, Christine and Michael, Daron and Precious, Dr. Young, Margie, Kelly, Toni, Lillian, Shirley, Sonya, and Maurisa—your material and moral support kept me afloat as I navigated creativity's choppy and often desolate waters.

And to my muse—my wife, Angela, and my incredible children, Lee, Jean-Angel, Truth, and Justice. Were it not for the lively and often raucous home environment, how would I have gotten anything done! Bill Reilly, thanks for teaching me so much about writing, characterization, and subtext. Your legacy will live on in my work and in my teaching. Rest in peace, my friend.

Finally, and most importantly, to the Ancient of Days. You are faithful even when I am not. What's next? I'm eager to hear.

Booker T. Mattison is an author and filmmaker who wrote the screenplay for and directed the film adaptation of Zora Neale Hurston's *The Gilded Six-Bits*, which aired on Showtime. His debut novel, *Unsigned Hype*, has been optioned, and he is currently writing the film adaptation of the book.

Mattison has taught literary criticism at the College of New Rochelle in New York, film production at Brooklyn College, and advanced directing and actor coaching at Regent University in Virginia. *Snitch* is his second novel.

Man, I Just Want to Make It . . .

"A great story. . . . [Tory's] life, music, and personal situations were stepping-stones to becoming someone great in hip-hop music. That's a beautiful thing."

—**Pete Rock,** legendary hip-hop producer and DJ